OBELISK

OBELISK

GEORGINA FATSEAS

CITIOFBOOKS, INC.
3736 Eubank NE Suite A1
Albuquerque, NM 87111-3579
www.citiofbooks.com
Hotline: 1 (877) 389-2759
Fax: 1 (505) 930-7244

Ordering Information:
Quantity sales. Special discounts are available on quantity purchases by corporations, associations, and others. For details, contact the publisher at the address above.

Printed in the United States of America.

ISBN-13:   Softcover   9978-1-963209-88-4
               eBook   978-1-963209-89-1

Library of Congress Control Number: 2024904480

TABLE OF CONTENTS

Author's Notes.

I thank the three Austrian World War Two Veterans who inspired this book.
May these men rest in peace and the world thanks them for their bravery and sacrifice.

Towns.
The town at the start of the story, Weghaltz, is a fictional location in Austria. Other mentioned Austrian towns or villages exist. Many villages and small towns in Europe mentioned in this book have merged in what appears to be one lager city or town. This is the result of the vast population growth causing an urban sprawl. Some places have retained their names to become suburbs or part of the sprawling cities. Others have simply disappeared or given new names in the urban sprawl.

People and Organizations.
All the people, but two, Hitler and Pope Pius XII, have fictional names. This is to protect their families living in Europe and other parts of the world.
If an organization existed, the name could either be altered for the story or left as is. People working within an organization have all been fictionalized.

****

A special note to all veterans from all wars at any place in the world. Your stories are important and should be told. Hold your heads up high and tell the world what you experienced in combat. That is the only way to make war the ultimate last resort.
There are no true winners in war- just displaced placed people with displaced souls.

In parks and memorial sites around the world, there are obelisks. Some places have memorial walls which have a similar function. They stand alone with inscriptions of names of the fallen etched onto their exteriors. The combined message is 'lest we forget'.

Europe Before World War Two (1939)

Note: Boundaries were constantly changing and are approximate for this year.

Courtesy: Arizona Geographic Alliance
School of Geographical Sciences and Urban Planning
Arizona State University
Cartographer Becky L. Eden
http://geoalliance.asu.edu/azga
EU_BeforeWW2.PDF10

AUSTRIAS AND NEIGHTBORING COUNTRIES IN 1938.

Chapter 1.
Weghaltz, 1938.

As Valetin Karner's car neared the town of Elsbethen, in east Austria, he pulled over to the side of the narrow winding mountain road. The gunfire below drew his attention. Cautiously he got out of the car and climbed onto its roof. He climbed halfway up the up the nearest tree that partly obscured his car from the unfolding events below.

From this vantage point, he could see members of the German army forcibly taking residents out of their homes and into the street below.

The women, children, and boys under sixteen were pushed to one side of the street close to a personnel carrier. The men and the older teenage boys were lined up on the other side of the street. Loaded rifles were aimed directly at their heads. The men in their later years of life were shot on the spot. When one of the women or children screamed, the major swung around and shot the person. It silenced the cowering fearful group.

The major bellowed a count, "One, two, three, four five." He raised his arm and pointed at the fifth person. "Are you going to join the Great German Army?" The scared young man in his late teens shook his head. Bang. The man dropped on the ground. The process was repeated. When no one volunteered to join the army at the point of the gun on the first round, the process began again with the first round of survivors.

Disgusted and despite being fearful of his own safety, Valetin looked at his pocket watch and noted the time. He pulled out a notebook and entered the time and date:

9.30 a.m. 12th March, 1938.

German soldiers killed 20 men, women and children on the outskirts of Elsbethen.

Valetin knew he had seen enough. He climbed down from the tree he was in, turned the car around and drove back to his village of Weghaltz. As he was driving, he knew as the town's mayor, he would need to draw up a survival plan for his people. His mind tossed various ideas around. He drove back to his village as fast as he could. What troubled him most for his planned defense was the lack of armory. He had driven to Elsbethen to buy more bullets for the hunting rifles. Wolves had moved closer to the village and were attacking livestock. With no extra bullets and now no extra anything to arm the village, he knew his people at any time be the next group to face the invading German troops.

When he arrived at Weghaltz, he drove to the village square and continuously blew the car's horn until most of the villages had come out to see what the urgent need was. Standing near the three-metre-tall pink granite obelisk in the centre of the square, Valetin ordered two teen boys to go to the fields and bring back their fathers and anyone else missing from the gathering.

When all were gathered, he waved his arms to quieten the voices. Valetin described what he had seen. Looks of horror and disgust appeared on all their faces. He sighed heavily. "I have a plan to defend ourselves, but it will be short lived. I couldn't get any bullets for our rifles. However, we can do limited things. We have shelters in the forest which are used by men for hunting the wild animals. We will begin to reinforce them and make them more weatherproof. We need teams of people to make more shelters and animal enclosures. The women will gather beddings, some household items, food and clothing to be taken to the shelters. I want the younger teenage boys and girls to stay behind for a special task." Valetin divided the 85 villagers into groups and gave more details of their tasks.

As the people were leaving the square, their eyes were drawn up to the sky above. The German warbirds, the Dornier Do 17 circled above. The people ran to their homes and drew the curtains.

When the planes disappeared towards the direction of Salzburg, they ventured out again. Satisfied the planes were not going to return, they hurried themselves to do the set tasks.

Outside of each of the homes, beddings consisting of a set of sheets and a few blankets were first placed outside. Then there were a few stools and a small coffee table or two. Then followed one pan and one pot with one set of cutlery for each household member.

The teenage boys rounded up the livestock and herded them into the square into makeshift pens set up by teenage girls. Cows, hens, roosters, goats, pigs, horses and sheep packed the enclosures. Hens and roosters were immediately caged, and the cages stacked in one corner. The horses and goats were tethered for both control and for later movement into the forest. The pigs and sheep were contained in pens.

Valetin looked at the progress of the evacuation. He nodded his approval. Things were moving as he had planned. The three cars communally owned by the villagers were loaded with goods. The cars would ferry the items to a clearing over three kilometers away. The path was barely wide enough for the cars to drive through. The clearing was the limit for vehicle transport and the only place where cars could turn around for a return trip. Two round trips of goods were made before Valetin called it a day.

The next morning, not long after dawn, the people gathered near the obelisk. There was still much work to be done. Overnight, Valetin planned more of the evacuation and strategies. The elderly, expectant mothers and mothers with babies under a year old would be driven to the clearing with any goods that could fit in the cars. The rest of the population would walk. Eighty-five people were on target for evacuation. The last of the group were the teenagers who were assigned another special task. They would follow as soon as each of their assigned task was completed.

The grass around the obelisk was carefully cut to be ready for replanting. A hole in the ground was made. A chest was lowered. The chest was lined with a blanket and baking pans with lids. As each baking pan was filled and covers placed on them, they were lowered into the chest. Inside were placed a mixture of documents showing land ownership, birth certificates, marriage certificates, jewelry and most of the chapel's nine carat gold candle sticks. Valetin removed one candle stick, the cheapest of them all, a gold-plated candle stick which had clearly seen better days. He told a teenager to place it on the alter with an open bible. The other instruction was to collect four bibles and 4 hymn books for the chest. When the chest was nearly full, a tablecloth was placed on top to help prevent dirt entering the chest in case it collapsed from the weight of the dirt being replaced. The ground was returfed with the original cover. Water was poured over the patch to help the grass regrow. The excess dirt was distributed into the nearby gardens. At the end of the task, newcomers to the village would have to thoroughly examine the ground for any disturbance.

Valetin watched as the teenagers walk away down the path leading to the shelters.

Now by himself, Valetin read the inscriptions on the obelisk. He had read the inscriptions before, but now he wanted to remind himself of the sentimental words which were in memory of past lost villagers: 'In memory of those who died in WW1.'

Initially, he wanted the chisel the words he wanted to add onto the obelisk, but the granite was too hard. He settled for some paint. He added, 'And in WW2'.

He tossed the can and brush into the rubbish bin outside one of the shops. As he walked to the path, he looked back and wiped tears from his eyes. He wondered if anyone would return and if they did, what would be the state of the homes, the very few shops and farms.

Chapter 2
Weghaltz

The next day, Valetin led his two brothers, Moritz and Max Karner, to a knoll to observe the village. Moritz directed attention of Valetin and Max to the obelisk. "Do you think the NAZIS will discover what is buried near the Obelisk?"

Max, the youngest replied, "They just might destroy the obelisk because of the inscriptions."

"They may. My added words may make them angry. 'and in World War Two'"

"War hasn't really started," replied Moritz.

Valetin scoffed. "It has for us. It maybe localized. Killing unarmed people is a war in my eyes. It won't be that long before the rest of the world will join us. The NAZIs marched in Austria in the 12th of this month. Salzburg has fallen. We are close behind."

Another German plane flew above and circled the village. Max looked up. "It has only been two days since they invaded us. Now, they've sent spy-planes. The circling indicates they have found our village."

They watched as the plane circled the area a few times before disappearing. "Now we move," said Valetin.

The three men ran down the knoll and entered the village. Between the walls of each house they placed, crude homemade explosives. With a stick which lightly scored the ground, the detonation cords were laid. The dirt was replaced to conceal the cords. It took three hours for the village to be covered in the crude bombs. Valetin and his brothers rested back at the knoll. Each took turns watching Weghaltz. Night came. No movement.

About seven in the morning, the men were woken by the sound of vehicles entering the village. Four trucks entered the square. One was parked directly over the buried chest. Troops poured out of the next two trucks. The last truck parked itself at a distance from the other three. Shortly, they were followed by a tank.

A major who was leading the assault surveyed the village. It puzzled him that no one could be seen. He guessed they were hiding in their houses or took to the farms. He ordered a search. "Find the people. Bring them out! Rip up the floorboards as well. They could be in cellars and look in roof cavities."

After several minutes, the soldiers came out empty handed. No one could be found. Frustrated! the major ordered half of the men to comb the fields and the surrounding areas to look for traces where the people could be hiding. An hour later, the men returned empty handed. The major swore, "The bastards have moved out. They have deserted their homes." The major ordered a NAZI flag be erected on the obelisk. The major looked proud and saluted the flag. "Hail Hitler."

Night fell. The German soldiers decided to sleep in the houses using the made beds- a night of unusual comfort for many. Six guards were stationed around the village. Moritz tapped his resting brothers. "The guards have just about nodded off to sleep. Time for the fireworks."

The men looked at the three detonators. "On the count of three, push down the levers," said Valetin. "One. Two. Three." Seconds later, the houses in the village exploded. Fire and fumes filled the air. The guards on duty snapped to attention and looked around for the invaders. One by one they were shot. Valetin, Moritz and Max picked them off and any injured soldier trying to escape the inferno.

Weghaltz burned to the ground. Slowly the fires died out. No movement could be detected in the smoldering ruins. Valetin and his brothers waited. It was mid-afternoon before they ventured to the destroyed village. The only thing standing in the village was the obelisk.

Valetin climbed into the truck covering the ground with the chest. It contained some medical supplies and some food. Valetin smiled at the haul. The truck which was beside it had seats and had some personal effects looted from the village. The next truck had tents under the seats and more food. Valetin grinned. *Useful*, he thought. The final truck which was parked slightly away from the first three offered rich pickings. This truck was loaded with guns and ammunition. He told Max, "Go to the shelter and get the cars and men. We are going to unload these vehicles." He pointed to the truck carrying precious goods.

Two hours later, all the useable items were removed from the trucks. The four trucks were stripped clean. Over the NAZI emblems were painted the Austrian flag, red, white, and red in equal horizontal widths. The vehicles were driven to the further-most outlying farm and placed in a barn. The wheels were removed, and the keys pocketed.

The tank's cannon was stuffed with dirt pushed down and compacted with the back of broomsticks. Petrol was poured inside and set alight. The escape hatch was slammed down. Valetin and the others ran for cover. The heat inside the tank would make the remaining ammunition explode. The escape hatch lid flew at least ten metres into the air while the rest of the tank exploded into the surrounding area. Valetin asked Max, "Didn't you remove any of the ammunition in that tank?" "No. Why?"

"I think the explosion was loud enough to be heard in Elsbethen. Did you feel the ground shake?"

"Yes. It was spectacular," replied Max. Valetin gave him a friendly clip on the head. "Let's get out of here. Company will be coming."

Chapter 3
Weghaltz.

The next day, the village people carried the supplies from the clearing to the shelters. The goods were separated into their groups. Tents went up immediately. Food was placed in of the new hastily built shelters, guns and ammunition distributed within the camp and fuel was hidden in another section. Valetin explained, "If the soldiers are not heard from by their commander, more soldiers will come. Don't get too comfortable. I want all people from the ages of fourteen to twenty-two to build another camp. The camp will be headed by Jonatan Huber. There was a grumble of discontent. Valetin explained further, "A separate camp higher in the mountains is needed as insurance that some of us will survive this potential massacre."

He handed them a rifle each. "Three people will come down daily for food supplies. This is to make sure we check on each other. If the youth groups cannot take supplies back, then the youth group knows the adult and children's group has been attacked. If no youths come down, the rest of us know the teenage group has been attacked. Whatever group survives any attack, they will travel further into the forest under Huber's or my guidance whatever the case maybe. Is that clear?"

Valetin knew the concept was unpopular. He offered others for suggestions. No one came forward with an idea.

A week later, German troops were at the decimated village of Weghaltz. The new major in charge shook his head as the smell of the charred body remains filled the air. Blackened statues glared back at the newcomers. Dead soldiers littering the town square were visible from his car before he attempted to get out.

His chin dropped when he realized the tangled broken mass, he was standing beside was the remain of a tank. Anger boiled inside him. He clenched his fist, and his face went red. He instantly knew there was resistance from the villagers, and they would pay for the damage. He took a few deep breaths then proceeded to the remains of what appeared to be buildings.

As the major inspected the site in greater detail, he held his nose. He wished he hadn't seen what he had. He was beginning to wonder if the bodies were soldiers or villagers. He soon got his answer. Badly damaged helmets confirmed his nightmare. The remains of the guards bearing bullet holes rotted in the spring sun. Maggots feasted on the bodies. He looked around for the trucks. He cursed. None were to be seen. *Obviously driven away and hidden somewhere*, he thought. Furious at the situation, he ordered his men to search the surrounding area. "Pay attention to the farms outside the village. Look for pathways into the forest. Look for anything that could be a clue to the murderous people."

Six troops spread out from the village on the western side. They followed a road out to the main fields. The group split into two when there was a fork in the road. The sign directing the way to the farms were on the ground and the directory pointers were removed and strewn nearby. One group of four continued on the main road. Two others took the smaller rougher unsealed road.

The group of four retuned to the junction two hours later. Nothing. No side roads. No signs of vehicles departing the main road to go across land to any destination hidden from view. They waited for the small group to return to the junction. When the sun was beginning to set, the group of four reported in claiming two soldiers had not returned to a certain point. The major surmised that would be the starting point of tomorrow's search.

A half of soldiers led by the major returned to the fork in the road. They drove on the bumpy road and came to a stop. The two missing soldiers were hung and swinging from a tree on the left side of the road. Their armory were removed. A sarcastic note was pinned to a uniform. '*Hail Hitler.*' The major grew furious. He ordered the men be cut down. He yelled, "Search the area. The bastards are here!"

The men spread out. The major watched the search. Nothing could be seen. He ordered the men back. "We will continue along this road. They must be hiding further along."

The vehicle came to a stop. A cut tree blocked the road. The major cautioned his men about getting out. "It's an ambush," he warned. The men were alert with guns ready to shoot. They sat in position for about three hours. Nothing happened and time has been wasted. When the vehicle was ordered to turn around, the wheels didn't move. The tires had been punctured with sharp objects hidden between stones in the bumpy surface. The major cursed as the objects were removed - nails, broken saw blades, broken farm tools and glass bound on sticks pressed firmly into the ground. "We camp here for the night. Don't sleep in the trucks. They risk being blown up. Sleep in the long grass for protection."

The soldiers walked into the tall grass lining the dirt bumpy road. All were cautious and worried if they would be picked off like ducks at a shooting range at some carnival. Sleeping there would be better than walking in the dark to the village and be bigger easy targets. The long walk back to this location in the morning also played on their minds.

The major woke at the crack of dawn. He blew on the horn to wake the soldiers up. Half of the soldiers who were sleeping on the left side of the road did not respond. The major and the other soldiers walked over. Feint groaning was heard. Seven of the men had fallen into a ditch. Two were impaled on pointed sticks and obviously dead. Two had recently died after bleeding out from the puncture wounds which struck assorted blood vessels. Two were caught in animal traps. One of the men had one arm and leg in two different traps while the other found himself trapped with one arm locked in the steel jaws. Infection was raging through their bodies. The other, much younger soldier was dead after bleeding out after his arm was snapped off at the wrist and his trapped leg was now showing colliquated blood attracting flies.

The major did not hold back his anger. "Find the bastards now!" In a softer voice, he commanded a youth, "Get them out of the ditch and load them in the truck." The youth obeyed. The youth took his rifle and slowly edged his way into the ditch. No traps. Confidently he entered the ditch of death. With the assistance of another soldier, he removed those still alive and took them to the truck for crude first aid. It was obvious, these two injured men were on their way out of this world. The other bodies were slowly removed and laid at the side of the road for collection.

At the start of the search along the road, some soldiers climbed over the downed tree trunk and landed on more animal traps hidden in the foliage of the tree. They screamed their pain as others ran to their rescue. The major ordered, "Everyone come back. Move the truck back. Pull by hand." The soldiers obeyed the order. The truck was moved back several metres. The major ordered, "Blow up this tree trunk."

Minutes later the tree was decimated by an explosion. The major sent half the soldiers back with the dead and injured to the village. They were to return with a new truck and extra tires to repair the stranded truck. The other half were ordered to walk with him on the bumpy road.

The remaining soldiers started again. They spread out and hesitated about walking on or on the side of the road. More traps could be hidden in the dirt road or in the tall grass. With their rifles they pushed the grass aside or jabbed the dirt inspecting every inch before taking a step.

With eyes focused downwards, the soldiers navigated the road with no drama. They reached another fork in the road. One was a rough path and the other not much more than a goat track. No signage could be seen. The major was wary. More traps could be possible. "We take the wider track."

The men walked on the wider track. After an hour, they were back where they started, a circle. The wider road turned narrow to be the goat track at the fork of the road. They headed back to the two trucks. "There is nothing this way," said the major. "Let's head back. I have had enough of these farm folk." The major ordered the truck drivers to drive the trucks back to Weghaltz.

Back at Weghaltz, the soldiers erected tents in the only clearing, the square. The weather worn flag on the obelisk was replaced with a new one. The taskforce for removing the dead soldiers had completed their work. Shallow graves were marked with a piece of timber. Their names if the dog tags were readable were painted on the timber. The dog tags would be sent back to their families with a piece of propaganda, and information regarding the location of their son's burial location.

Later in the day, the major ordered a search further into the forest. One path which seemed to have had foot traffic was found. The soldier called in his discovery. The soldiers converged on the path. No other path appeared. The major surveyed the countryside with a set of binoculars. He pointed to the knoll. He sent two soldiers to that vantage point and report back if there was evidence of anyone one using the location.

They reported in the negative. They were ordered to return and keep watch. The village of Weghaltz was now secured in German hands. The surrounds were not. The major surmised the villagers were higher in the mountains and were watching them.

Early the next morning the German patrol walked along the path which led to the clearing. They were confident the villagers had come this way. Car tracks were noted. The cars were no longer visible, obviously hidden somewhere close by. The search revealed nothing at first. No indication as to which way the village people went. The soldiers sat down to eat some food. When they were about halfway through the snack, gunfire opened. From the trees the villages shot the soldiers. The gunshots were heard by a group of soldiers heading towards the first group. One soldier ran back to the town square. He puffed, "We were attacked." The major ordered more troops to the mini-battle zone.

More soldiers came, but they only reached the halfway point when they were mowed Down. The major ordered more troops and this time he was going to go with them to see how many villagers were killed. He wanted to see their faces. When he arrived at the scene, he was horrified. The second group of soldiers were dead. He looked up hoping to spot any person in the trees. He couldn't see them. They were well hidden. He cursed.

He signaled for the soldiers to continue along the path. The clearing contained dead soldiers who were stripped of their clothes and boots. All were naked except for the dog tags and helmets. The major screamed his frustration. A noise was heard above his head. Instinct took over. He aimed his gun in the direction and fired. A bird dropped out of the sky almost hitting the major.

The stripped soldiers were carried back to Weghaltz. They were buried alongside their other fallen comrades. The major counted his losses. Nearly fifty per cent of his soldiers were down. He radioed in the pocket of resistance.

Chapter 4
Weghaltz.

More troops arrived. More guards were on night duty. More care was taken with everything. A plane flew overhead surveying the area. Nothing. The new troops were cautioned about the attacks and booby traps. They were warned, expect anything and everything and if nothing is happening means something was happening.

Valetin watched the village from a new vantage point higher up the mountain side. He noted the mobilization of the troops towards the main shelter. He sent Niko Huber, Jonatan 's brother, back to the camp with orders to evacuate further into the forest but away from the youth group. Only after the evacuation had occurred, then it was time to tell the youths.

Niko puffed as he relayed the instructions. The camp went into a flurry. They would head further west and up the mountains. They would be further away from the youth group. The villagers barely had time to settle in their new location when word was sent to Jonatan Huber. The teen camp was to move further up and east. They were to go to the top of the cliff which dominated the landscape.

From that point, they would be able to see all who was moving around in the forest, and who was moving around Weghaltz. The Germans now resembled ants scurrying around a nest. Jonatan rostered two teenagers at a time to watch over the surrounding areas. The rest were hidden behind the cliff, deeper into the forest with orders not to light any fires for any reason. Any light or smoke on top of the exposed cliff was like a beacon. Orders were to crawl to the cliff face and lie down. Wear brown, black and grey clothes to blend in with the rock face. It would be much harder for those on the ground to spot them crawling in dark clothing.

Two girls, Rayna and Miya were on watch. The girls spoke about when times were less complicated and good. In mid-sentence, Rayna stopped talking. "Oh, shit. I see some NAZIs coming up this way. I will keep watching. Go tell Jonatan." Miya wriggled back halfway and then ran to the camp. Jonatan ordered all to pack up the camp as previously drilled and to head further up the mountain path going to the peak. That would be a steep kilometre climb.

Samuel who knew the path well from past rock-climbing trips, would lead the way. He was armed with a rifle and ammunition. Jonatan signaled to the remainders to follow him in the opposite direction, down the mountain. Hidden in the trees and camouflaged as best they could, the teenagers stood their post with guns pointed onto the crude path. Four soldiers were headed their way. On Jonatan's signal, they fired their rifles. Three soldiers dropped but were not dead. Jonatan finished them off. One of them has escaped.

Jonatan ran down the path to follow the escaping soldier. The soldier disappeared. Jonatan froze. He recovered too late. The German soldier shot him in the head. The soldier scrambled down the mountain. Another shot rang out. The German soldier was dead. Niko checked the soldier to be sure he was dead. He removed the rifle, a pistol and a knife. He ran to Jonatan. He closed his eyes and cried. When he pulled himself together, he noticed he was not alone. Two of the teenage boys had joined him. They helped Niko to his feet and dragged Jonatan to the camp where he was buried.

Niko stayed with the teenagers that night He noticed the food supply was low. He ordered three teens to go to the new campsite to collect more rations.

Niko looked at the group. "I will lead you over the mountain. There is a cabin used by hunters staying overnight. We move now. It will be night time when we reach the camp. Also, you will be pleased, there is fresh water. A small stream caused by melting snow trickles down that side of the mountain just by the cabin. Maybe some of you can do with a major bath." He heard the group chuckle.

After two days at the cabin, food was dangerously low. A deer was caught. Niko gave them a quick lesson on how to skin an animal. He showed them how to carve up the animal before cooking. The deer meat lasted two days. Niko ordered two teenagers to search the area for ground berries and mushrooms. Three others were dispatched for the main camp for more rations and an update on information.

The three teenagers returned quicker than expected. They reported the main camp was deserted. All the animals were taken. No food. No people. Niko was concerned more than ever."We pack up and keep moving. Pack up tonight. We leave in the morning," he ordered. "It is berries and mushrooms for a meal. Sorry."

The group followed a rough path going down the mountain and then it started to climb again. There was another cabin- not as large and more dilapidated. Niko examined the structure and decided it was too risky to go inside. They would have to rough it out with sleeping bags only.

Morning came. The group left the site. Empty stomachs rumbled. Discontent but all were silent. Niko told them to conserve their energy and that meant silence. At midday, the group rested. Scraps of anything were consumed. Jaro and Oskar who were sent to search for berries were asked to do so again. Kiana, Oskar's younger sister demanded to go with her brother. Niko gave in. Oskar offered little protest. Then he thought, *little sister had grown up fast in the last month.*

Chapter 5
Leaving Weghaltz.

The trio were less than a kilometre away when they heard a volley of gunshots. Oskar held his hand over Kiana's mouth. "Shh. We can't do anything. Hide," he whispered and pulled her to the ground.

Jaro wept and shook with fear. Oskar extended an arm over Jaro in a bid to comfort him. Jaro's brother and sister were in that group. Now he had to presume they were dead with the others. Oskar kept Jaro and Kiana down on the ground. He hoped the Germans would think they had captured and killed all the villages. They stayed put until nightfall.

At dawn, Oskar ventured towards the camp. Everyone was dead. Bodies were left to the elements. Rifles were gone along with the ammunition. He zipped up the sleeping bags with the bodies inside. He dragged each to the side of the path. He found some red and white material to make rolls. A crude flag of Austria was draped over one body. He walked back to Jaro and Kiana. "Let's get out of this place," he whispered as tears rolled down his face. He wiped them away with a shirt sleeve.

"Where to?" asked Kiana.
"Liezen," said Oskar.
"That's a hell long way. Just how do you think we will get there?" asked Jaro.

"Walking. Hitch hiking. On back of farm wagons," said Oskar not really sure if the suggestions would be possible. They were physically dirty. They smelled. No one would give them a ride looking like that. We take two changes of clothes. That is it. Any food we scavenge, we share. If you have any other ideas, let me know," said Oskar.

For two days, they walked. They ate some herbs, berries and mushrooms. Jaro caught a rabbit. He tried to kill it. He couldn't. Oskar took the animal and turned his back. He closed his eyes as he twisted its neck. He felt sick in his stomach. It was the very first creature he killed. Recalling the technique Niko had shown them, he skinned the animal and gutted it. Jaro managed to make a fire. The rabbit was rotated over the flames and the white-hot coals. Thirty minutes later the rabbit was cooked. It wasn't tasty as they recalled their grandparent's method of cooking. They had pots and certain herbs which were denied to them on this trek. The meal did its job. Full stomachs.

As they walked down the mountain, they came across trickles of water slipping over a few rocks. They took turns sipping the precious commodity. They moved on. When they were at the bottom of the mountain, they had no idea which way to go. Jaro faintly recalled Liezen was south-east from Elsbethen. He asked the others, "Which way is south-east?"
Oskar and Kiana looked blank. They sat down on a rock. After a while Kiana said, "The sun comes up in the east. But these mountains don't let the sun in until nearly midday. I am going to guess." She pointed along the valley floor. "That way."
"Are you sure?" asked Oskar.
"No. Absolutely not. But it is better than sitting here," she replied.
"The sun will be over us soon. That will be east." She drew a cross on the ground and marked the points. They waited.

The sun rose over the mountain. Kiana smudged out the directional points to adjust them to the direction of the sun. She groaned. "Over another mountain."

"What if we go along the valley as you said, where do we end up?" asked Oskar.

Kiana drew a mud map of the surrounding countries of the time. "East. I don't know if we will hit any town in Austria. We could end up in Hungary or Slovakia. North will take us to Czechoslovakia and north-west is Germany. I don't think it is such a great idea. The other ways is west. That would take us to the edges of Germany or into Switzerland and from there into France. France sounds okay. South will take us to Yugoslavia and south-west takes us to Italy. Problem. What I hear and I am not sure if it is true, in Italy the King and the nutcase, Mussolini are not getting on. Mussolini is running rampant. He is not much better than Hitler. They are the choices we have. The major problem is we have no passports. Dad said we needed passports to travel but he never got us one."

"Wow. What a choice. If we cross the borders, we could get arrested for having no passports," said Oskar.

"What is a passport"" asked Kiana.

"I think it is some special kind of book or papers which says who you are and where you are from," said Oskar.

"Well that kills border crossing unless we smuggle ourselves somehow," replied Jaro.

Oskar said, "Yeah, we end up in jail."

Kiana looked around. "Maybe it is safer in jail than the outdoors. Since we don't know for sure which way Liezen is, this is our jail because there is no food and no water. At least in jail, we get a bed, water and food no matter how bad it is."

Oskar said, "We should go for Liezen. Let's travel east and then turn south. We just may be lucky.

We travel along this valley for about ten kilometres. When we see what an easy mountain climb, we turn south. Is that a plan?"
Kiana and Jaro nodded. Kiana looked at the crude compass. She pointed the way east.

Chapter 6
The Trek to Liezen.

After three slow days of travelling the unforgiving valley floor and stopping to examine the mountains on south side, the trio rested. Hunger made itself known. Their stomachs growled in protest. Kiana commented, "I am feeling weak. The hunger is burning my stomach."

Both Jaro and Oskar agreed. "I think we should rest under this tree." He brushed away the pine cones. He wondered. "Are these cones safe to eat?"

Jaro shrugged. "I am not too adventurous to find out."

Kiana picked up a cone which had its woody petals opened. She hit the cone on a rock and shook it every so often. "What are you doing?" asked Oskar.

"I saw Solea do this," she said. "The pieces that fall out can be cleaned up and reveal the nut."

Oskar and Jaro looked on. Kiana peeled back the long taper and then rubbed the small black end in her fingers. After test tasting the first nut she smiled. "Yum. Just like the bought ones in the shops in Elsbethen." She handed the boys a few each for them to peel for themselves. They gathered more cones and repeated the actions. Oskar puffed. "Now I see why these nuts are so expensive in the shops. It requires intensive labour."

Before they moved on, they gathered more cones and removed the seeds with the tapers. An empty container measuring about 300gram was filled. As they walked, they had their eyes peeled for more possible food items. Oskar held up his hand for the others to stop. He nodded towards a rabbit sitting beside its burrow. Stealthily, they approached the animal. Jaro was about to pounce when the rabbit darted away towards Oskar. Oskar shot the rabbit. "Food. At last." He smiled at the catch.

They walked for two more days. The supply of nuts had depleted and very few pines trees could be seen. Jaro studied the mountains. "I think we can cross over here." He pointed to a gap halfway up. Kiana grinned. "I think we should try to climb that. If we keep walking in this valley, we may end up in Hungary or Slovakia."

In silence, they moved towards the perceived gap. Oskar pointed. "Over the next ridge and hope for the best that we can see a town or two. They climbed over the ridge. Oskar tried to get his bearings. "I am not sure if we are achieving anything. Up! Down! Up!. Down!" He was about to add more when they all looked up to see a German plane flying overhead. Jaro called out "Duck!" Immediately they all hit the ground. The plane didn't circle but continued flying south-east.

Kiana whispered, "The bastards must have beaten us to Liezen or some other village."
Oskar placed his arm around his sister's shoulder. "We need to keep going. I hope we come across a farm. I really could do with a bath, clean clothes and a meal."
Jaro clowned around lifting his arms and trying to smell his armpits. "I got used to this bad smell. I have forgotten what clean is. We could all do with a major clean up."

Two more days of foot travel had them go up and down two more lower mountains. The terrain was difficult. Sharp large rocks were threatening to pierce them if there was a slip. Others were polished by melting snow which made them tread equally as cautious. One slip over the polished stones and rocks and it was goodbye. After the third day, they looked down from their new vantage point. In the distance was a village. Three dwellings were well back from the village. The farmhouses were all surrounded by farmland. Kiana gave a sigh. "At long last. A hint of civilization." Then she added in jest. "Or is it a mirage?"

Oskar confirmed, "Not a mirage. Let's study the place first before we go in. I really don't want to see any more Germans."

For half a day, the trio watched over the village and the farms. Crops on the farm were squashed to the ground. Parts were burned. Jaro said, "I think the Germans have been here. They have damaged the crops. They could be in the village and in the farmhouses."

Night fell and the trio were about to sleep for the night when the sound of vehicles floated towards them. The trio snapped to attention. German soldiers raced into the nearest farmhouse and dragged the occupants out. They systematically ransacked the houses and then a small barn. A couple of cows, a horse and a pig fled the opened doors. One soldier took it upon himself to shoot all the escaping animals. Then the gun was aimed at the occupants.

The German soldiers said something to the farmer and his family. The trio were much too far away to hear but the movement of the held gun indicated a threat. One by one, the farming family members were shot. Their bodies were left to rot where they once stood. The German soldiers drove away taking one of the smaller cows and a pig. Oskar was furious at what he witnessed. "Bastards. That was murder. Just plain murder."

Kiana's eyes welled up. "They are wiping out our people. Why? What did we do?"

Jaro held back his anger. "Nothing. For months they have been wiping us out. Genocide, I think they call it."

The next day, the trio watched the village and the farms. There was no movement. "Shall we try to see what is inside the homes?" asked Kiana.

"I think we need to see who is alive and who is dead. We bury the dead. If that is possible."

Chapter 7
Donnersbach

The trio advanced to the closest farmhouse where they witnessed the murder. Oskar approached first. He went around the outside of the barn and peered in the only window before approaching the door. Empty.

He signaled for Jaro and Kiana to go to the barn. "Wait here. I want to check the house." Carefully, he walked across the open area to the house. The odour of the bodies instantly hit his nostril. He gagged. He continued to look into each window before venturing inside. The house was empty. He signaled for the others to come.
"We bury those people. We leave a sign up as to where they are. Go through their belongings and see if there are any names to put on the notices."

Jaro found a letter lying on a sideboard. There was no envelope. "I have something. The letter is addressed to 'Mum, Dad, Elsie and Elio.'
"That should be enough." The trio found shovels and dug up the soft earth between the barn and the house. One by one, they placed the bodies in two shallow graves. Two crude cross was erected.
Above one shallow grave was marked 'Mum' on one side and 'Dad' on the other. In the smaller shallow grave laid the bodies of the two children with their names added in a similar way, 'Elsie' and 'Elio'.

"I am going for a bath and then I am going to wash my clothes," said Kiana. She went through the cupboards to look for clothes which may fit her. An old fashioned and worn skirt and a blouse from 'Mum's' cupboard was the closest fit. She took the clean clothes and her backpack into the bathroom and emptied out the few contents. After her bath, she put on the new clothes and washed all of hers in the tub. To her horror, the clothes which she rotated over the last few months released so much dirt. When she pulled up one dress to examine it cleanliness, the material ripped. It was less than a rag. She binned it. Carefully she examined each item from the now muddy water. They held together but the dirt was too ingrained to be removed. She cursed. She held them up to her nose. They smelled a lot better. She then looked at her backpack. *That could do with a cleaning as well*, she thought. She drained the mud from the tub and did her best to revive the bag. When she considered herself finished, she washed the tub down. As she carried the wet clothes out of the bathroom, she said, "Whoever is next, can go in. Clean the mud off the tub for the next person."

Oskar looked at her new set of clothes. "Yes Mum."

"Raid the cupboards for fresh clothes. You won't be able to get the grime out of the old clothes. One of my dresses fell apart. The mud was holding it together."

Jaro grinned as he nudged Oskar. "Just who is that pretty girl giving domestic orders?"

Oskar played along with the jesting. "She looks familiar. I really can't place my finger as to where I saw her before."

"Very funny. I can't wait to see if I have been walking and living with two Africans or two Austrians."

Oskar's and Jaro's mouths dropped.

Kiana tried to prepare a meal with the meagre food items left behind by the German soldiers.

She gazed at the large dead cow and wondered of the meat was too far gone. She played it safe.

The animals would have to be buried as their stench was creeping into the farmhouses. She wondered if there were any eggs in the barn. She left the safety of the house to go to the barn.

She went in. It was quite dark except where the only window shed some light. She rummaged around shifting hay and objects around. Nothing. She went up to the loft. A chicken was there. It was nearly dead. It looked at her with lifeless eyes. Kiana carefully picked it up and carried it down and back to the house.

Jaro looked at the humble meal. He pointed to the unidentifiable mass on one side of the plate.
"What is this?"
"My attempt to cook chicken. It was very scrawny to begin with. I think it would have died by tomorrow." She pointed with her knife. "Eat or I will eat it for you."
"No. No. No. I'll eat it regardless how bad it tastes. I just forgotten what chicken looked like on a plate."
"Stop teasing. I know I am not a cook. I did my best," said Kiana.
Oskar ploughed into the meal. "Actually, it is just bland. Some salt and pepper would help." He looked around the kitchen for the condiments. None could be seen.
With a mouth half full of food he said, "We sleep here tonight. Beds will be a luxury. Then we move on and check the rest of the place out. I want to know what the name of this village is."

The next morning, the trio walked cautiously towards the next farmhouse. This farmhouse was closer to the village. They looked around looking for a hint of German soldiers. None were to be seen. They entered the house. Dead people were on the floor. Their bodies were attracting flies. Oskar sighed. "Another burial is needed."

Again, they searched the house for any identification of the deceased occupants. A marriage certificate was found for the adults. Birth certificates were found for the three children who were all under ten years of age. The young family had been wiped out. New graves with names painted on crude crosses would need to be erected.

Kiana looked around the farmhouse searching for anything of value. She found a necklace, a silver chain with a silver disk. She looked at the disk. It was a coin, an old Austrian coin. She pocketed it. In a drawer near one of the children's beds was a coin box. She shook the small box before opening it. Ten low value coins tumbled out. She pocketed them as well. However, she wondered what could be purchased with the coins. Her only thought was an ice cream cone at the most or a few hard-boiled sweets. She was about to investigate the last bedroom when Oskar called out.

"Hey! Everyone! I found a cellar!" As Jaro and Kiana entered the room, Oskar had already moved the kitchen table and chairs. He had inserted a knife into what appeared to be floorboards. The only clue it was a cellar were the holes in the floorboards. The broken ring handle had been removed and was lying on the kitchen bench near the sink. It was a clue to Oskar that a cellar was hidden somewhere in the house. The door squeaked open under protest. The short ladder was the only way in and out. Slowly he went down while Jaro searched for a torch or lantern. An old lantern was found in a cupboard which stored crockery. Jaro lit it up and handed it to Oskar.

Oskar looked around the cellar. Jars of home preserved fruit and vegetables lined one side of the small cellar. On the other was a rack of wine and a table and two chairs. He called out to Kiana and Jaro. We have food. I am passing jars up."

After ten minutes, the cellar was emptied out. Two bottles of the ten bottles of wine were placed in the centre of the kitchen table. He opened one bottle. He spat it out after taking a mouthful. "It's really off. It's rancid." He washed his mouth out to get rid of the lingering flavour. The trio opened two jars at a time: one vegetable and one fruit. When they were emptied, the next two were opened. Their stomachs were full for the first time in months.

"We sleep here tonight and then move on. Is there any information as to which village we are in?"

Jaro shook his head. "Maybe the village centre will give us a clue. We move on tomorrow. We take some food with us just as precaution."

The next morning, they packed their backpacks and added an extra bag for the extra food.

They were nearing the village when they heard heavy vehicles coming their way. They took cover behind a stone wall which had bushes growing in front of it. With eyes barely reaching over the wall and through the bushes, their obscured vision was still enough for them to see what was going on.

Soldiers rushed out. They searched each building and dragged out anything what appeared to be of value. An old lady was found huddled under the counter of her wrecked shop, a survivor of the first invasion. The woman protested. She was hit in the face with the butt of a rifle. She fell to the ground screaming in pain from a broken jaw. She was silenced with a bullet.

Orders were bellowed by the sergeant in charge. The soldiers searched continued for more valuables and people. Nothing. The soldiers went to the farmhouse where Jaro, Oskar and Kiana had been the night before. "Someone was here. There is a grave and empty food jars on the sink. There has to be a cellar somewhere. Search the place."

The sergeant ran over to inspect the find. He looked around. They can't be that far away. Search everywhere including the surrounding bushes."

The trio watched as the soldiers moved into and around the farm and the surrounding land. Oskar, Kiana and Jaro adjusted their position to avoid detection. It seemed forever for the trio for the cat and mouse game with deadly consequences to come to an end. The Germans pulled out of the village taking what they considered valuable. Oskar said, "We stay here for a while just in case they have soldiers hiding in the buildings waiting to catch us. Keep quite."

It wasn't long after Oskar had uttered the words, four soldiers appeared. Their conversations were as casual as their stance. They walked around each building in the village. They opened and closed doors at random. Nothing. One soldier dragged the dead old lady by the feet and dumped her at the front of the church door. The men dragged a table and a few chairs to the centre of the square. They began to play a card game while smoking and drinking some beer they found in one of the buildings.

Oskar, Jaro and Kiana slowly crept away from their hiding place when they noted two of the soldiers were inebriated. The other two were not far off. They moved out of the village and back to the mountains where they once came. "Let's bed down for the night. Oh, I miss the beds we slept in." said Jaro. He looked around to see the agreement on Kiana's and Oskar's faces.

The next morning a German jeep had returned to pick up the four soldiers. The vehicle sped away. Jaro tugged at Kiana and Oskar who were still sleeping. "They have gone," said Jaro.

"I think we can move on to another village. This place is history."
"Which way do we go?" asked Kiana. "I am completely lost."
"Are you sure you saw all four leave?" asked Oskar.
Jaron nodded. "I saw them eating breakfast. They just got in the jeep and left. There were no soldiers in exchange for the four who stayed overnight. It is all clear."

Cautiously Jaro led the way down the slope and into the village. They went to the town hall, hoping to see the village's name and any map of the country. Kiana went to a clerk's desk. She rummaged around looking for a clue. She found what she was looking for. "We are in Donnersbach. Liezen is north-east. We overshot."

Oskar thought about the information. "I think the Germans are already in Liezen. This is only a village where Liezen is a town. Germans are more interested in towns. Villagers are just loose ends that need to be extinguished. Well, that is how I read the situation. Is there a radio? Maybe some news will give us a clue as to what is going on in the world. We left Weghaltz on the seventeenth of March, just days after the Salzburg invasion. We have been hiding and travelling for months." Jaro looked around the room. Then left to go into the mayor's office. He turned on the old radio. The reception crackled.

Oskar and Kiana joined him in the room. Between the static was an announcement by some official in the German army.
Today we celebrate a great victory. All of Austria is now in German control. This is a reminder for all males who are between seventeen and forty-five to enroll in the German army. All men must go to the city hall in their town or city and register. Those refusing to register will be punished.

The German orders repeated themselves. Then it was followed by German music heralding the greatness of the Fatherland. Jaro turned off the radio in disgust. "What the hell! Coscripted to the German army? No way."
"Hitler knows what he can do," said Oskar in disgust as the images of murdered farmers filled his mind. "Do we head for the hills again and live there or do we join some resistance groups?"
Kiana recalled the heady days of hide in seek in the mountains behind Weghaltz. "I think I would rather hide and live off the land. May be come to the farms for clothes and other essentials."
Jaro looked at Kiana. "Are you serious about staying in the mountains?"
Kiana nodded. Oskar looked around the room. "I Think we are done here. No Liezen or any other place. We just have to live through this situation."

Chapter 8
Donnersbach

The trio made a camp in the mountains behind Donnersbach. It was a six-kilometre hike from the camp to the first farmhouse they entered. The lookout they established was on the crest close to half a kilometre from their camp.

Each day, they would go down the slopes and into the farmhouse to retrieve any required items. First were tools to make a permanent shelter. Timber was cannibalized from the barn. It wasn't perfect but it did keep out the cool night winds and morning dampness. Two rugs roughly the same sizes were thrown on the ground to help stop the rising damp. The structure was barely enough for the three to squeeze in at night.

Next were the blankets and pillows and then the coffee table with one round of cutlery, plates and cups for each person and any food that could be scavenged. The farms started to regrow some grains and different crops. They tendered to what was growing wild. Baths and clothes were washed once a week. Water had to be conserved.

Once a week they would go to the mayoral room to listen to the radio. They were shocked to hear World War had been declared. On the second of September 1939, the world exploded. There was nowhere to hide. Nowhere to run. It was now a survival of the smartest and the cunning.

Jaro, Kiana and Oskar were in the mayor's office listening to the radio. They didn't hear the solitary car coming into the village. It wasn't until they heard a car door slam and they looked startled. The radio went off instantly. They hid in predetermined locations in the building.

A German captain walked into the building. He looked around. He was suspicious as he thought he had heard sounds as he approached the building. He examined each room. Nothing. He shrugged. He went to the closed shop which once sold assorted products. The shelves were empty. He went to the next building, a café come restaurant. He went inside the unlocked shut doors. He made himself a cup of black coffee. He spat it out. The coffee was off. The bitter taste laced his mouth. He washed his mouth with some water. Some packets of biscuits were still on display. He opened a packet. He closed it as fast as he opened it. Molds. He tossed the packet on the floor. He moved on to the next shop. The last shop in this village was a drapery shop which also sold a few premade items of clothing. A child's dress was on a mannequin. He examined it. It looked about the right size for his five-year-old daughter. He removed the dress. He was chuffed with the find.

As he returned to his vehicle, he thought he saw movement at the corner of his eyes. He turned. Someone was there watching him. He took out his gun ready to shoot. A dog limped into sight. The animal seemed to be begging for food. He shot the dog. He got in his car, circled the village before driving away. Something nagged at him. He had a gut feeling he was being watched. He dismissed the dog. He looked at the dress he stole form the shop and smiled.

Kiana, Jaro and Oskar left their hiding places at dusk. They met at the first farmhouse they ever entered. "That was a bit close," said Jaro. "I have a feeling the bastard is going to come back. I don't think we should come down here for a few days."

Two days later, two personnel carriers full of soldiers emptied out into the village. The soldiers entered each building, checked them out for any occupants and then stayed guard of that building. Oskar watched the occupation. He crawled back to the camp.

"No fires. The NAZIs are in the village and are occupying it."

"Fuck," swore Jaro. "What do they want from this place? There is nothing of value."

Kiana nodded. "The farms are left wild. Crops are growing back. Mr. Hitler doesn't have enough food for his soldiers. They have to scavenge like us."

"Come off it!" scoffed Oskar. "What war leader would not supply his army with food or other basics?"

"If the supplies are having trouble getting through, then that would be a problem," said Kiana.

She continued. "To quote Napoleon or was it Fredrick the Great, 'an army marches on its stomach,' or something like that. Hell, we were drained from not eating food. It is a weakness. How long do you think they will stay here?"

Jaro shrugged. "No idea. They must have a reason for coming to this place. We just have to wait and see. Keep alert and heads down. We don't want to end up in their army or be dead."

About mid-morning the next day, three personnel trucks rumbled into Donnersbach. The drivers and four soldiers per vehicle climbed out and stood guard. There was a hive of activity by those stationed in the village. Men were scurrying around while those higher up in command bellowed orders.

From their observation point, the trio could see boxes were being transferred from the less guarded transport vehicles to the new arrivals. Within an hour, the new arrivals drove off. Two hours later those stationed in Donnersbach were reduced in number by half. Jaro cursed in a whisper, "Get the hell out of Donnersbach. Count up how many soldiers are left." The group focused their attention on the German soldiers. Kiana said, "I think there are ten."

"I got twelve," said Jaro.

Oskar was quiet for a while. "I got about twelve. There could be more stationed inside."

"What did they load into those trucks? But more important where are they headed?" asked Kiana.

Oskar and Jaro shrugged. "What was in those trucks was important and where they are headed is unknown. We will never know."

The sound of twigs cracking behind them caused a startle. The trio spun around. A young German soldier no more than twenty had a gun pointed at them. The soldier held a finger to his lips. "Shh. I don't want to shoot my own countrymen." He ducked down and started to rip off his uniform showing signs of disgust at the same time.

"There are fifteen down there. Three are very forced conscripts like me. They kept on shooting people in my village. My mother pushed me forward as a volunteer in hope they would stop killing more of us. It worked. They stopped shooting the rest of my relatives. Bastards."

"What village was that?" asked Oskar.

" Loeben. It is to the south-east from here," replied the soldier. "My name is Lori. Lori Binder."

"I am Oskar Grat and this is my sister Kiana. And that is Jaro Bauer."

"Nice to meet you," said Lori. "How long have you been here and where are you from?"

Jaro wasn't sure if he should answer. He slowly volunteered the information. "We're from Weghaltz." Then he lied, "We have been here for two days."

Lori accepted the information knowing the stay was actually longer. He had walked past the camp and noted the equipment. He didn't argue. He was a newcomer to the group."

"What was in the guarded trucks and what was loaded into them?" asked Jaro.

Loris said as bitterness entered his voice, "Anything that looks like gold, silver and works of art. I overheard that Hitler gave orders for each village to be ransacked. The gold and silver are to be converted into bullion. They are thieves stealing anything and everything. Bastards."

"Where are they going with all of that?" asked Oskar.

"I wish I knew. But they are going west. As a guess to Switzerland. Who knows. They may even divert to somewhere else. For now, I know it is west. Switzerland has remained neutral so far in this war. I guess it is Switzerland; a safe haven for now. They will most likely change direction and go into Germany or some other unknown location. Whatever!our national treasures are disappearing. Bastards."

Kiana asked, "Won't you be missed if you don't go back?"

"For now, the others are making excuses for me to escape. If I go back, I am dead. They could also be killed for covering me. If an opportunity for them arises, they may join me later. Do you have any spare clothes? I hate this uniform."

Oskar pointed to the camp. I think my size is closest. The brown bag."

Lori slipped away and changed clothes.

The following morning, Lori spotted two soldiers leaving the camp. Both were headed in their direction. Lori whispered to Oskar. The soldier on the left is Austrian. His name is Paul. Another person from my village. The other is a NAZI. Be Careful."

As the two soldiers approached the camp, Paul looked around. After checking the surrounds for anyone on watch, he knifed the German soldier in ribs. The soldier fell to the ground gasping for air. Paul held his hand over the German's mouth and snarled. "You killed my wife and son. Now I kill you." Paul held the other hand over the German's nose until the soldier stopped moving. Paul stood back and rammed the German soldier's bayonet into his heart.

Lori came forward. He greeted Paul. "Nice job. One down and far too many to go."

Paul looked up in surprise. "I thought you would have gone further by now. Where did you get those clothes?" Lori pointed towards the farmhouses. "I stole them from a farmhouse. I knew they would come in handy."

"What did you do with your uniform?" asked Paul.

"It's still with me. Why?"

"Help me bury this shit and I want you to come back with me….in uniform. We are going to say, Herman deserted. This will cover your absence as well. The higher ups are getting suspicious. They won't expect you to be visible again. Then you can come back here and for God's sake run."

Under Paul's direction, Herman was stripped of his clothes and buried in a shallow grave not far from where he was murdered. "Take his clothes back to the village. When you get to the first farmhouse, take a piece of civilian clothing. We make it look like Herman stole the clothes and was careless to leave a piece behind."

Lori and Paul headed back to the village and reported Herman deserted. Paul placed Herman's uniform on the table which was now being used as a desk. "Herman deserted. He left his uniform and dropped an item of clothing in the rush to leave. We chased him for a bit, but he was too fast for us. He is injured from a fight we had before he ran away." Paul pointed to the blood. "He still managed to escape. Sorry."

The Sergeant screamed his disappointment and then swung around to Lori. "Just where have you been? You have missed two rounds of duty."

Lori looked at the sergeant square in the face. "Searching the hills for escaped villagers. No one is hiding in the mountains."

"What made you take on that initiative?" asked the sergeant who was slowing calming down.

"I saw some footprints behind a barn, so I traced them back to the foothills. I found the farmer dead.

He died of some gun wounds," lied Lori.

The sergeant nodded. "That is only half the time. What happened next?"

"As I said, I searched looking for more clues of escapees. Nothing. My search was thorough. I also helped Paul to search for Herman when he escaped."

The sergeant waved his hand to dismiss Lori and Paul. The sergeant cursed under his breath, "He isn't the first and he won't be the last. He will be shot when captured."

Late in the night, Lori and Paul headed for the hills. Lori led Paul away from the camp. They rested until the sun woke them up. Standing over them was Oskar holding two cups of water. Paul recoiled in fright. "Morning. Sorry no coffee or tea."

Lori introduced Paul. "I saw your handiwork yesterday. Nice," said Oskar. Jaro came towards them holding two changes of clothes. "Sorry, not much choice," he said. "Get the uniforms off.

We are packed and ready to go."

"Where are we going?" asked Paul.

"To Italy. The Fascists run the place, but we can pretend to be civilians and if you wish Germans.

Keep the uniforms. They may come in handy. That will depend on the situation we are in," said Oskar.

Chapter 9
Klagenfrut To Villach, Austria.
To Undine, Italy.

The group of five began to cross the country by walking parallel to the roads. This permitted cover for a quick response to any passing vehicle. Ducking down and observing what was coming in either direction was a survival tactic. German vehicles laden with soldiers and equipment often drove past. It was rare to see any civilian vehicles and when they did see them, they were loaded with people escaping with limited private possessions.

Fruit trees growing near the roads were thinning out as they moved further south. The fruit from the sparsely spaced trees were collected for a later time. Small stray farm animals or rabbits were caught and consumed as the group walked along the uneven and bushy ground.

A house or two in the distance were observed before approaching. Most times they were deserted. The houses were checked for clothes, food, water and money of any denomination. Any new clothes which fitted were kept, and the old ones washed or discarded as the situation dictated. New clothes and baths recharged restored their spirits.

With extra warm clothes and fresh and thicker blankets, they headed over the Alps and into the town of Klagenfurt, one of the largest towns in southern Austria. From here, they hitched a ride on the back of a train wagon which took then to Villach. Villach was the largest town closest to northern Italy. In Villach, they rested from their travels.

Sleeping under cover through the mornings, they broke into isolated homes and stole cash and food at night. Clothes left overnight on a line, at times disappeared with them. In the afternoons they scouted for information regarding transport out of Villach. Luck would have it, a bus going to Udine in North Italy. The bus was going to leave the following day at eleven in the morning..

On board, they sat in different seats. It was a security measure. Oskar sat in a seat behind Kiana to keep watch. Lori sat directly opposite her across the aisle. Jaro sat opposite Oskar. Paul sat in front of Kiana. Kiana's and Oskar's hearts took a leap when a uniformed German soldier sat beside Kiana. She turned her head to the scenery outside: people bustling past doing their everyday chores were a distraction to her sudden stress.

The German soldier was silent until the bus had exited the town's perimeter. Oskar kept glaring, almost drilling a hole with his eyes into the German's head. The Soldier turned around sensing someone was watching him. Oskar offered a smile and nodded. The German just nodded back Then he looked in his backpack for something to read. Lori looked across the aisle in anticipation something would happen. Nothing did. He relaxed. He looked to Kiana. Another set of protective eyes.

After twenty minutes, the soldier tried to make conversation with Kiana. Oskar's, Jaro's, Paul's and Lori's ears pricked. Kiana kept staring at the window refusing to look at the soldier as he spoke. He eventually got the message. He was silent for a while. The soldier stood up and brought down his travel bag. After he removed a pen and a notebook, he settled down again.

From his position, Lori could see the soldier writing on the pad. The first page was an address. Nothing else. The next page contained a start of a letter. The soldiers continued the unfinished task. When the letter was finished, the soldier tore out the address and tucked it away in his pocket. The notepad and pen went back into the overhead bag.

Again, the soldier tried to engage in a conversation with Kiana. The soldier didn't want to be ignored this time. He said softly but not soft enough not to let Paul, Lori, Jaro or Oskar to miss what he had to say.

"Fräulein, we have been sitting side by side for closeto an hour. I just want to make general conversation. My name is Louis." He held his hand out for a shake.

 Instead, Kiana turned her back
and kept looking out of the window. "I am not interested in any conversation with any strangers.

Please leave me alone."

The soldier shrugged. "Okay. Here take this." He handed her the address on the paper. She returned it and placed it on his lap. He picked it up and said, "This is an address to a party. We need more girls to come. Take it. You can make up your own mind. The party is tomorrow night. It starts at seven p.m. I would like to see you there." He placed the address on her lap. Kiana knocked it to the floor where it stayed for the next thirty minutes. In that thirty-minute period, the vibration of the bus going uphill, slowly moved the note towards Oskar.

Using his left foot, Oskar dragged the note towards himself, before picking it up. He opened the note and memorized the address. He displayed the note across the aisle to where Jaro was sitting. Jaro copied the address onto a wrapper from a snack he purchased before getting on the bus. He shoved the wrapper into his pocket. Oskar stood up to lean over the seat in front of him. He acted innocently. "Sir, is this yours? I found it on the floor."

The German looked at the note. Gave a nod and said, "Thank you. How careless of me."

Oskar gave a quick glance to Kiana who continued to exercise great control by continuing to look out of the window. As he sat back in his seat, Oskar thought, *Kiana. Well done. It could have been a disaster if this jerk decided to be forceful. You didn't give him a chance.* Oskar gave a slight smirk.

Lori and Jaro turned to look at Oskar. They had blank faces, but their eyes said it all.

The bus pulled into the centre of Udine. Everyone alighted taking their belongings with them. The group of five still pretended not to know each other. With most of the other passengers, they moved down the street. The German soldier again approached Kiana. He handed her the same note paper and tried a bit of flattery. "Please come to this address at seven p.m. tomorrow. It is a party."

Kiana refused to take the note. "No Thank you. I have other arrangements. She looked around as if trying to see anyone she knew. Paul took a gamble. He dropped his bag and walked towards her. He gave a big smile. "Ah! There you are. I couldn't see you. Did you have a good time at your mother's home?"

Kiana played along. "Yes." She gave him a hug and planted a kiss on his cheek. "Have most of the wedding arrangements been finalized? Mum helped me make the dress over the last week. She is going to do the final touches and bring it with her in two days' time."

Paul played along. "Yes. The chapel is booked. Flowers are organized and the venue for the small reception has been confirmed."

The German soldier muttered to himself, "No wonder she ignored me. The pretty fräulein is getting married." He looked at Paul and thought, *he looks a bit old for her. What a shame she is wasting her youth on that man."*

Watching on were Lori, Jaro and Oskar. They stared at the event. Both acted so well, that Oskar had to shake himself and wandered if Paul had really set his eyes on Kiana. The soldier moved on. Lori picked up Paul's bag that was dumped on the ground just over a metre away. The group reformed after checking the soldier was well away.

Oskar gave a sigh of relief. "That was close. Darn good acting you two. I almost believed it myself."

Paul grinned. "I did some amateur stuff. Some plays for the local villages. Entertainment is self-made in Loeben. That is a small town where Lori and I are from." Lori nodded his agreement. "It is doing art, playing music and a bit of stage stuff at Easter and Christmas. The usual thing is to entertain the children. Over the years, Paul has been in every show and been in every role over five years. Costumes were just a mish-mash of anything that could be found."

Lori said, "I think we should get the hell out of here. There is a German jeep coming down the street with you know who inside." The group went into the nearest shop, a barber's shop. Kiana felt a bit uncomfortable.

The barber looked up. "Hello. Gee all you men could do with a professional shave and cut. This is the right place. Thank the young lady for dragging you in. You really need a tidy up."

"How much for cuts and trims?" asked Oskar.

"One Reichsmark for the beards. Two for your long hair," said the barber.

Oskar sat down first. "I have three Reichmarks. The small beard I am starting to grow and a trim to the collar."

Next was Lori, followed by Paul and Jaro.

The group was about to leave when the barber said, "The young lady brought you all in. I will give her a free hair wash. Do you want a free wash?"

Kiana hesitated at first. She glanced to Oskar and then to Jaro who was nodding approval.

"A free wash it is. Thank you."

When they were finished, the barber ushered them out. He noticed them loitering, deciding what to do next. He opened the door. "If you have nowhere to go or don't know of any place, may I suggest the hostel two blocks down. But be careful. German soldiers frequently go there. If that does not appeal, there is a large house just two blocks away from the Casello, on the other side of Udine. It has been converted into a guest home since the war started." The barber gave the addresses.

The group moved to the hostel. Through the timber and glass doors, German soldiers were seen, two were pawing local girls. The group agreed it wasn't the place for them. They walked for nearly twenty minutes to the guest house. "Much better," said Paul. "Let's check it out first and the cost per room."

Lori and Paul checked the surrounds while Jaro checked out the costs of the rooms. Jaro returned. "A room for each of us will drain all our finances. We will have to share one or two rooms."
"How much for the rooms?" asked Kiana.
"A double is five Reichsmarks or ten Lira. A family with two beds – one single and one double, is six Reichsmarks or twelve Lira."
"We are used to bunking in together. We take the double and the family rooms." They looked up when they saw Lori and Paul returning.
"All clear. No soldiers. Apparently, they do come for overnight stays and bring their lady friends with them. It is random. If we stay in our rooms after a meal, we should be able to avoid them," said Paul.

The group were in their rooms. Lori, Paul and Jaro were in the family room while Oskar and Kiana were in the double. The place was quiet until nine-thirty. German soldiers noisily walked down the passageway while singing as loud as they could. Third Reich songs blared out of their drunken mouths. Oskar held onto Kiana's arm pulling her back from any temptation to go to the door to voice her annoyance. There was loud knocking on the door. The handle was twisted. The sound of a key trying to enter the lock was heard. Failure. Swearing filtered through the door. Kiana gasped in fear. Oskar held a finger to his mouth. "Shhh. Quiet. The bastard will go away."

The drunken soldier swore louder, banged the door a few more times before another drunken voice distracted him. All was quiet after a few noises that sounded like a person stumbling.

Early in the morning, the group met behind a fountain in the medium sized, well maintained rear garden. "Where do we go from here?" asked Jaro.

Paul looked at the crude tourist map he took off the front desk. "We go to…. Let's look around before deciding. "

SWITZERLAND
AUSTRIA
VILLACH
LAKE COMO
LECCO
UDINE
CHIASSO
CERNOBBIO
MASLIANICO
COMO
PALMANOVA
SAN
BARTOLOMEO
PORTOGUARO
MEDA
MILAN
VENICE
FARRARE
SAN MARINO
BOLOGNA
MARCERATA
ITALY
TERMI
ADRIATIC SEA
ROME
VATICAN
BARI
GROTTAMINARDA
MONOPOLI
BRINDISI
NAPLES
ITALY AND NEIGHBOURING
COUNTRIES IN 1938.
SICILY
Switzerland
Austria
Hungary
Roma
Italy
Yugoslavia
Bulga
DURESS
Albania
VLORE
Greece

Chapter 10
Udine to Rome.

With meager belongings, food and water, the group explored the town of Udine which is set in the mountains. Lori pulled out a compass to help them navigate the town when they came to the realization, the tourist map was next to hopeless as most of the nearby streets were not marked and tourist sites were misplaced. Armed with a compass stolen from a drunken German soldier lying on the passageway floor of the guest house, Lori laughed when he recalled how he obtained the compass. He saw a soldier holding the compass in his hand. He told the others, "The soldier was so drunk, he was trying to navigate his way to his room. He didn't even budge even when others stepped over him to continue their way down the passageway."

The group ventured towards a park and found a bench. Here they sat looking at the unfamiliar surroundings while eating their rations. Passers-by would give them a wide birth as they looked very much like the unwelcomed gypsies that filtered through the town. Strangers were rarely approached unless they exuberated wealth displayed by expensive clothing and cars.

After eating, Jaro laid down on the patchy dirt and grassed ground. He looked at the sky as he said, "We better get some money. Earn it somehow. I don't think we could or should break into houses. They are too close to each other for a start. No cover."

Paul agreed with the assessment. "I don't think basking will do the trick either. People are avoiding us. Look how they divert their paths away from us." The group watched.

A policeman approached. "You gypsies have to move on. People are complaining."

Paul was taken aback. "We are not gypsies. We are Austrians. We are broke. We have chewed through all our finances just to get here. We want to work."

The policeman asked, "Can I see some papers?"

Jaro said, "We don't have any." Then he added a lie, "At the last check point at the border, the soldiers didn't return our papers. Other people lost theirs at the same time. The driver asked for the papers to be returned, but the soldiers refused and threatened the driver with a rifle. The driver drove off with all the passengers inside."

The policeman rolled his eyes and whispered under his breath, "So much for the alliance we have."

Lori said, "We have no money and nowhere to go."

The policeman sighed and looked around. "This damned war is making everyone destitute. Still, you can't stay here." He pointed to the other side of the park. Go that way. There is a place where other homeless people live. Look after your belongings as they tend to disappear."

In the makeshift refugee camp, the conditions were bad. The lucky ones had a tent. Most were sleeping and cooking anything in the open air. The smell made the group gasp. Lori pointed to a small clearing slightly away from the main group. I think our best chances are there."

When they tried to settle in for the night, Oskar decided to take the first watch. People were always milling around, thieving when the opportunity allows. Whispers at times turned into shouts of rage and accusations. The pit of society displayed itself.

The following morning the group heard the sound of a train whistle. Lori said, "It's a train ride out of this hell hole."

Paul made enquiries about trains going further into Italy. "One cargo train having three carriages will be coming through close to eleven p.m. It is a short stop to refill with coal and water, the necessary fuel for the old-style trains." Jaro thought, every mode of transport in Udine was at least twenty years behind the rest of the world. The next stop was Palmanova. Jaro hoped that this town would be more modern.

At ten-thirty, the group was at the station. They took position close to the refueling siding. The train slowly puffed its way to a stop. Station hands busied themselves with the usual tasks. Lori was first to venture out. Then one by one the group approached the train. The doors were securely locked. They were never going to enter any carriage. Paul pointed to the roof. It was going to be a roof ride. Each positioned themselves along the roof and then laid flat. The train gave a departure whistle. The wheels clunked into motion. Oskar was thankful all were on board, and no one spotted them going on top of the carriage. If they did see the group climb up, they ignored the incident. No challenges and now it was time to hang on for dear life.

It was hours later when the group climbed down from the roof of the carriages. When the train came to a stop, they crept away hoping no one would spot them. Their luck didn't hold out.

They had just jumped the fence when armed Italian soldiers pointed their rifles at them.

The corporal spoke. The group didn't reply. Only Jaro understood isolated Italian words but not enough to make any sense as to what the soldiers were trying to say. The soldiers signaled for them to raise their arms. They complied. Another patted them down and said to the corporal, "They are unarmed."

The corporal looked at the group. "Where are you from?"

No reply. One soldier stepped forward and spoke in broken German. "Where are you from?"

Oskar replied, "Austria."

"Take them to the police station. Let the police handle these people," said the corporal.

With the guns nudging them for two blocks, they were directed into a building. The corporal gave a quick explanation and left.

The police captain looked the group up and down. He guided them into a cell which was designed for two people. The five were cramped into one. After an hour, Paul was removed and taken into an empty room. A middle-aged woman wearing a grey skirt and a blouse sat across the table. Her long hair was done neatly tied into a traditional bun. Her thick black glasses dominated her face.

She sat beside the captain.

"I am an interpreter, German and Italian. I advise you to answer the questions truthfully. It will save time and pain. Do you understand?"

Paul nodded.

"Where did you all come from?"

"Austria."

"Where in Austria?"

"Three are from the village of Weghaltz near Salzburg. Myself and the other one further south in Loeben"

"How did you meet?"

Paul hesitated. "By accident in Donnersbach. We literally ran into each other while trying to scramble for fruit on a tree. We were all starving. At first, we fought over the fruit but then we realized we were just as hungry as each other."

"Where are your families? Surely you could have stayed with them instead of running away."

Paul became annoyed, but he knew he had to control himself. "They are all dead. Shot."

The interpreter relayed all she heard. The captain asked, "What are you doing in Italy?"

"Trying to find work. There is no work in Austria. All the jobs are gone. Farms are not producing. Factories are closed. Many shops are closed. So, we thought we could try our luck here.?"

After the captain heard the translation he said, "Get your friends together, including the girl.

Tonight, all of you will be transported to the Royal Guards or the new National Army as they now call it. You have just joined the Italian army. The girl has just joined the army nurses. It appears you didn't want to join the German army, so you can join the Italian one." Paul gasped. He wondered if the German uniform still in his bag would be discovered. A deserter here would be returned and then either interned or shot by the Germans. The captain called the police officers standing guard outside the room.

Within minutes of returning to the cell, Paul gave them the news. The looks of horror were written on their faces. Kiana was going to be separated from Oskar and God knows where. They were going into the Italian army. Paul was upset as he mentioned, "The Royal Guards is a good way to be killed. They are not trained in war and the army is ill-equipped. We are doomed."

Lori added to the doom and gloom. "If we are assigned to Africa, namely Egypt, we won't last more than a week. The French and the British are superior in arms and training."

"Do you know anything about the nurses?" asked Kiana.

"Not a thing. At least you will be slightly away from the bullets," said Lori.

"That is not much comfort," she retorted.

Under guard and with several other people, the group was herded onto a train. Soldiers acting as guards, supervised the new recruits which were no more than a bunch of foreigners who were in the wrong place at the wrong time. Other rounded up foreigners were with them in the same carriage. One French man who could speak some Italian explained though broken German. "I overheard, we get trained up and go to Ethiopia. Mussolini and King Emmanuel began a war in Ethiopia, Africa. For what reason, I don't understand. The place is a hell hole of jungle and wild animals."

Lori wasn't impressed with the thought of going to war in a far-off place which met nothing to him or the others in his group. The person trying to explain their fate added as he looked at Kiana, "I am not sure to pity you or feel happy for you. Your chances of going to North Africa is slim. You could end up in a field hospital or be stationed at a fascist home serving the upper echelons of their society. They like pretty servants. That is the worst scenario for you."

Oskar suddenly became hyper protective. Little sister forced into whore service disgusted him to the core. Fear for his sister's safety filled his eyes. He held her close fearing if he would let go, she would become an instant victim.

The train came to a stop in Portogruaro. It was a refueling station. Soldiers alighted first for a short break. The rear carriage was decoupled. The people inside were ordered out and piled into the very few Italian People carrier trucks. They disappeared.

Refueled, the train snaked down to a town, Marghera, the western outskirts of Venice. Marghera was just another fuel stop. No soldiers or enforced passengers got off the train. There were two more fuel stops. The first was at Ferrare and shortly after, a city called Bologna.

Then the train travelled to San Marino. Soldiers alighted; new ones climbed on. The second carriage was decoupled. Again, the passengers disappeared. The carriage which had Oskar and his group were ordered to rest on the carriage. Through one of the other passengers, they learned they were heading to Rome.

Two more refueling stops. One at Marcerta where Italian soldiers climbed on board a passenger carriage. Two carriages of men sat almost silent. Whispers of their discontent at being conscripted in a war they didn't want or understand, filled the carriage.

The next stop was Termi, a city which was almost in the centre of Italy. More soldiers in passenger coaches were added with a carriage full of armory. The train puffed on to Rome.

In Rome, the soldiers were driven away in army transport vehicles. The carriage with the armory disappeared with them.

The men in the now smelly carriage where Oskar's group was herded into one building. The few women into another. All the men were processed; given documents of their recruitment into the Italian army where they would receive rudimentary training before being shipped off to wherever they were needed. The group split and fears of not being united became very real.

The women left with another set of papers indicating they were either nurses or hostesses. Kiana cringed. Her nightmare was realized. She would become a hostess and be appointed to a motel in Rome, just three blocks away from the Colosseum. All hostesses would be escorted by armed guards. Being separated from Oskar gave her no opportunity to tell him where she was going. Like the other women, she sat in silent fear all the way to her Italian posting.

At the Royal Guards barracks, Lori, Paul, Jaro and Oskar underwent training. They were horrified at what they saw. The barrack buildings contained fifty men per dormitory with only two bathrooms per building. The food was all pasta based washed down with either water or old red wines. Lori referred to the wine as the gut rotter. The training consisted of no more than vigorous physical exercise due to a lack of equipment and qualified staff. They were given guns to shoot at targets but there were no bullets. The Italian army was short on ammunition and what was available was reserved front line.

Chapter 11.
Front Line, Albania.

After training, Oskar, Jaro and Lori were assigned to Albania. From there, Italy launched attacks on Greece. It was one of the first attacks ordered by Mussolini. The superior British air force bombed the Italians on the front line. British and French ships bombed the area form the ocean. The British army more so than the French, sprayed their more modern and much superior machine guns in the ill-equipped Italians. Again, Mussolini requested German assistance to win this battle. He had to save face. The British and the French were winning to leave the Italians with heavy losses and Hitler fuming at the ill-conceived attack on Greece.

In the battle, Paul, Lori, Jaro and Oskar just sat down in the trenches holding their rifles across their chest. Popping your head up to try to shoot was a guaranteed death sentence. Paul crawled a few metres away reach a dying Italian soldier. He tried to take whatever bullets the dying man had. A grenade blasted. Paul was gone. Lori looked on in horror. His long-term friend who he considered as an older brother had died. Mud and blood splattered onto Lori's face. He wiped it away. It was then what he saw, Paul's body minus some parts. He was shocked and silent for a few seconds then tears poured down his face. Then anger spread throughout his body. He tried to stand up to take revenge, but Oskar and Jaro pinned him down. Lori screamed out, "I want to kill those bastards. Get off me!"

Jaro said between gritted teeth and fighting to keep Lori down. "He will go to heaven for sure. We are in hell. We got to sit tight and wait until dark to get out of this place." It took Jaro and Oskar all their strength to keep Lori down. They stayed down. The three men huddled together with arms linked over each shoulder. Not a word was spoken as artillery fired overhead. As dusk came, the artillery slowed down. Isolated gun shots and a blast from a grenade pierced the air. Flashes of light in the growing darkness made sure the trio stayed put until there was unguaranteed silence.

Oskar whispered as he slowly released his grip on Lori and Jaro, "Let's get the hell out of here. Desert. This is not our war. Get your bags and check for civilian clothes. Take the uniforms off as soon as we get to some place that looks safe. Get Paul's bag. I want the German uniform. It could come in handy."

On their stomachs, the men crawled in mud and over numerous dead contorted bodies. Anything that looked like ammunition was pilfered until they could carry no more. Containers of water were taken and consumed. The empty container was discarded beside the owner. For nearly two hours, the group slid over the landscape towards a farm. The Albanian farm was long abandoned. Carefully the trio searched the premises, taking small denomination coins and any hint of jewelry which could be pawned later. The Italian uniforms were taken off. New civilian clothes which had an approximate fit were put on after a bath. All the Italian uniforms and the German uniforms were washed and dried.
Their army issue backpacks were cleaned and stuffed with the uniforms. Rested, cleaned and fed, they planned their next move.

While they were making their plans to desert, Jaro heard on the radio that the Germans were going to assist the Italians with the campaign. "I didn't get all the information. My Italian isn't that great yet. There was something about Germans coming this way because of some alliance with Germany. The bungling Italians have basically forced the Germans to help them out."

"That is all we need," said Oskar. "We need another German uniform, just in case things get problematic."

 "The closest seaport is Durres. It is still in Albania. If we can get there, we get a boat and sail down to Greece."

"How do we get a boat? I doubt any fisherman would hire any out to us?" said Jaro.

"We steal one," said Oskar.

"And what do we do in Greece?" asked Jaro not really sure if that was a good plan since the British, French and the Italians had bombarded the place and with the Germans on the way. It would be rougher and no doubt more dangerous.

"We sail across to Italy and find Kiana. I am not going to make anyone come to look for her. We can go our separate ways. I just have to get Kiana to safety."

"Exactly where is safety?" asked Jaro.

"Hiding in the mountains, any mountains and living off the land like we did before," said Oskar.

Chapter 12
Durres, Albania to Italy.

The trio sneaked out of the farmhouse in the early evening. While walking parallel to the road to Durres, they only paused when they saw or heard any vehicle. They only took cover once. It was an jeep chugging along. Black smoke poured out of the muffler. It was some Italian colonel being chauffeured. A German colonel was beside the Italian colonel. The trio glanced at each other. As if reading each other's mind, they squatted down behind some bushes, raised their rifles. Oskar, Jaro and Lori took aim. The driver and the two colonels each took a bullet to the chest. The car veered out of control to hit a tree. The tree in response dropped some flowers and immature fruit over the dead.

The trio advance with their guns pointed at the jeep. No movement was detected. The bodies were removed. They tried the uniformson. They didn't fit that well. Too big. They were discarded after all military emblems were removed. The car was pushed away from the tree and examined. The only damage was the passenger side doors. The front had a minor dint. The engine was tested. It clicked over. The jolt the car received somehow dislodged some dirt clogging the internals. No smoke poured out of the back. The car purred its way towards the coastal town of Durres.

The trio drove the car to the small fishing town of Duress. A small crowd gathered around the car, a novelty for the town. The trio alighted and pushed through the small gathering crowd.

They approached several boat owners and tried to make a deal. Only one person was interested.

The car and a necklace found in the Albanian farmhouse was swapped for a small boat complete with a small outboard motor and sails incase the fuel ran out. The trio paid extra for the rare fuel commodity, bought food and any other provisions before heading down the coast towards Vlore, the largest of the southern coastal villages in Albania.

They pulled into port. Rations needed to be purchased. The small outboard motor was pawned. Fuel too expensive to purchase. It also required maintenance and none on board knew how to fix the engine. With not quite enough provisions, it was supplemented with a few stolen items from the back of some shops. The trio set sale across the Adriatic Sea towards the closet Italian coastal town of Brindisi.

Halfway through the voyage, a storm raged. The trio fought the powerful winds and the waves that
washed over the boat creating slippery surfaces. At one point, the boats threatened to capsize but the combined strength of the men straightened the boat. For twelve hours the men battled the sea. Then calm. The sails were damaged along with the cabin. Water in cabin was painfully bailed out a bucket at a time. The food supply was diminished. Two of the three storage cupboards had busted open and the contents mixed with the ocean water.

Jaro tried to get a reading as to where they were. "Lori. Do you have that compass you stole form the German soldier?"
Lori searched his belongings and found the compass. "Here."
Jaro did some calculations. The storm blew them off course. They were further north than expected. "I think we are now closer to Monopoli than Brindisi." He checked the map. Oskar and Lori gathered round. Oskar said, "Put on Italian uniforms. The cover

story is we were doing coastal surveillance for Mussolini. The storm damaged the ship."

Chapter 13
Monopoli, Italy.

The boat limped into Monopoli. The trio in Italian uniforms alighted and did their best to look very official. They strode to the nearest bar in a bid to glean information and a drink or two. The locals watched on with curiosity and nudged each other who was going to approach the three out of place soldiers.

Jaro spoke the best Italian of the trio. He asked a local if there was any transport to Rome. The bar tender looked at the trio and shook his head. He felt something was off. He couldn't put his finger on it. He replied, "The train to Rome leaves every day at one p.m." The trio looked at their watches and guzzled their drinks. Jaro asked, "Which way to the station?"
The bartender asked, "How did you three get here?"
Jaro quickly explained, "We were at sea for Mussolini. Our boat is almost wrecked in the storm. We need to get to Rome as fast as possible."
The bartender spat at them. "Mussolini is one big bastard, and you work for him?"
Jaro quickly added, "Unfortunately, he is our leader and stuffing up because he isn't getting good information. That is why there are so many deaths."
The bar tender was skeptical. "The station is three blocks down on the right side of the street when you get there, turn left for three more blocks. You can see the station."

The trio walked quickly through the door and down the street. They found the station with ten minutes to spare.

They approached the railway guard who looked the trio up and down. "The train comes in ten minutes. I advise you to buy some food. Your passage maybe free but there is no food or drinks available." He pointed to the only café on the platform. It was doing a roaring trade as there was no competition. The trio bought a standard snack pack which consisted of a piece of fruit, two small tomatoes, buttered bread with a slice of salami. It came with a mini-bottle of local wine. When the train arrived and after refueling, the passengers were checked for tickets, but the soldiers were ushered on. no ticket required. Lori, Oskar and Jaro found an empty cabin and settled in.

The train did a 'milkrun' as Oskar called it. It stopped at nearly all stations going from Monopoli to Naples; refuel, passengers got on and off at the different stops. The trio bought some food at Grottaminarda, was the only town with a small café on the platform. It was the last of their finances.

The train pulled into Naples. The civilians and soldiers bustled about. The trio spoke softly in an alcove close to the men's restroom. Oskar spoke first, "We need to get some money. Do we pick-pocket or rob a few places?"
"Well, we know soldiers travel free. If we stay a day or two, we rob a few places. It is annoying that the town is bigger than the others we have been to. The buildings are so close to each other. We have to be very careful on what we select to rob. I am not comfortable about pick-pocking unless it is a situation which reduces a capture risk."

The trio left the station and stood on the street trying to decide what they should do. While they were waiting an army transport vehicle pulled up. They were ordered to get on board. They were driven to an army barracks. Now among so many new soldiers, they felt quite at home. They joined in with the usual physical training, the fake gun practice and slept on bunker beds. At least this barrack had only thirty people per room but still only two bathrooms.

A major noted the trio were different. They showed some experience. He called them over. "You three which stick together like glue, where have you served?" Lori answered, "Albania. We are survivors of Albania." The major smiled. "Good. You can teach these soldiers how to survive. Tomorrow, you take over the fitness classes. The other trainers will try to get some ammunition for target practice. I will see you on the assembly area with the other troops at six a.m. After one hour, they can have breakfast. Then more training for three more hours."

Lori, Jaro and Oskar walked quickly away from the major. The trio discussed what they would do in training.

At six a.m., the men assembled on small assembly area. The major bellowed the introductions and what was expected. Lori took one third of the group to the far side of the facility. Jaro took another group to the opposite side. Oskar's group stayed where they were. Each gave the usual exercise drill for the first twenty minutes. Then each gave them specific skills, crawling on their stomach, climbing walls, camouflaging. After breakfast, the groups rotated but only focusing on the extra skill for ten minutes. Then it was another rotation. After that the groups united.

Lori explained the final two and a half hours. "This time we are going to mix you into two groups. One group will be the enemy and the other our side. At random, Lori asked forty soldiers to take their hats off and to stand aside. He said, "You are the enemy. Your leader will be a Corporal." Jaro stepped forward. "I will be supervising. The home group is to try to stop the enemy. When you capture someone from the opposite team, tie up their hands. Then at eleven o'clock, march your prisoner to this courtyard. The team that wins will have the most captured soldiers." The soldiers before them looked a bit blank and wondered what these three people were talking about or knew about war. Each soldier was given a piece of rope to bind their prisoner. The two groups dispersed for the bushland at the far end of the grounds.

While the two groups under supervision played war games, Oskar reentered the barracks and rummaged through as many wallets in as many barracks as possible. He was careful not to remove all the cash. He aimed for the smaller notes and the larger coins. It wasn't enough to be greatly noticeable but enough to make all think they had less than what they thought. He stuffed the loot away in a calico bag similar to what the banks were using for coins. He would be sharing the loot with Lori and Jaro.

After one and a half hours Oskar was outside again waiting for Lori and Jaro with their charges to return. It didn't take long for men to appear. He counted the groups of two. All were accounted for. Oskar looked at the results. He shook his head. Only four 'enemy' were captured. Ten 'soldiers' were captured by the so-called enemy. The entire group looked exhausted. Looks of pointlessness were written across the faces of all. Oskar said, "That was not even a test or survival. All of you have failed. The captured people on both sides, did you try to escape?" All he could see were people shaking their heads. Oskar shouted at the group as the major returned, "That was appalling. We will do this again tomorrow. Dismissed for lunch."
The major asked Oskar, "What was appalling?"
"We did a mock-up battle. The home defense team lost with ten captured. They only captured four of the pretend enemy."
The major looked at Oskar. "They are here to learn, not play games. You and your friends were supposed to keep their fitness up!"

Oskar looked the major in the face. "Battle requires thinking to stay alive. That is how we survived Albania." The major didn't like the retort. He had never heard such an idea. He yelled back, "You three will be assigned a different task- shooting. You are incompetent at drill work. You take over shooting tomorrow. Each soldier will be allocated ten bullets. Make sure they hit the target. Can you manage that?" Lori saluted and said in a sharp manner, "Yes Sir!" Oskar and Jaro copied.

The next morning the soldiers assembled in the usual area. Jaro, Oskar and Lori were absent. The major looked around and sent a trainee to search their barracks. The soldier returned and said sheepishly and knowing he would get an earful, "The instructors from yesterday are not in the barracks. Their belongings are gone." As the major yelled his disgust and annoyance, the assembled men cringed knowing all too well the day ahead was going to be punishing. The major's anger would be taken out on them. The major made all to do star jumps non-stop until he returned from his office. From his office he could see which men were slacking off. He used a loudspeaker to remind the men not to stop jumping. In his office, the major issued three Absent Without Leave notices to the handful of military police.

When the military police received the order, they reluctantly began gathering their equipment and a rundown jeep to travel through the city. The jeep was an unreliable car and fuel was short. If they ran out of fuel, they would have to pay for the refill out of their own pockets. They knew from experience, they would never be reimbursed. They would have to search the city knowing there was only half a tank, and the base was dry. No prefilling. In case the jeep stopped, the box of tools on the back seat was supposed to help to restart the jeep if any mechanical problem arose. That was often.

When away from the barracks, one of the policemen took out a cigarette. He offered one to the driver who was more than happy to receive it. The one who brought out the cigarettes said, "Pull over at the coffee shop. The escapees are long gone. Good luck to them. None of us want this war. Mussolini should get off his own backside and go to the colosseum and fight it out with whoever rubs him up the wrong way. Just like they did in ancient times. At least the rest of us can live in peace." He blew out a stream of smoke. "The coffee shop there will do. Pull over but park this heap around the corner."

Three hours later and only going to a handful of places and spending an hour of that time at each, the two military police returned to base. They reported back that nothing was found..
The major huffed and muttered, "Fuck. Those men will go to prison when captured." He stumped out a cigarette on his desk in the ashtray overflowing with ashes and stubs. "Fuck," he whispered to himself. "I have better things to do than chase after run-aways."

Oskar, Jaro and Lori had changed into civilian clothes. They found a rundown market and purchased supplies for the next trip. They moved freely in the crowd knowing all too well, they blended in and only speaking when necessary. When they had finished, they went to the train station to check out times for trains to Rome. The train was going to leave in one hour.

Ten minutes before the expected departure, the trio switched back into their Italian uniforms. The train pulled in ten minutes late. The trio climbed on and found two seats facing each other. Not a word was spoken.
The conductor walked by and ignored the trio. It was free passage for soldiers. He didn't even approach them. He felt sad that so many young men had gone to war and so many have never returned. He gave a faint smile as he walked past.

Chapter 14
Rome, Italy.

The train pulled into Rome's largest station. People were moving about at a much faster pace when compared to their country cousins. The trio looked at the crowd studying which way they were moving. Oskar pointed. "Over there. The exit." They quickly walked in that direction. No one bothered to stop them or speak to them. That suited the trio.

Outside on the street an army jeep pulled up. The trio were waved over. "Can I see your transfer papers?" asked the sergeant in the passenger's seat. The trio looked at each other. Oskar said in broken Italian, "Got none. The barracks didn't give us any."
The sergeant rolled his eyes. "Slack bastards. Get in. We will drive you to the barracks."
Jaro said, "No we are on leave. We are going to the bar across the road. We have three days off, so we are going to use them."
The sergeant nodded as his brain ticked over, *I don't blame them.* He drove off.

Jaro, Oskar and Lori walked across the road and looked in. The place was busy. They could hide in the crowd while watching every female going in and out and going in any direction. Two German soldiers sat in a corner talking softly between themselves. They looked at the trio and hailed them over. Soldiers on the same side were welcome. Uniforms didn't matter.

One German introduced himself, "I am Hans. This is Walther. Come and join us. Err sorry, our Italian is not that good."
Jaro smiled. "That is okay. We speak German reasonably well."
Jar, Oskar and Lori sat down. They swapped war stories. Except for Paul, the trio had survived the badly thought-out attack on Greece from the borders of Albania. The Germans were on rest and recreation leave after spending six months on the Western Front, South France. The group disbanded after an hour.

Oskar approached the bar for details about hostesses in the place and in surrounding hotels, motels, and bars in general. He was given a rough list of likely locations. Oskar wrote the names as the barman named them. Oskar made up his mind he was going to visit all on the list and any new names which pop up either by being named by the bar tenders or if spotted in the streets.

When they visited each of these locations, they would ask of other possible locations where hostesses were available. With each visitation, the trio were edging closer and closer towards the centre of Rome.

At one of the most prestigious motels in Rome, The Albergo Maestoso, in the neighbourhood of Villa Ludoiusi, the trio arrived at the front doors. They stood there with mouths wide open. A doorman approached. "Move on. This is only for the well-to-do." Slowly the men took a few steps back and then crossed the street. They sat on chairs of an outdoor café wondering just how they could get inside this prestigious hotel.

For two days they sat in different shops offering outdoor settings. They were looking at the clientele arriving in fancy cars and expensive clothing. No soldiers of any description entered the place. Jaro summarized it was politicians, aristocracy, and royalty. There was no hope. Oskar could not help but note most of the people entering were men; the men outnumbered the women by ten to one. The women were lavishly dressed and dripping with jewels and giving pretentious airs. Oskar screwed up his face at the opulent misconduct. "How do we get in the place to check it out?" "Through the back door," said Lori in jest. Oskar grinned. "Not a bad idea. Let's check out all sides of the building. It occupies an entire block.

Two side doors opening directly on to the street were studied. One had a bellhop guarding the flow of clients utilizing the short cut. The second door was more obscure. Staff were seen going in and out. No one was observing the flow of traffic. Oskar looked at the possible entrance. With his head, he nodded to the entrance. "This is the way in. We do a quick survey and then get out as soon as possible. Stick together."

They entered the unguarded door. There was a small alcove with an unattended desk. Jaro thought it was for staff to check in and out. The group continued before the entrance came to an end. The hall split into two passageways all with multiple closed doors on each side. Oskar turned left.

He opened the first door. It was a storeroom full of clean aids. The next door contained cleaning equipment. In here, bottles of cleaning aids were in use. The third contained female cleaner's uniforms. All were neatly stacked or hung and labeled with the owner's name. Kiana's name did not appear. The next room was a laundry. In the brief moments of opening the door, it was obvious to Oskar, this is where the women uniforms were washed. Rows of washed uniforms were hung on a clothes hangers before pacing on one of two lines. The window to the street had open to air the clothes and assist the drying. The next room had a set of cubicles where staff changed their clothes from street wear to the required uniforms. Then it down the other side of the corridor.

Oskar opened each door as he returned to the starting point. The first door was directly opposite the women's changing room. This was the men's changing room. From what he could see, the bellhops changed here. The next room was a change room for other male staff. The final and largest was a storeroom with neatly stacked or hung uniforms. Again, the men's names were printed on the uniforms. The next was the laundry for the uniforms. The smallest room contained drycleaner machinery for the suits required for the men. The machines were operating but no staff was present.

Oskar, Jaro and Lori slowly opened the doors to the right side of the divided passageway. Jaro noted it was a first aid room complete with a doctor's examination bed. No doctor was on site. The next door opened to a nurse's room. The woman looked up from her novel she was reading when the door opened. Jaro quickly said, "Sorry. Wrong door." The nurse gave a nod. She didn't offer any assistance but went back to her reading.

The next door had opened by Lori. It was directly opposite the nurse's room. The room was completely bare. The next set of rooms were a series of staff showers and toilets. This was the end of the passageway in that area. Then there was a turning right.

The trio walked down the new longer passageway. It opened to the ground floor of the motel. The dining room was to the left; a lounge occupied the main central area, and the foyer desk dominated the right side. They were in. They walked through the area checking out what was around them. A large staircase led to the upper floor. A small lift, which looked likea cage but the most modern of its time, was snuggled between the stairwell and an opulent gift shop.

When the trio were looking around, they were approached by a man who was dressed in a very formal suit. He coughed. "Excuse me gentlemen, may I enquire about your business here?" Lori was quick to respond. "We are new staff. We just wanted to see where we will be working. We just want to get an idea of the guests and the layout. We are supposed to start tomorrow but we decided we should familiarize ourselves so we can be more efficient when we start." The man gave a broad grin. "We don't frequently get enthusiastic staff. Not a bad idea to look around. What shift are you on?" "In the evening. We start about six p.m." "Oh, the busy period. That is when we could really do with the extra help. I won't be on duty. My colleague will be on duty then." "May we look around upstairs?" asked Lori. "Just the first floor. That is also a busy floor. All the rest are guest rooms." Lori, Jaro and Oskar nodded "Thanks," said Oskar.

The trio went upstairs. There were a series of large rooms all designed for functions. There was a clear sign for male and female rest rooms. Down another passageway was a huge dining room encased by glass French doors. Staff were setting the tables, white tablecloths, wine glasses, silver cutlery, fine china and a single stem flower in a narrow crystal vase. Lori stared. "I wonder what stories waiters overhear? I bet there are some juicy stories." Oskar tugged at his arm. He pointed to a small semi-obscured lounge with a mix of partitions and visible areas. "I bet that is where hostesses meet their sleezy customers. The lounge is quite close to the cashier. That makes for a quick exchange of keys and payment." Lori nodded. "I bet the cashier here sees and hears everything in that corner. My ears burn just at the thought." Jaro tugged at Oskar's arm. "We better get moving. Let's see what is above. Is it really the start of the guest rooms?"

They moved towards the stairwell. They reached the top of the stairs. More doors with no numbers.

Oskar slowly turned the handle of the closes named room, 'The Gardens'. As he opened the door, he said, "Look at this!" He went inside with the others following. True to the name on the door, the place was a horticultural centre with an odd addition. A double bed was placed to the wall close to the opened balcony. Lori jested, "Make love in a garden, eh?"

Oskar frowned. "The outdoors is in-doors with maximum privacy. I wonder who uses such a room?"

Jaro was quick to answer. "Wealthy pricks with stuffed up egos."

They left the room. The next room was labeled, 'The Music Room.' A piano and a violin each had a chair, and a gramophone were to one side. The gramophone was on a cabinet with a series of long-playing records with the latest singers and musicians of the time. A table for two was elaborately set in the centre. Behind that was pale blue sheer fabric curtain with an oversized four-post bed covered in opulent coverings. The sheer fabric curtain which was now secured to posts with red ribbon only required the slightest tug to release the curtains. Oskar groaned. "Disgusting. Feed the woman and then make her pay in bed. The richer you are the more morally bankrupt you are." The trio left the room.

The next named room was called 'The Smoking Room'. They entered the room. On a set of custom-made shelves were tiers of assorted cigarettes and cigars. The shelves were placed on a bench where matches, cigarette lighters, ashtrays and cigar clippers were neatly arranged. Bottles of spirits and wines graced the walls on the same side. On a table nearby, were sparkling glasses to suit every beverage. In the middle of the room was two three-seater sofas divided by a narrow coffee table. The other side of the room were two double beds squeezed together. They were more simply dressed in fine sheets, a plain bedspread, and six pillows. Jaro said, "Sleezy. It makes my mind rattle as to what happens here."

He held up a box which was sitting on the bedside table near the pillows. "Jesus. Condoms. They must expect a lot to go on. I guess babies are excluded."

"Let's get out of here. This is supposed to be a prim and proper motel. It is not much more than an expensive sleaze joint," commented Lori.

The next door, named 'The Daylight,' was locked. The room was occupied. They placed their ears to the door. A male voice was clearly heard. The much softer voice of a female was muffled. Jaro said, "Very occupied. I wish I could see the prick who is trying to relieve himself. I would like to post his picture up for all to see." Lori pulled him back. "Shh. They could hear us. Let's go." The noise in the room stopped for a second as Lori's voice filtered through. Then whoever was inside continued.

The final room was called 'The D Room'. "I wonder what D stands for?" asked Oskar. Oskar turned the handle and slowly entered. His jaw fell to the ground. The others who followed looked equally shocked. Oskar barely got the words out of his mouth. "D is for Danger." "No," said Lori. "D is for dungeon. A mediaeval dungeon." To the right of the room and fixed to the wall were shackles for arms and feet. On the rack in front were a series of shelves adorned with masks and short-handled leather whips. A bed occupied the centre. Again, shackles were fastened to the two bed ends. Then over to the far left was a private bath surrounded by candles and assorted bottles of fragrances. On a small table nearby was a small first aid kit. Lori looked inside. It was very basic, a few bandages, some disinfectant and cotton wool. "What the hell?" said Oskar who was totally disgusted with the imagined concept flooding into his mind. "This place caters for the most perverted creeps. I wonder if the hotel staff provided the specialized staff for this kind of activity, or the people bring their own partners. I want to vomit. Let's get out of this vile place."

"We will come back tomorrow. We have to find Kiana."Oskar was looking green. "I hope she is not working here." He gestured to the rooms as they were leaving.

When they were halfway down the passageway, the door to the locked room opened. A man in his late forties walked out. He was well dressed in an expensive suit. He gave a nod as he passed them. The door to the room remained closed. The trio waited near the restroom area to see who was coming out. They didn't have to wait long. A lady in her mid-twenties walked out as if nothing happened. She was respectfully dressed; some modern accessories trying to update a season old dress. She walked down the steps with her handbag slung over her arm. She looked as if she didn't have a care in the world and nothing had happened. The epitome of discreteness..

The trio followed her at a distance but stopped at the bottom of the stairs. They moved slightly to the right to allow guests to pass. They observed the lady entering the foyer. She sat in the lounge area, drew out a pouch of cigarettes, lit it up and puffed a few times before placing the burning cigarette in the recently cleared ashtray. She opened her handbag and pulled out a notebook. She wrote something inside. The trio could only guess what she wrote: the amount of money and or the person's name and time with location. The little black book was causally returned to her handbag. The lady finished her cigarette and then left the motel through the main entrance. She disappeared into the crowded street. At six p.m. Oskar, Lori and Jaro were outside the servant's entrance of the hotel. Oskar drew in a deep breath. "Let's do this." Through the unguarded side door for staff, Lori, Jaro and Oskar entered the Albergo Mastoso for the second time. They went to the uniform storage rooms and donned any uniform that fitted.

Lori went to the front door to assist at that location. He watched every person coming and going, and assisting the patrons as required.

Oskar went to the restaurant on the first floor. He pretended to be the water boy carrying jugs of water and refilling the glasses of the customers as their drinks disappeared down their throats. Jaro placed himself in the downstairs restaurant. He also played the water boy running and taking pre-paid cups of coffee or tea to the patrons.

By ten p.m. the trio had completed their shift and met again outside the hotel. They swapped notes. Jaro said he had heard of hostesses being escorted into the Vatican to serve as waitresses in the all-male domain. "That is the next stop," said Oskar. He looked at the others and said again, "You don't have to come with me. These trips are dangerous." Lori retorted, "Dangerous yes. But the risk is worth it. It is too hard to do this task by yourself."

Chapter 15
The Vatican.

Oskar, Lori and Jaro stood in Saint Peter's Square and gasped. In silence, they slowly rotated to take in the scenery. People around them walked with purpose and ignored the newcomers. Oskar broke the silence. "Where do we start?"

Lori replied, "Maybe we should get some information about the place."

"We should get some information about the cardinals and the Pope as well. I have a hunch this place holds many secretes."

"What makes you think that?" asked Jaro.

"Just look at this place and the surrounding buildings. Christianity expounds humbleness. This isn't exactly humble. Grandeur or opulence generally screams corruption. Well in my view, it looks and smells that way. It is not my idea about Christianity." Oskar was trying to be neutral in the growing debate. "I think we better find a place to stay. This could take some time. We need to get some money." Jaro eyed a wealthy looking woman. "Yep, you are right. And here comes lunch." He tossed his head towards the woman.

The woman was fashionably dressed and wearing a string of pearls decorating her neck. Her handbag was firmly secured on her arm. Her small dog was cradled against her bosom with her arm holding her handbag tucked round her beloved pooch. Tailing behind her were two well-dressed children who were protesting about the venue. They were whining the need for food, drink, and a rest for their aching feet. The young madam tugged on her mother's arm. "My feet ache. We have been walking all morning to see some old buildings with bird pooh covering them." The lady gave a stern look. Before she could respond, the boy who was much younger said, "I'm hungry and tired. Carry me instead of 'Amore'."

The woman's eyes widened with anger. "Don't tell me you are jealous of a dog? Are you?"

The boys looked down at the ground to avoid eye contact. He was furious. He wanted to lash out but that would bring on more trouble especially in a public place. He slowly looked up with a scowl.

"I am not jealous of a dog. Just hungry and tired. These shoes are starting to hurt my feet." He sat down on the ground. He was quickly joined by his older sister who crossed her arms and pouted her support for her younger brother. Having no choice, the lady put the dog down and used her two hands to pull the children up. They initially resisted until Amore darted off towards the fountain.

The lady and the children gave chase. The dog scampered away yapping the joy of his freedom and ignoring calls of its name. When the dog reached the fountain, he jumped in the water splashing his delight. The girl took off her shoes and jumped in to catch the dog. The boy followed while the mother yelled her dismay and tried to call the children back. The boy caught the dog which was wriggling to regain his freedom. The dog succeeded. The lady looked at the children. She sat down on the fountain wall yelling directions to the children until the dog was caught. "Hand me Amore. You have just caused a major embarrassment. We are heading back to the café to meet your grandparents. What will they say when they see you like this?" Both children shrugged. Shyly, the girl said, "Mama Mia. Look at you two."

Jaro and Lori had followed the children to the fountain. Purposefully they took off their shoes and wadded in the cold water. Jaro offered a cheeky gin to the girl and her mother. He said in a loud voice.

"Ma'am relax. If you are on holidays, let the children have some fun. It is good for children to play in water."

Distracted by the remarks, the lady and her children looked at Jaro who was joined by Lori. Lori splashed water on Jaro, the start of a water fight. The children joined in and laughed while the mother held onto Amore in disbelief.

With the attention fully focused on her children playing with the strangers, Oskar took the opportunity to open her handbag. A change purse was lifted, and Lira removed. The purse was quietly slipped back into the handbag. The money disappeared into Oskar's pocket. Oskar casually moved away before reapproaching from a slightly different direction. He joined Jaro and Lori in the water. They played around until the lady and the children moved on.

Instead of continuing the visit in St. Peter's Square, the lady marched her children out of the area. As the children left, they peered over their shoulders and gave a wave accompanied by broad smiles.

Jaro, Lori and Oskar climbed out of the fountain. They shivered as water dripped off their clothes. "How much did we get?" asked Jaro. "Fifty Lira. That is enough for two meals and one night's accommodation at a guest house. I saw a guest house with a vacant room sign one block away. We better book in before it goes."

In the guest house, the trio shared one family room. The room had a bunker bed and a double bed. The room was slightly over packed with furniture.

Jaro spread out brochures and the newspaper over the lower bunk. Oskar sat on the double bed with Lori beside him. Jaro handed one brochure to the others. "This is a rough map." The trio studied the map. Lori commented, "This doesn't really indicate much other than the names of the buildings. The Swiss Guard are placed at each entrance. Problem number one. There has to be accommodation quarters somewhere, but I can't figure it out." He twisted the map around, studied it further before handing it to Lori. Lori looked at the map. "As a guess, I think the quarters are over here, behind these main buildings." He put the map aside.

The next brochure contained a brief history on the making of St. Peter's Square.

The other brochures gave less information about the remainder buildings. The last brochure Jaro read out gave a brief history on the current Pope, Pope Pius XII. Jaro stopped reading aloud. "I see something interesting. It says when Pope Pius was still a cardinal, Cardinal Pacelli. He lived as the Vatican's ambassador in Germany. He noted the aggression against the Jews. He was instrumental in drawing up a treaty with the Germans to protect German Catholics and to respect the religions and races of all people. It also condemned the deportation of Jews to prison camps. Strange. The newspapers have been saying, the Vatican has been vocal but in reality, has done nothing to stop the slaughter or aid Jews. Maybe they saved a few living in Italy, but they have done zilch to save Jews in other countries."

Oskar leaned back on the bed and stared at the ceiling. The paint was peeling and threatening to drop flakes as he stared at them. He drummed his fingers on his chest. He sat up again. "Okay. They are hypocrites. Words only. The opulence of the place, at least from the outside, smacks of past financial greed. If Kiana is in this fake place of reverence, then we got to get her out as soon as possible."
Lori frowned at Oskar's expression. "Fake reverence? What do you mean by that?"
Oskar said in a matter-of-fact way, "They say they obey the command of God and live a righteous life etcetera. I doubt that. Something smells rotten. Just a brotherly feeling towards a vulnerable sister.

They are like rotten apples, nice outside and but the worm is inside. Someone tell me I am wrong."

He took another brochure and read it before putting it down in disgust. "What my scant history is of Christianity is, the Catholic church broke away from the Greek Orthodox Church about 200AD. The group wanted someone to represent God but the conservative Greek Orthodox didn't want anyone to represent God. To the Greeks, no one could or should represent God. That makes it from the start the Catholic Church set out on a power grab. It was built on the desire for power and along with that came the grab for wealth. I would love to get into the archives and read what is hidden deep in the vaults. I bet embezzlement, illegal land annexation and sex scandals are the main mix. Yep, I bet some mistranslations of the bible were also included so to push the male dominated hierarchy. I bet celebrate was change to celebrant to keep priests in line. I bet that didn't work."

Lori looked at Oskar. "Shut up. That sounds so heretical."

Oskar grinned. "Is it? If they are as pure as they try to say, then why aren't records on public display? That is just my thinking. Don't let my thoughts cloud our mission to find Kiana."

After a brief silence, Jaro said, "Okay. Suppose we say the old men are angels, then they won't have any issue for a brother to visit his sister. Bureaucracy may step in. We can gauge that by simply just asking and see what the response is. If they carry on about zero visitors, then something is off. Shall we try the straightforward approach to test the waters?"

The following morning, the trio approached the doors of the Basilica. As expected, they were stopped at the door. A priest of lower rank and acting as a clerk asked, "Good morning. May I be of assistance?" Oskar replied, "I was informed my sister was working as a kitchen servant here. I would like to see her." The priest looked Oskar up and down and then inspected Lori and Jaro with the same disapproving glare. "There are no women in the Vatican other than visiting nuns. Is your sister a nun?"

"No. I was told she was recruited for kitchen duties."

"That doesn't sound right. There is an elderly married couple who cook for some of the staff. They do not have any children in the Vatican."

Oskar saw the polite refusal. He decided to stretch his luck. "Is it possible to talk to the elderly couple? Maybe they can shed some light and explore all avenues on my search. We were separated by the National Guard almost a year ago. She and a few other women were assigned as hostesses and the rest to be nurses for the injured soldiers."The priest looked sympathetic. Oskar added a lie, "Our mother is gravely ill. It is her dying wish to see all her children before she passes on. There is not much time. Maybe a month at the most." The priest nodded. "What I will do for you is to ask the couple to meet you at the other city entrance. It is called the Porta del Perugina. There is a side road called Italia. It branches off Via di Porta Cavalleggeria." The priest pointed to the general direction. "They will be at the gates at two-thirty this afternoon. Is that any help?"

Oskar smiled and thanked the priest. "I will certainly be there. Thank you again."

At two fifteen Oskar, Jaro and Lori were at the gate of Porta del Perugina. A man and lady in their sixties met them at two thirty-five. The man told the guard, "Let them come in. We were expecting them." The guard nodded. "Come over here." He pointed to a tree with a bench. "Visitors sit here all the time. We are just out of ear shot of the guards, but we are still very visible."

"Now young man, how can I assist?" asked the man. Oskar gave the same story as he did for the priest. The elderly couple nodded as they absorbed the information. The lady said, "We are training young people to do our job. We will be retiring in a couple of years.

However, it takes a couple of years to bring staff up to scratch. Your sister may be one of a couple assigned to serve the cardinals their food. I did hear that one young lady was always dropping plates of food and full wine glasses over the cardinals. She was shifted to other duties."

"Like what?" asked Oskar.

The man gave a cough before trying to answer. "Err. There is a place deep inside the Vatican, I am not exactly sure where it is. We are restricted in our movements on the premises." The man pointed to a distant location where other buildings were clustered. "We can't go beyond that." He pointed to road separating the permitted side and the buildings on the other side. "Some young ladies are in that location and that includes the accommodation for the visiting nuns."

"Where are the nun's quarters?" asked Oskar.

The man and lady pointed to another distant cluster of buildings. "Somewhere over there. Which building, I can't tell you for sure."

"Exactly what do the young ladies do if they are there?" asked Lori who asked the question without taking his eyes off three possible buildings.

"Maids. Cooks. Laundry. Maybe a few other tasks which we have no privilege to know. It is generally the rejects as the cardinals call them that end up in the nun's quarters. That is all I can tell you."

Oskar asked, "How do I get a message to her? Our mother is very ill. Also, she will need leave time."

The old man and lady stood up. "You have to approach the enquiry desk at the Basilica. Some priests are helpful while others are not so. You must have struck Father Vincent who is a man who is very soft hearted and very family-oriented. If Father Dominic is on duty, he can be very abrupt and is suspicious of all. Good luck." The couple stood up and walked away. Oskar, Lori and Jaro watched the couple leave. Their eyes flashed over to the distant group of building which could be harbouring Kiana.

The trio returned to the Basilica. As luck would have it, Father Vincent was still on duty. Oskar explained that Kiana could be in the nun's accommodation section. Father Vincent pulled out a book. He quickly flipped through the pages. He came to a section marked Nun's Quarters, List of Servants. His finger went down the page. It paused at Kiana's name. "Ah, yes. Here she is. Kiana Grat. Now called Sister Gertrude."

"Sister?" chorused Oskar, Jaro and Lori.

"Oh yes all women are called Sister." Father Vincent grinned. "And we are called Brothers."

"Did she take vows to be a nun?" asked Oskar.

Father Vincent looked the trio directly in their eyes. "That I can't answer. I have no information."

"How do I get to see her? But more importantly, how does she get to leave to visit our dying mother?"

"Just a minute," said Father Vincent. He picked up a phone behind the main counter. He asked questions to someone who had greater authority and nodded a few times before returning. "I send a written application to the nun's quarters. Then I get a reply. Come back tomorrow. Father Dominic will be on duty. I will leave a note so you can immediately have the request. Now, what day are you leaving and when are you returning?"

Oskar replied, "Tomorrow afternoon at one. We need to catch the train to Bologna. That is where our parents live."

Father Vincent wrote on the paper. "I will leave it open for a month. It will take over a day on the train just to get there."

"Can you make sure she has her travel bag? She doesn't have any clothes at home."

Father Vincent made the note:

Her brothers will pick her up from the front desk. One bag with a few changes of clothes.

Father Vincent smiled and bid the trio good-bye.

The following morning, Father Dominic was manning the desk. Oskar introduced himself and mentioned he was there to pick up his sister, Sister Gertrude. Father Dominic looked at the notices in a folder. "Ah! Yes." He looked around but Kiana was not to be seen.

A nun approached the desk. She had come through the main doors. She said, "I believe someone is looking for Sister Gertrude."
Father Dominic pointed to Oskar. Oskar spoke, "We are her brothers. Our dying mother wants to see her before she dies."
The nun gave a cough and looked skeptical at Oskar. She gave all three men a once over. "She is waiting outside. You can take that insufferable girl. Don't bring her back."
The nun asked for the paperwork regarding Kiana's release. She scrawled over it:
This young lady is not to return. She is permanently dismissed. Unsuitable for this establishment.

She slammed the folder down. She looked at Father Dominic. "Don't ever let that child back into these holy walls ever again." She turned to Oskar. "Take your sister and leave. Don't come back. I will be happy to see the last of her. She is waiting outside." The nun strutted out.

When Kiana saw Oskar, she ran to give him a hug and then extended her arms to embrace the others. She couldn't wipe the grin off her face. "I have missed you all so much. Let's get out of here. I can't wait to join the outside world."

When they were well away from St. Peter's Square. Oskar asked, "What exactly happened in there?"
Kiana smiled dropped. "The lecherous bastards, well some were. Some were very polite and nice. There were a handful who should be tried and shot. Just because they are high up in the church, it doesn't mean social rules or morals should be dropped. Hypocrites.

They give the church a bad name. The good guys are muted from doing anything while the handful of bullies prevail. Anyway, where is Paul?"

"Unfortunately, Paul was shot in Albania. We all ran out of ammo and he tried to get us some," said Lori.
Kiana felt tears well up. "He joins thousands on the field. Some of the women who were taken away with me were placed as nurses. They didn't last long either. Some, I was told were captured and are now prisoners of war. Others were shot. It is a cruel senseless war." Oskar looked around at the street. "Let's get a meal and have a detailed catch-up chat."

At a small non-descript outdoor restaurant, they slowly consumed their meal. Kiana elaborated on her experiences after the men had completed theirs. "I was first sent to a building where a so-called high-class lady lorded over everyone. She trained about ten of us to be puppets to men: smile, thank you, obedient servants no matter how dreadful you were treated. I played along with the so called 'schooling' as they termed it. I needed to get away from that slavedriver as soon as possible.

"My first assignment was to a big motel on the south side of the city. I don't know the name of it. I was blind folded to the venue and entered through a side door like all other staff. I was told to be a bartender at the main bar. Naturally, I assumed I was only to pour beers and get what drinks they were requested. That was the good side. I can pull a good beer and serve wine the right way. The bad side was, I was expected to accept tips and go with men whenever. The tips were more than generous for a reason. Sexual services were expected. I was given lots of money, all shoved down my bra. The money was quickly removed and returned with excuses; monthlies or already booked out for the night. The regulars started to see through the excuses and tried to force the request with higher amounts of money or just violence. The violence was grabbing my arm and pulling me down across the counter. Them on one side and me on the other. The boss ignored the actions. Actually, he laughed. I was their entertainment. The guys often ended up with their drinks thrown in their faces or me serving a punch. One creepy regular who grabbed me several times got a major lesson. It just happened the bar tender left his ice pick close by. When this prick grabbed my arm, I grabbed the ice pick and slammed it into his arm. His arm was like a fountain. He let go of me faster than he grabbed me. Naturally, the bar tender reported me to the agency. The dragon queen reassigned me to the Vatican thinking I would behave there.

"At the Vatican, I was one of three females serving meals to the staff working there. The guys were generally well behaved. It was just delivering the same meals to all the staff. No brain power required to recall who wanted what. Then someone decided I should be 'promoted' to serving the priests and cardinals. It was more cardinals than priests. That was when the fun and games started.

"The first week all the cardinals behaved themselves, polite and respectful. Then it started the sexual frustration. Hands started going up my skirt. At first, I just stepped away. If their feet were in view, I would step on their toes and I pushed down hard as I could. The hands disappeared. Those who persisted found I dropped food over them and a few times I poured water or wine over their heads. Of course, I apologized profusely for my clumsiness. I was kicked out and sent to the nun's quarters.

"Mind you, I did overhear some dreadful things going on. Hypocrites."
"Like what?" asked Oskar.
"Well that treaty Pope Pius XII signed was totally ignored by Hitler. He didn't care about anyone or anything except himself. That is nothing new. Interestingly, the Pope and the Cardinals only helped any Italian Jews but wouldn't help any Jews from any other country.

I saw delegations getting refused assistance. To quote one cardinal, 'they are not our problem'. There was a flyer which was placed on all the tables. I couldn't read it that much but, I lingered around one of the cardinals who I knew he wasn't an octopus. He read out what Pope Pius XII had sent to all and to the general public. The words burn in my head. 'It is impossible for a Christian to take part in anti-semitism. Antisemitism is inadmissibly spiritually. We are all Semites.' There was a lot more but that is what stuck in my head. And yet, they refused to help Jews coming from other countries? It is beggar's belief. There was an address to the Italians and to the politicians. It took me a long time to work out the gist of what he was saying.

"Okay. I get the Vatican had to give a neutral stand. But the address was evasive. Sure, the Pope didn't want to stir up Hitler or even Mussolini. I am sure the cardinals felt the same way. I understand caution. They hid their views by the words 'justice and clarity'. Which means, we do stuff-all. You know what makes me boil?"
Oskar gestured for her to continue as he sipped on a very cold coffee. He waited until Kiana took another sip of hers. "The upper cardinals, oh yes, they are ranked. The upper ranked ones call themselves 'The Holy See'. A blind person can see more than they do. As for the nuns? They are equally as blind.

"When I was in the nun's quarters, again there were a mix of very nice ladies and bats from hell who always reigned. They held up the patriarchal system with blind obedience even to their own disadvantage. At first, I was assigned to the visiting nun's quarters. It was good there. You didn't have to put up with horrible people for that long. They came and went. Then I was placed in the permanent quarters. I was fortunate to meet some beautiful nuns. I will always give those ladies my greatest respect. I really liked working for them. It was a pleasure. Then I was transferred to the so-called mother superior section. Ugh. Bitches. Only two were nice. Two others were okay, but the rest were Satan's wives.

"The lady who brought me to the desk was, okay you can call me harsh for saying this, she was the queen of the bitch group. She must have been a slaver trader in her past life. I had to get up at five each morning. Go to prayers for one hour. Then prepare breakfast for twenty of them. Breakfast was always at seven thirty. It just wasn't toast with some Italian spread, it was eggs poached or fried, and pasta of all things. Fruit had to be served with tea or coffee. Then I had to clean up by nine-fifteen to get the food for lunch. They expected three courses all the time. Soup, more pasta, some red meat except on Fridays and assorted vegetables. Then dessert on top. Meals were served at twelve thirty. I had to clean up after that and that also included doing the floors. Then afternoon tea had to be Italian style biscuits with tea, juice, water or coffee. Then it was preparing for dinner which could have extra guests. I was never told how many extras even when I asked. I had to read their minds. That was when I got into trouble most. Volumes of food were over supplied or under supplied, not enough setting and so on. When I tried to defend myself, I was slapped across the face for being insolent or some other excuse.

"One evening, I didn't serve any meals. They were cooked but were in pots. I was so exhausted; I really needed a rest. I was reprimanded for sleeping. I wasn't permitted to go to bed before ten. I was required to do another stint of prayers for thirty minutes before retiring. As punishment, I had to polish their shoes, all 20 pairs."

"That is a bit too much," said Jaro who was slowly shaking his head. "I got back at them. I just laid all the polished shoes near the entrance to the hallway which led to the bedrooms. Next, I purposely mixed most of the shoes up when I had to deliver them to their rooms. The shoes did not have any names on them. I did that three-times and sat back and watched their annoyance. The nuns I did like, always got their shoes. Actually, one of them burst out laughing. I guess she also had her fill of their rotten behaviour toward the others.

"Just recently, I was giving myself a day off and an afternoon off. I was worn out doing the work seven days a week and no assistance except from the good nuns who came in and did a few simple chores here and there and a short chat They made me feel a little human. Giving myself time off didn't wash well with the bitches. I started to cut prayer time out. Then going to bed at nine at night meant some of these nuns had to get their own glasses of water or wine or whatever they fancied. At times they would barge into my room and drag me out of bed to get them what they wanted. Hell, if they can drag me out of bed, then they can save energy and time getting those items themselves. There is no sign on the kitchen door banning them from entry. It was a horrible display of power.

"One thing that did puzzle me and I saw it a few times. When I was supposed to be in prayer mode in the small chapel for the nuns, I heard the noise of trucks pulling into the place. From the window, I could see they were German trucks unloading crates of all sizes and what appeared to be covered paintings. The soldiers carrying the goods went into a covered walkway. The men returned empty handed each time. When I sneaked out from the chores, I went to the tunnel-like structure. There were two doors. One was just an entrance to the men's quarters. The other had a locked door. The door was old, heavy and triple bolted. I guess the items disappeared into that area. I did some snooping and kept my ears open. I am not one hundred per cent sure if my Italian was getting all the information right. I still fumble with the language. I am sure one of the senior cardinals who was walking around said to another equally senior that the Germans delivered cultural items for protection from the war."

Lori frowned. "You mean that some of the looted artifacts of Europe were stored in the vaults of the Vatican under the pretense to preserve them? The Germans used that as an excuse to hide the loot?" He blew out a puff of air. "The Germans must have filled up their hiding places for the plundered items and did a sweetheart deal with the Pope or other officials. I bet after the war, the Vatican keeps the loot and denies their involvement in the looting."

Jaro chipped in. "Those trucks that were guarded in Donnersbach went to Switzerland, or did they? Switzerland could be the innocent exchange venue: trucks in, items categorized and then moved on. The thought horrifies me as to what was stolen from anywhere and what could be hidden in the Vatican vaults."

Oskar scoffed. "The Vatican has always been greedy. What I understand in the medieval era and the religious zeal of the time, people paid tax to the king or to the feudal system they were caught in and paid tax to the Catholic Church disguised as a donation. Taking bribes is entrenched in their history. It is obvious, the greed continues today. The hypocrites call themselves people of God. Didn't the bible state that Jesus trashed a temple because of its misdeeds of wealth collection? And here is this institution doing the exact same thing." Oskar shook his head in disgust.

The group stopped talking when some Italian soldiers started to walk towards them.

The soldier who had harassed Kiana many times before, stopped and looked sternly at her. "Kiana, my dear Kiana, you wouldn't join me when I tried to pay for you but here you are dining with three men. I am somewhat upset."

Oskar stood up. His mouth tight with anger. "Keep your hands off my sister."

Lori and Jaro stood up ready to attack. Jaro lied and displayed equal anger. "Touch my cousin and you will know how my fist feels." The soldier backed away. "Maybe we can meet for a meal another day?".

Kiana looked at him up and down. "Dream on. I am not for sale."

"Ah! You're for free!" said the soldier. Lori, being slightly further away, took a step closer. The next thing the soldier knew he was on the ground. Oskar and Jaro punched him at the same time. The soldier struggled to get up. He held his hand for Oskar and Jaro to stop. Lori raised a fist ready to punch the soldier again. The soldier cowered. "I get the picture. I have to go through you two."

Lori's voice rang out as he lied, "And through me. You don't touch my girlfriend."

The soldier slowly stood up. "Three bodyguards who get on so well, I get the picture. Hands off."

Oskar said, "Eyes off as well." The soldier looked around to see three fists ready to punch him again. Oskar turned to the others and said in a much quieter voice, "Let's get out of here. We have to catch a train."

Chapter 16
Vatican City to Bologna

At the station, Oskar, Jaro and Lori went to the men's room to change into their Italian army uniforms. Kiana took the opportunity to change into a habit and veil.

Kiana approached the ticket office. The man looked at her. "Why would a pretty lady like you hide away in the church?"
Kiana just smiled back. "It has its good points and like every profession has its bad points. One ticket to Bologna please." The man at the ticket box nodded his agreement. "Tickets for nun's are half price. To Bologna it is twenty Lira."
Kiana looked at her purse and pulled out all she had. It was fifteen Lira. She looked around to see if Oskar was close by. He and the other two were buying food at the stall quite a distance away. Kiana said, "I will come back with the rest of the fare." She was about to leave when the man in the ticket box said, "Fifteen is close enough." Kiana smiled and handed over the money. She took the ticket. "Thank you so much." Playing the part she added, "God bless you and your family." She quickly gave the sign of the cross and hurried away.

The train made several refueling stops. It took twenty-four hours to reach Bologna. When they arrived, they changed into civilian clothes and Kiana into normal street wear. The uniforms were all stuffed into the bottom of their bags. They walked to a nearby park.

"What do we do from here?" asked Kiana.

"Get some cash and find a place to stay. We need to hear some news to know what is happening in this war."

They moved slowly away from the park. Three blocks away they saw a sign on a house. 'Accommodation Available.' Kiana said, we should check this out. As she walked up the narrow path leading to the house, she couldn't help but notice the unkept front garden and the front door was needing repairs. She knocked. A voice deep inside called out, "I am coming!"

The lady was in her mid-sixties. Her greying hair was tied into a tight bun at the back of her head. An apron covered her floral dress which had seen better days. She greeted Kiana, "Are you coming about the room?"

Kiana nodded. "Yes. I need a room." She turned to the group waiting at the gate. She added, "My three bothers also need a place."

The old lady frowned as deep in thought. "I have only one room. Two single beds. One brother can sleep on the floor and you, may sleep on the lounge couch. The room is ten Lira. Do you want it?"

"Just a minute. I will speak to my brothers," said Kiana. Kiana walked back to the gate and told them the deal.

Oskar opened his wallet. "I only have eight Lira and two Reichmarks. See if the Reichmarks are acceptable. Ask her we can do some work for her to make the up the difference." Kiana walked back to the waiting lady. When she heard Reichmarks were the balance, she screwed up her face in disgust. "Lira only. But you people can do some work. I will agree to that. Come." She looked over Kiana's shoulder and waved to the trio.

She led the group to the back room. "You three sleep here. One of you will sleep on the floor. I will get some extra blankets. Young lady, you sleep on the lounge sofa. When you put your bags away, I will tell you what work needs to be done. I will take the eight Lira." She held out her hand. Osaka dropped the last of the money into her hand. The lady clutched it and walked away.

Ten minutes later she gathered the group around the kitchen table. "You men can start fixing the shingles on the roof. Start at the back. The room you are in is like a strainer. There are holes where water and wind come through. It needs to be fixed first. I will show you where the shingles are stored with the tools. My husband used to fix things after work or on the weekends. He passed away three years ago. He bought the shingles but never had a chance to nail them to the roof. He became too ill to climb to high places. I forbade him from going up there." The lady looked up to the ceiling and did the sign of the cross. "For a while, my sons would come over and do the gardening and minor repairs. Then Mussolini had this bad idea that my boys should fight for Italy in Ethiopia. My daughter was helping me out, but she was told to be a nurse in Yugoslavia. She was badly injured. She was shot in the legs. One bullet in each. Now she is crippled. Her children do their best to help her. I go once a month to help with the cooking and laundry." The lady directed her gaze to Kiana. "Kiana, your job is to help with the housework. The bathroom and kitchen need major cleaning. I have trouble doing that. My arthritis in my hips and knees stops me from doing some jobs well. My hands are starting to show signs of arthritis." The lady gave a sigh and tried to joke about her ailments. "When you get to sixty, the body starts complaining and wobbles like a loose wheel on an old cart. You try to fix one part and another part starts squeaking."

She nodded her head for Kiana to start in the kitchen. "Do under the sink as well. Pull out everything and clean the shelves." She turned to Lori, Jaro and Oskar. "Come with me to the shed at the back."

The trio followed the old lady to the back yard. She pointed to the shed. You will find a ladder, hammer, nails and shingles inside. You

can start now." She walked away leaving the trio to work out how to do the repairs. Oskar said, "I will go up and look at the roof and see how other shingles are nailed. You two start bringing out the shingles out of the shed. Ten minutes later Oskar reported, "I've worked out how to fix the shingles to the roof. I think the whole roof needs replacing. Some are looking very dodgy. Jaro, pass up the hammer, nails and a shingle. Then keep passing the shingles up. Lori, just bring them over to Jaro." All afternoon the trio worked on the roof. Most of the roof was repaired. Oskar counted how many more were required to complete the job the next day. "How many do we have left?" Lori counted the ones still in the shed. "Three."
Oskar replied, "We need fifteen more. Let's do the last three and tell her the bad news."

By the afternoon, Kiana had completed the kitchen, ceilings, walls, inside cupboards and old stove. The bathroom wasn't even touched. It was close to six p.m when the old lady came in with a load of vegetables. "Take a rest. The kitchen looks wonderful." She walked around and noted the paint was beginning to peel on the wall behind the cooktop. "I think this needs some paint." She sadly looked at the wall. "No money. No paint. It has to stay that way." Jaro and Oskar entered the room after a quick bath. They told her of the need for extra tiles. The lady rolled he eyes. "No money. No more tiles. It stays. What room will be affected?"
Oskar replied, "The front section above the patio."
"Ugh. Not an important area. Now rest all of you. I got the newspaper. It is yesterday's newspaper if that is okay. We get the papers a day late here."

By lunch time the next day, all the tasks the lady had asked for were completed. Oskar asked, "If we can find work at another place and get paid, can we stay another night?"
"Of course. Leave the bags in the lounge. You can let me know by five thirty. I don't think there will be more people looking for board."

She muttered to herself as she turned her attention to preparing food, "They better find work. I need the income."

In the afternoon, the group went to a nearby park. They sat on a log swing discussing their options. Kiana's and Jaro's eyes were constantly looking at the houses surrounding the small park.

Jaro nodded towards a medium sized house. He noted the owners had just left the premises. They had driven away in a flashy new car. He commented, "That house may have some cash and other items. I just saw the owners leave in a flashy car. We better go now before the owners return."

The group followed Jaro to the house. They studied it for a while. Kiana went up the small flight of steps and knocked on the door. No reply. She listened again. She turned the knob. To her surprise the door was unlocked. She signaled for the others to follow.

The group entered the living room. A stylish lounge suite took centre stage. The sideboard was decorated with family photos. Jaro stared at the man in the uniform and the flag behind the man.
Jaro called the others over, "Hey we better be quick. The people here are Mussolini supporters. He seems to be of high rank. I think the man is a two-star general. There has to be a home office. Head there." The others walked quickly around the house. They found a locked door. "I think this is the office," said Jaro. Oskar picked the lock. The door opened to reveal a desk stacked on one side with papers. Oskar rummaged through the drawers before looking at some of the paperwork. Lori peeked behind the painting on the wall. He found a safe. "Does anyone know how to open a safe?" he asked the others. Oskar and Jaro shook their heads.

Kiana left the room and went for the bedrooms. She found some loose change in one of the children's rooms and a total of twenty

Lira tucked in a wallet in a dressing room drawer of the master suite. She pocketed the cash along with a couple of rings and a gold chain. She left the room to go to the kitchen.

 Just near the door she grabbed three bags which were used for shopping. She helped herself to the pantry. She filled the bags with bread, vegetables, and fruit. It was enough for two meals for all of them. On one side of a cupboard, she spotted a bottle of red wine. She took that with four cups and entrée plates which were washed and left to drip dry on a rack by the sink. She met up with the others.

Their search had turned up little. Oskar went back to the drawers in the desk. He examined the depths for matching heights. One drawer was shallower than the others. He took the contents out and pushed around the edges and then the centre. Eventually, the false bottom popped open. Cash in both Lira and Reichsmarks were lifted. Everything was carefully returned. He said, "Time to leave we have enough money for now." Lori assisted Kiana with her haul. The group carefully shut the door before leaving. They were about to turn the corner of the street when the owners returned to their house. Their car was parked outside. The family slowly climbed out. They entered their home.

Oskar and the others hurried away. "They may not notice the theft for half a day. The big tell sign will be the kitchen. I just about emptied the food supply out. That is when they will start hunting to see what was taken. It may take a day or two for the lady to realize the gold chain was taken. I took the more modest looking rings. She had some very nice rings, but I thought they would be too hard to sell off. Let's get our stuff and go to another guest house. If we get caught, I don't want the old lady involved." When they reached the house about four in the afternoon, the lady wasn't home. They collected their bags and left a note telling the lady they were leaving. Kiana placed two small tomatoes, a bread roll and two Liras with a note on the table. "That should keep her happy." They all walked out.

When they reached a larger guest house several blocks away, they noted several German soldiers were in the area. On a closer look, they were people of higher rank. Lori said, "Let's try somewhere else." They moved on.

A few more blocks away, the group entered another guest house. They checked the surrounds for Germans. None were to be seen. However, an Italian colonel appeared before them. He beckoned them over. "Young men and young lady, what brings you here?"

Jaro responded, "We are taking a travel rest. We are on our way to Venice to attend funerals. Many of our family members have died in the war. "
"Then attend and go back to the front line. We need more men." He looked at Kiana. "We need more nurses too. You are a nurse, are you?"
Kiana gave a smile. "No Sir. A nun on leave to attend the funeral of my relatives."
The colonel nodded. "A nun? That is good enough. I hope to see you attending to the injured men and giving them their last rites."
The desk attendant called the group over. He handed them two sets of keys. Kiana accepted the keys. The colonel frowned. "Only two sets?"
Oskar replied, "We are on a budget. Funerals can be expensive. Multiple funerals more so." The colonel seemed satisfied with the reply. He walked on.

The next morning the group were huddled around the radio in the common lounge room. They listened with intent to the various news flashes.

Mussolini had become the sole 'ruler' of Italy after King Emmanuel was forced by Mussolini into exile in Egypt. The pacts with Germany remained on shaky ground but the Germans cooperated with Mussolini and put up with his failures. The Italian campaigns into Greece and Yugoslavia via Albania continued causing thousands of lives to be lost. The situation in Africa was not much better.

The campaign in Egypt was going badly. The British, Australians, New Zealanders and the French had combined forces. Superior everything saw the Italians take a severe hammering. Due to the Italian-German Treaty, the Germans offered some relief. Still the truth did not filter to the Italian public. More troops were sent. Half battalions were united to enforce numbers. All failed to conquer Egypt.

The truth of the Ethiopian and Egyptian failures and all other failures were never mentioned to the public at home. It would have caused a major morale slide or a riot or mass desertion in the fledgling army. Mussolini didn't want to acknowledge he was the failure. He kept the propaganda going on the radio and newspapers.

Very little was mentioned about the German push on the Western Front which snaked its way from the Swiss border to the North Sea, above Holland. After the broadcast, Lori said, "The world has gone mad. There is no real safe place to be."

Just then the colonel walked in. He greeted and smiled at the group to hide his depression and concern. He invited himself to sit on the vacant two-seater beside the group. He took out a cigar and lit it up. He drew in a breath of tobacco and exhaled. "By the way, I am Colonel Luca Morelli. That news flash was hiding half the truth. Mussolini likes to omit details and mixes bits of the truth with lies. When that happens, things sound accurate, speak no evil, and be selectively deaf and blind."

Oskar asked, "I am sure you know more than what is being permitted on the radio."

Colonel Morelli nodded. "I sure do." He looked firmly at the group. "I sense you three men have deserted. Good for you. I will keep it a secret. Young lady, if you want to survive, stay with this group but you may be forced to break up as the war continues. I don't see the world settling down for many years to come. Now let me tell you where it is safe to go." He puffed more on the cigar.

"Go to Switzerland or to Sweden or Norway. Maybe if you can afford it, to Australia or New Zealand They are at war, but their homelands are not getting bombed. The Pacific Islands and other Asian countries are not safe. The world is culling its population. Next disease will follow because the dead can't be buried fast enough. Just hide wherever you can."

Oskar interjected, "Why has Italy invaded Greece and Yugoslavia via Albania?"

The Colonel looked up to look Oskar in the eyes. "The fascist government made King Emmanuel the Emperor of Ethiopia and King of Albania. I suspect they wanted him to take the blame for the fascist's colonial drive, especially when things go wrong. It is going wrong in every aspect of the war. King Emmanuel was against the war against Greece and Yugoslavia and for his efforts was sent into exile in Alexandria in Egypt. Delegations of us have been begging the King to come back. He may return. If he does, as an educated guess, he will be on the side of the Allies. He hates Mussolini and his thugs. My brother, General Paco Morelli lives in a flashy Mussolini house. He has a fancy car, an over indulged wife and two spoilt brats. To him Mussolini is God." The Colonel gave a spit. "My brother and I do not talk to each other anymore. The war has split us and the rest of the family. It is sad. It is the reality. Many families are split. Not just in Italy but in every country. War only divides. In my observations, wars run by politicians are doomed to failure. There is no respect for the soldiers but above all no pre-planning for a war and even less when it ends. They create defeats, not victories.

"I am guessing now, and I could be wrong. Italy will fall twice. The Germans are getting sick of coming to Italy's aid in botched up, badly planned attacks. When that happens, Italy will become a puppet to Germany. Ugh. That will give the Allies an incentive to invade Italy. We fall again but the Allies will eventually save Italy from further demise. They will help us regain our freedom. I can't wait for that to happen."

Lori asked, "If that happens, what do you think will happen to your brother?" "I have to make guesses here. He could commit suicide before facing any courts for war crimes. He could face war crimes and be imprisoned. He may run away like a coward. All bullies are cowards when the tables are turned, sheep in wolf clothing. He has made his destiny. Now you young people, I congratulate you on you willingness to desert. Run and don't get caught." The Colonel was beginning to stand up when Oskar asked, "Your brother, does he live in the house with the statue of Venus in front?

"The Colonel frowned. "Err yes. Why."
"I just thought it may make you happy to know he was robbed. He will never say it of course."
The Colonel's face broke into a grin and then he began laughing. "Well done. You should have burnt his house down. That would make him realize how others feel when he destroys their homes. He has a safe somewhere. It could be full of interesting things besides money. When we were still talking to each other, he gave me the combination as a safety measure. He wanted to make sure the contents were distributed to where they should be."

"We found it," replied Oskar. "Where is it?" asked the Colonel.

"Behind an ugly painting by Salvador Dali," replied Oskar.

"Uphmm. Probably stolen. Thanks for the information. I have seen that picture. I do agree it is ugly. No finesse. By the way, how are you going to get into Switzerland. You need some form of documentation. Passports are the best. I have a contact who works for the immigration office. He takes a few blank passports for those wanting to escape to anywhere. If you need his services, let me know."

Lori jumped at the idea. "We will be wanting four. We have the pictures done already. How much will it cost?" The colonel was standing at this point.

"I will cover the cost. It is a reward for robbing my dangerous brother and telling me where his safe is. I am just going to return the favour. I will contact the man within forty minutes and arrange a time to meet here. I will leave a message at the clerk's desk. I must be off and go back pretending what I am not. I hope one day we meet up again, maybe in Switzerland. That is where I will be heading when I have two weeks of service leave. I have had enough of this war." The Colonel tipped his hat and walked away.

"Is he to be trusted?" asked Jaro.

"We will scatter outside and see what happens. If the military police come or the local police come, then we know." said Oskar.

Lori jumped at the idea. "We will be wanting four. We have the pictures done already. How much will it cost?"

The colonel was standing at this point. "I will cover the cost. It is a reward for robbing my dangerous brother and telling me where his safe is. I am just going to return the favour. I will contact the man within forty minutes and arrange a time to meet here. I will leave a message at the clerk's desk. I must be off and go back pretending what I am not. I hope one day we meet up again, maybe in Switzerland. That is where I will be heading when I have two weeks of service leave. I have had enough of this war." The Colonel tipped his hat and walked away.

"Is he to be trusted?" asked Jaro.
"We will scatter outside and see what happens. If the military police come or the local police come, then we know."

The group scattered themselves in different locations outside the building. True to his word, the Colonel returned, went inside and left as fast as he entered. The group waited for an hour. Lori went in the guest house to collect the note. He was on guard, ready to be jumped by any type of police unit. Nothing happened. As arranged, he walked to an outdoor restaurant and waited. Still, no one came. He gave a signal to Kiana. She relayed the signal to Jaro and then he relayed it to Oskar. The group reformed but kept on high alert. Their eyes were constantly watching the surroundings.
They met the contact two hours later. The man in his forties wore thick glasses. He positioned himself in a corner of the store run by his wife. He greeted the arrivals with a warm smile.
"Welcome to my office. Please sit down. Show me the photos." He took the photos one by one. He asked the relevant questions of name and date of birth. The next of kin he wrote 'deceased'.
He handed each book back in turn. He stood up and left without a word. The group walked out slowly spacing their exit as a precaution. In Italian army uniforms and Kiana in her nun's habit, they boarded the train to Milan. There was no need to remain in Bologna. Now that they had stolen money and pawned a ring, it was necessary to get out of town.

Chapter 17
Milan to Meda.

As soon as they got off the train, they immediately changed into civilian clothes. Oskar entered a small motel. He went to the check-in desk and asked for a tourist map. The young teenager on the other side barely looked at him. Mechanically, she handed over the map. Oskar thanked her. The girl almost grunted a word of acknowledgement.

Outside the motel, the group looked at the map. The front page just had a few streets of the city centre. The back page proved more valuable to the group. It was more of a map of North Italy to the shores of Lake Como. The groups smiled at the find. They could plan their movements. They spread out to scout for information to towns north and be a step closer to Switzerland. They would meet up at the park across the street in two hours' time.

Kiana returned last to the pre-designated location. She said to the others, "There is a man who drives a bus. He does round trips to a small town called Lecco. Lecco is north by northeast. It is about twenty kilometres away from the coastline of Lake Como. The cost per person is ten Liras. I was also told on a good run, the trip will be five hours but on a bad run, it could stretch to six and a half. Then we have to walk to the border going over the rest of the cold mountains. What did you find?"
Oskar said, "Nothing much." He pulled out another few Liras. "Just this."

Jaro said, "I saw Germans loading a personnel carrier. I heard them say they would be crossing into Switzerland via the towns of Como and Maslianico. Como is a port for Lake Como. Maslianico is the largest town on the Italian border before crossing into Switzerland. For us, it is by boat to either San Bartolomeo or Cernobbio before going to Maslianico. The question is, do we follow the Germans or travel a day or two later taking the same path or by boat?"

Oskar was hesitant. "If we walk to Como, it will take days to reach Como or Lecco for that matter. If we make a wrong turn we could end up in Austria, or some other country at war with the Germans. Let's look around for more transport to Como."

"Let's find some accommodation first," said Jaro. "We can then sort ourselves out later. Anyone for a drink?"

They found a small rundown motel having no more than twenty rooms. The unpainted walls were paper-thin. Voices at normal volume floated through. It was whispers only. The group looked at each other when they realized the walls were so thin. Oskar said, "We talk outside in the street. This place has too many ears."

That night they scouted Milan for more information. Travel to Como by road was by bus or Train. Travel to Lecco was by bus only. Lecco offered more safety and away from the Germans. They would be further away from Switzerland but a step closer Austria. Como would be that much closer to Switzerland. No matter which way, mountains were an obstacle especially if they ended up walking. The group voted. It was going to be Como.

Dressed in their uniforms, they went to the train station in Milan. To their dismay, no trains were going to Como. A small avalanche blocked the tracks at Meda. The road was not passable.

Kiana looked at the station clock. "We have missed the bus to Lecco. It leaves in three minutes, and we are at least twenty minutes away."

Lori looked around and noted other passengers were equally inconvenienced by the closure. "Let's try tomorrow. There is a small café across the road. Let's go there and plan what we will do."

Again, they searched for information regarding transport to Como. Oskar found a police station and risked entering. After ten minutes he got some information. There was a bus which goes to Meda every day. It leaves Milan at eight-thirty in the morning each day. It returns at six p.m. Oskar asked for directions. There was no official bus stop. People had to go to the driver's home.

An elderly man escorting his equally elderly wife were on their morning walk. Kiana approached them. "Excuse me. Can you give me and my brothers directions to this address?" The man read the address. "Ah! Yes. That is across the road from where we live. You are close by."

The old man pointed up the street. "Go all the way to the end and then turn left. Then all the way to the end of that street. Then turn right. There are four houses and a shed. Wait for the bus outside the shed." Kiana thanked the couple and relayed the instructions.

At eight in the morning the group were at the designated shed. The bus slowly emerged from its overnight shelter. The bus was in a bad shape; dints and broken or missing windows made the bus look untrustworthy and cold for the trip. The driver greeted the group. "I am not ready yet. The windows need fixing." He pulled out sheets of cardboards and taped them to the inside of the bus. When he had finished, he proudly stood back. "Perfecto." Three other people had joined the group.
Cheerfully the driver said, "Climb in. My wife will collect the fares before we leave." When all were seated, a middle-aged lady entered carrying a bag. She said quietly to all, "Ten liras please."

Oskar gave her forty Liras. He pointed to the members of his group. She nodded and took the notes. She left the bus.

After thirty minutes, the bus pulled into a non-descript village. Here four more people got on and each paid the driver the same amount of money. The new travelers sat down as the bus pulled away. Twenty minutes later the bus stopped again.

German and Italian troops stopped the bus. The driver cursed as he came to a stop in the middle of the road. A German held the driver at gun point while one Italian spoke. "Where is this bus going?" The driver mustered up as much calmness as he could. "Meda." The Italian soldier looked at the travelers. He ordered one man to vacate the seat and move down to another spare seat. The German then lowered his gun. He also ejected the person sitting directly behind the driver. The person found another seat further back. Oskar moved to sit beside Kiana. Lori moved to sit beside Jaro. The newcomers noticed the shift. The Italian asked, "Why did you move?" Lori said, "Just in case more soldiers get on. Are more coming on?" The Italian soldier looked blank and didn't respond. The passengers were now distinctively quieter; whispers replaced near audible soft voices. One traveler put away his harmonica. The driver was fuming. He got out of his seat and asked for the fare. The soldiers laughed and pointed their guns at the driver. The driver returned to his seat to continue the journey to Meda.

At Meda, the passengers got off the bus. The soldiers were the last to leave. Oskar and Kiana headed directly to a tavern not far from the bus depot. Lori and Jaro followed minutes later. In the tavern, they sat in separate groups chatting quietly. They wanted to make sure the soldiers didn't appear. They never surfaced. Uneasiness remained as the two groups united.
"Those two soldiers on the bus were serious," said Lori.

"Too serious. Maybe a power trip," said Kiana. "I saw people like that in the Vatican. Creepy. Self-absorbing devils. They speak with twisted tongues; they say one thing and do another. Yuck." "I think we need to be extra careful. The border is just over sixty kilometres away. So close and yet so far. We need to buy warmer clothes for the journey and a few blankets will help.

The small town only had two taverns with accommodation. The one which had a vacant room had a sign which said, 'Couples Only'. Lori and Kiana entered and posed as a couple. When they were in the room, Lori slipped out and smuggled Oskar and Jaro in.

 Later that evening, Lori and Kiana left the tavern. Lori and Kiana returned two hours later with four blankets, three of which were taken off clothes lines and one they purchased. Oskar returned from his night of scavenging with two thick jackets he stole from the tavern and two he bought at a shop. The shop was closed but the owner was still working. He had tapped on the window to gain the owner's attention. The owner was pleased with the extra sale. Jaro came back with an assortment of gloves and thick socks he stole from a shop. He added, "I was at the front and noted the back door was open. The owner was working in the back area. I could see the top of his head. By the time I went to the back door to gain his attention, he was nowhere to be seen. I think he went to the toilet at the back. The back door was still open. I just helped myself and hoped the man stayed in the toilet block long enough for me to escape. We just need to get some food and that will be it. We should make a start in daytime. Crossing at night will be too dangerous. Just thinking about the cold makes me shiver."

Chapter 18
Meda to Como.

At the crack of dawn, the group set out to cross the mountains. They were walking along the road when a farmer drove past. The farmer stopped by the group. He asked, "Where are you going?"

"Como," replied Oskar.

The famer looked concerned. "Just how are you going to cross the mountains? The cold will kill you."

Oskar said, "We have warm clothes and blankets."

The farmer shook his head. "My farm is halfway up the mountain. I can take you all to where I must turn to go to my farm. Do you want a ride?" Without a second thought, the group clambered into the old large car

It was nearly forty minutes before the farmer stopped driving. There was a side road. "I turn here. Time for you to get out. Don't walk for more than an hour. You need to find shelter. A storm is coming. There is an old cabin used by herdsmen on the left side of the road. There is a track leading to it. It may be covered with snow. If the track is covered, you may miss the cabin. There are no signs to show the way." The group thanked the farmer before heading further up the road.

After an hour of walking, the sky became dark. Kiana looked at the foreboding clouds. "We better find shelter, and fast. Do any of you see a cabin?" Lori climbed a tree to the first branch.

"I see it. We walked past it. It sure looks old." He pointed to the direction of the cabin. "I can lead the way."

After five minutes of backtracking, Lori said, "This way." He shuffled some snow away with his feet. Evidence of a muddy track was revealed. When the group reached the cabin, they looked at its condition. Jaro asked, "I am not sure this wreck will stand up. The wind is increasing. Let's look around and see if there is anything else."
Oskar pointed to a cluster of rocks. "I will check that out." The rocks were in a rough u-shape. One rock had fallen over a part of the u to make a crude roof. He muttered to himself, "This will be a backup if the cabin begins to shake."

The group entered the cabin and looked around. Gaps in a timber wall allowed the wind to whistle through. There was a fireplace made from stones. No wood. "Well do we stay here?" asked Kiana feeling the cabin was just as cold as the outside.
"If we sacrifice one blanket over the wall where the wind blows most, and huddle together, I think we will survive the night," said Oskar. A blanket was erected on the wall which cut out most wind filtering through. Lori and Kiana gathered some wood hoping it wasn't too moist to be lit. They tried a few times to start the fire before giving up.

"It looks like a cold meal," said Jaro as his teeth began to chatter. "It is a choice of frozen vegetables and frozen fruit." He twisted an apple around on his fingers as he spoke and grinned. "Gelato, anyone?" He continued with his clowning. "Pure fruit or vegetable gelato." He placed the selection in the centre of the group. Slowly they reached out for an item.

Through the night, the wind became stronger. The cabin shook a little. The noise and the vibration woke the group up from their uneasy sleep. They looked around the cabin. Similar thoughts raced through their minds; do we leave or hope for the best. They had their answer seconds later. The group quickly gathered their belongs, ripped the blanket off the wall and ran outside. There was a loud noise. The cabin came crashing down. Oskar led them to the rocky outcrop where they sheltered for the rest of the night.

The next day the sky was blue. The raging winds of the night before had died down but still the wind-chill factor made things uncomfortable. The group packed their mere belongings and headed back to the main road. They walked for nearly a day; their heavy backpacks made the trek slow. It was very late in the afternoon before they saw the town of Como in the distance. Too tired to travel and worried about another possible storm, they looked for shelter. Lori found an alcove of rocks near the side of the road. He pointed. "This looks like home for the night. At least we are protected on three sides. The two bushes in front will act as a wind break." Finding nothing better, the group squeezed themselves into the rocky alcove.

Oskar and Jaro went looking for wood to make a fire. "Let's hope we can get a fire going. Even ten minutes will feel wonderful." They carried the wood back to the camp to find Lori and Kiana had already laid out the meagre rations. Kiana looked up from her food arrangement. "We have a tiny bit of frozen salami, frozen cheese, frozen nuts and frozen bread. That is it. I hope the wood is not too wet." It took Oskar several goes to get the fire going. At the end of their meal, Oskar placed the hot pieces of timber around the interior edges in their rocky alcove. The extra warmth wouldn't last long but while it lasted, it was a small luxury. Before drifting off to sleep, they planned their moves into Como.

The road to Como was uneventful. Very few cars or trucks of any description passed by. From their last camp, they took just over an hour to reach the outskirts of the town.

Chapter 19
Como.

Almost aimlessly they wandered through the streets of Como. They noted where any guest houses were, and which houses appeared as possible ones to enter for a cash robbery. Now and then they would pause and ask directions and distance to the lake shores. There had to be a boat for hire or to work on or just for the taking. When they reached the shores, they looked around.

The boats were moored on posts supporting two jetties. More boats, mostly smaller ones were pushed on the land. Most were covered with canvas which drooped with the weight of the recent snow. Kiana spotted a rundown kiosk. "Let's go there and ask for information."

As they walked the short distance Jaro commented about the lake's water, "The water hasn't frozen over. There are shards of ice. If anyone fell into that water, they would die from the cold in about five minutes. The chards may cause a few motor issues. Sailing will be the only short cut unless we walk to the Swiss border."

They reached the rundown kiosk. Although it was shut, Kiana knocked as loud as she could on the door. Eventually, a light at the back of the store came on. A tired looking middle-aged woman opened the door halfway. She rubbed her eyes and roughly asked, "What do you want?"
Kiana tried to smile as best as she could. "We want to hire a boat to Cernobbio."
The lady leaned one arm on the door. "Good luck. The army has taken control of the bigger boats and the owners of other boats refuse to set sail because they are pulled up by the army. The army thinks everyone is running away to Switzerland. If our army doesn't stop you, the Germans will. There are quite a few German boats

patrolling the lake. They shoot first and then ask questions. Many people have just disappeared, shot or taken to prisoner of war camps somewhere in Germany or Poland. I suggest you walk. I'm not risking any more boats." With that, the lady shut the door.

"Well, that was short and informative," said Kiana.
"We better head back towards the town," said Oskar. "Keep your eyes open for a place to stay or a place to work. We are low on cash and food."

When they came across their first open outdoor café, they stopped. Jaro looked at the menu on one of three empty tables. "Not much offering. Turkish coffee and Turkish coffee, and a choice of orange juice and apple juice for drinks. The food isn't much better. Half the menu is crossed out. It is pasta, eggs on toast, cheese on toast, Italian salad and…..that is about it."
Lori groaned. "A food shortage caused by this war. How much do we have?"

Oskar picked up another menu to look at the prices. "Well, we have enough for water and two serves of eggs on toast. Anyone for sharing eggs on toast?" "We better find us some work," said Lori.

The order for two servings of eggs was placed. The waiter-cum-owner frowned at the order. As two people began to split the servings, he frowned and shook his head. He decided to keep a sharp eye on the group. When they left, he watched them walk slowly up the street and turn a corner.

The group came across a guest house. Knowing they had no funds, they asked if they could work in exchange for accommodation. After a bit of haggling, the owner-cum-clerk gave them all clear. He showed them to a small back room with two single beds. They barely had time to put their belongings in the rooms when the owner said,

"You, young lady will work the kitchen. It needs cleaning." He pointed to Lori and Jaro. "You two come with me." He took them to another guest room. He slowly opened the door. Lori gasped at its state. "What happened here?" "Germans. They trashed the room and just about broke everything. Some people should never drink. They get violent. Fix and clean this room up. Put anything that is beyond repair along one side of the hallway. That needs to be disposed before five. New guests generally arrive about that time." Then he told Oskar to follow him outside. "Can you fix a shingled roof?" Oskar nodded. "I have done it once before. An old lady got me to repair her roof for two nights of accommodation. It took three of us to redo the entire roof. We did it in two days."
The man nodded. "Agreed. The holes are in back, above two bedrooms being used by other customers. I think about fifteen shingles will cover the holes. When that is done, let me know. I have another job."

By midafternoon, Kiana had completed her task. The kitchen sparkled. Lori and Jaro were still repairing the room that was trashed. Rubbish in boxes lined one side of the passageway. The owner looked inside to see the bed covered in old drapes catching drips of paint from the ceiling. The handbasin in the corner was shining as if new. The cupboard doors were reattached on to their hinges. The cupboard was cleaned up inside and out. The owner looked at the accumulating rubbish and inspected the contents. He then went to check on Oskar.

Oskar was checking the rest of the roof, looking for more damage or gaps. The owner called out to Oskar, "Are you finished?"
Oskar walked over to the edge. "There are three more suspicious spots which could develop into possible gaps in the near future. I will fix them now. I will need five more shingles. The owner replied, "I will have to buy more. Come down and take the rubbish out of the

passageway while I go and buy more." Oskar climbed down from the roof.

By the time the owner had come back, all the rubbish in the hallway was placed behind the front fence ready for quick removal. Oskar climbed back up the roof and began working. The owner then rechecked the bedroom. The ceiling was completed. The walls above the timber paneling were completed. The owner looked at the old drapes. Paint splatter had killed off any reuse. He reasoned, the curtains were old anyway so new curtains would be in order. He had noted there was less splatter than any tradesperson he ever had before. He nodded.

He met Kiana in the common lounge area. She looked up as the man approached. "Can you sew?" he asked.
Kiana put the magazine she was flipping through down. "Not well and I have never used a sewing machine. Why?"
"I need to get new curtains. Can you put curtains up?"
"I have never done it before. I can try," she replied.

Twenty minutes later the man returned with a bundle of material. "Put these pre-made curtains up. I couldn't get what would look very nice. Nothing much is getting through." He looked down at the gaudy red, black, cream and green abstract pattern. "Not my taste." He handed the curtains to her. "Put them up tomorrow. The paint needs to dry first."

By mid-morning the second day the group had completed their assigned tasks. The owner inspected all the work. He nodded his approval of the room's transformation and smiled. The gaudy curtains with the touches of cream didn't look too out of place. At least the cream matched the ceiling and walls. The owner said as he approached the group, "Do you want to stay longer? Trades people are hard to get, and you lot do a good work?"

The group flashed glances to each other. Oskar replied, "We are transient. Who would want us to do any work?"

"I have a friend who is nearly blind. Can't walk much either but he does have funds to pay for work. His house needs fixing. Again, the roof and the inside could do with a major clean up. He can't see the accumulating dirt and the locals are refusing to do it or think they can't. It will be two days of work and the man is willing to pay.

Oskar looked at the others for direction. There were nods to do the task. "When do we start?"

"Now," replied the man.

Two days later, the group had finished the major clean out and organized the rubbish to be carted away. The blind man paid the group enough cash to cover the accommodation and more.

The owner of the guest house smiled when he inspected the rundown house. The transformation was complete. He assured the blind friend the place almost looked like new on the inside and the money spent was worthwhile.

Oskar said, "We have decided to move on. We are going to walk to Maslianico."

"What a shame you are leaving. If the stories are right, walking will take three days and soldiers are guarding every kilometre. What is in Maslianico?"

Before Oskar could answer, Jaro blurted out, "Family. My aunts and an uncle."

The owner said, "Be careful. That is close to the border. The Swiss won't say anything, but the Italian soldiers will hold you up. Aren't you supposed to be in the army?"

Oskar replied, "We did our time. We were in Albania trying to fight the Greeks, but they were helped by the British who continually bombed us. One of our friends died in that war."

"Sorry to hear that. I think half the young men are buried over there. Politicians should never run wars. It is sad for me to see such hard-working and good workers leave. Good luck getting to Maslianico.

Three days later the group were two kilometres away from the outskirts of San Bartolomeo. They were held up by an Italian patrol group. Not satisfied by their replies as to why they were travelling to Maslianico, they were detained at gunpoint until a superior was informed. They were taken to a building for questioning.

When they saw Colonel Luca Morelli they met in Bologna, they were surprised. Colonel Morelli ordered the guns to be lowered. "I see we meet again, my friends," said the Colonel in a welcoming voice. The soldiers surrounding them looked surprised. The Colonel turned to the soldiers and ordered, "Give these people a meal and then have them brought to my office.

In the office, Colonel Morelli made sure the staff just outside were given time away. Then he said in a soft voice, "Thank you for the valuable information about my brother's safe. I made quite a tidy retirement sum. My brother was fuming about the robbery. His wife was ten times worse as I took most of the remaining jewels. Of course, no one nearby saw anything. Now I have a job for you to help me out. When you get to Maslianico, go to this address." The colonel handed him a piece of paper with an address. "I have two nieces aged ten and fifteen. I want them in Switzerland. I want you to escort them over the border where they will meet by my sister, Maria. Maria is one of my two sisters. The girls haven't seen Maria for five years. She was smart and got out early. I will phone Maria that you will be travelling with the girls and for her to wait one kilometre inside the Swiss border. There is a chalet which is used by all newcomers to buy food before going deeper into Switzerland. There are signs pointing to the chalet." The Colonel drew a mud-map on the same paper just in case the signs were pulled down.

"Tell Maria, I will be joining her in four weeks and that's when I will get official leave after a few delays. It is important to get the girls out. The war is deepening. Switzerland is the safest pace for them." He coughed and gave a wink with a grin. "As for now, you stay in the barracks. Put on your Italian uniforms." He turned to Kiana, "I am not sure what to do with you."

Kiana coughed. "I have a uniform now. I stole one off a clothesline in Meda."

Oskar looked surprised. "You didn't tell us that"

Kiana smirked. "I wanted to surprise you. I will stay with Oskar, Lori and Jaro. If we are together, I will be safe." The Colonel felt uncomfortable but there were no alternatives which he could think of. "It is settled then. Tomorrow morning after breakfast come to this office."

The next morning, they visited Colonel Morelli's office. The secretary held them up. "The Colonel gives his apologies for not meeting you. Things have happened overnight. He said for me to give you these instructions in this envelope." Oskar took the envelope.

Oskar gave a nod. "That is okay."

When they left the building, Oskar said, "We better find a place to change our clothes and read the instructions."

The group looked around. Jaro pointed to a public restroom. "Not ideal. It will have to do."

The streets were busy with army trucks from both Italian and German armies. As the trucks drove through the streets, people quickly stood aside crowding the edges. Lori asked a teenage girl, "What is going on?"

The girl gave a frown. "Didn't you hear? The Germans are taking over Lake Como to stop people using the lake. They said spies are using it to cross into Switzerland."

"No I didn't hear that. Thank you for letting me know."

Jaro returned to the group to report. "Traveling by boat to Switzerland is now out of the question. The Germans are patrolling the lake. We better find a newspaper for an update."

They found a shop which sold newspapers. The one sheet tabloid was light on details regarding the new lake patrols. The Italian forces were patrolling the land while the Germans patrolled the lake in confiscated local vessels. The bigger boats were converted to enhance the German war machine. Motors which were not powerful were upgraded. Guns were mounted at four locations; one at front and back and one on each side. Powerless and angry, the locals could do nothing but watch after a few owners were shot for not handing over their vessels. Their livelihoods of all were suddenly stripped and adding to the town's food shortage.

"What do we do now?" asked Oskar who, like the others, was frustrated at the events.

Kiana grinned. "It shouldn't be too much of a problem. We have German uniforms, don't we?"

Lori looked at her and smiled. "Unfortunately, only three and I doubt the nun's costume would wash with other Germans we will meet."

"Then we will get one," said Jaro as he looked around the street. There has to be a place where the Germans go. Keep your eyes open."

After asking some locals where the Germans were based or went frequently to, one directed them to a camp four kilometres out of town.

At dusk, the group walked along the main road pushing a barrel of scavenged assorted vegetables, bread, butter and wine. When they neared the perimeter of the camp, they were stopped by guards who questioned the group and inspected the wheelbarrow.

Jaro and Kiana who were in civilian clothes were directed to a location used for venders. Lori and Oskar who were in uniforms were automatically ushed through the gates. Two other vendors had already set up shop. The soldiers were inspecting the goods before making a haggled purchase.

Lori and Oskar walked freely through the camp. Occasionally they waved and nodded to others as they passed them by. When they came across a tent which was unoccupied, Oskar stood guard while Lori rummaged through the contents inside.

He stole one helmet to complete his uniform from one tent and from others he stole some cash but was careful to leave some behind to help disguise the theft. Overall, the uniforms were too big. He changed tact. One tent had a uniform which were obviously for a short person and was approximately the size Kiana could wear. The uniform was squirreled away into a German backpack. Lori then had an idea. "Let's go to the building over there, the bath house. I think we can get some more items from there."

They moved towards the bath house. Three men were in the showers. They were too engrossed in their conversation to notice a pair of hands removing a jacket, a belt and boots. From another location in the shower room three helmets disappeared. Oskar placed one helmet on his head. They carried the two extras to the vendor's location where Jaro and Kiana were selling their wares.

The stall was bare, but Kiana had kept the men entertained by singing a few German and Italian songs. Jaro passed his hat around for a collection. Coins were deposited into the hat. He thanked each who gave a donation. The crowd groaned when Kiana said, "The show is over boys. If I can, I will come back next week." The comment raised a few smiles and claps. She gave a bow with a broad smile.

The wheelbarrow was returned to the location where it was found. The owners would not be wiser. They found a gap between two buildings in the town. The rear gap was blocked by a rickety wooden gate. The alcove provided a makeshift dressing room with an old blanket being held by two of the team as each changed into German uniforms. In uniforms, they made their way to the harbour where most of the unused boats were anchored.

Lori got on one boat and checked the cabin. Then he checked the fuel supply. The tank was half full. He called the others on. Oskar released the boat from its mooring. At slow speed, the boat chugged its way up the lake for a couple of kilometres before turning to hug the coastline. When the engine started to give signs of low fuel, they diverted the boat to shore. The boat was pushed onto the shore and abandoned. Someone would eventually find the craft.

Chapter 20

San Bartolomeo to Maslianico.

Under the cover of darkness, they silently moved along the shoreline until they saw some piers. From there, they could see the streets. Dawn was beginning to break. They had to find shelter as soon as possible for a change of clothes. After not finding any suitable shelter, they found an alley where they changed from German uniforms into civilian clothes.

The group began walking down the street with the dawn rays lighting their way. They looked for a guest house as they walked to what they presumed towards the main part of town. No guest houses were open at this time of day, but they noted many had the 'no vacancy' signs pulled down. Kiana asked, "I wonder if the signs are down because they are genuinely full, or the owners didn't want early newcomers waking them up."
Oskar placed an arm across her shoulder. "Maybe it is a bit of both. I bet there are more German soldiers here than Italian ones. We are still in Italy. We have to keep moving. I wonder if we can find a map. We can't be that far away from the border."

By midday, the group had made no progress. Most of the shops were closed and the handful that were open looked almost bare. There was a supply shortage of everything. Jaro ventured into a shoe shop and asked the owner, "I see there are not many shoes in the store. Is there a transport problem?" The man looked up from his workbench. He was mending a pair of overworn shoes.

"Nothing gets through these days. Most factories are only supplying shoes for the war. What you see here are the rejects from the factory. They are badly made but I can fix them to be wearable. Also, making things hard are our Swiss customers don't come anymore. The Germans shoot their ships and pull people out of the lake to be transported to prisoner camps. Bastards. You're new here, aren't you?"

Jaro nodded. "Just passing through. How do I get to Chiasso?"
The cobbler put his work down on the bench and stood up. He whispered, "Not a good idea. From here to the Swiss border, there are a mix of German and Italian soldiers guarding every road. There are more German ones than ours. Mussolini," the man paused and spat to the side, "doesn't give our men any warm clothes. They die from the cold. They catch a cold and then it is good-bye. Bastard. Families pay the price. We always do and he sits in comfort while giving bad orders from his very bad ideas. To get to Chiasso, you need to go over the mountains and pray you do not freeze to death."
Jaro gave the cobbler a small valued Italian coin. It was the last of the coins he had. He nodded before walking out. The cobbler took the coin, gave a smile before pocketing it. His eyes followed Jaro out of the door.

He saw Jaro meet up with two other men and a lady. He watched as the group moved away. He went back to work and shrugged off the interlude. The man paid him. He thought to himself, *so what a bit of rare cash for just a bit of information. So, what if these were young people on the run from the war.* He gave a sigh and reflected. He would join them on the run if he had no family commitments. He whispered to himself, "Good luck crossing the mountains. If the cold doesn't get you, the Germans might."

Through the next day the group thought of ways to earn money in a town that was obviously financially crumbling. They entered a few homes but walked out empty handed. No loose cash. No jewelry and barely any food. The people were on the poverty line like they were. Kiana suggested, "We should head to the centre of the town. Maybe there are more opportunities. One idea I have is we or at least me sing, some busking."

Oskar, Jaro and Lori thought it over. "Okay. There is nothing here anyway. The people there may be more better off. No harm in trying," said Jaro.

When they reached the town square, they were surprised to see most of the shops were shut. The streets were bustling. The shop owners had created a market which seemed to have attracted town's people. The group mingled in the crowd and lifted a change purse or two and a few food items which were consumed as they walked around. They met outside a tavern. In a corner, they compared notes and how much was collected in the change purses; just thirty Lira. They had to do better. It was enough for one night accommodation in this town of San Bartolomeo, that is, if they could find any. The group went back to the market area.

Kiana and Jaro began to sing. Lori and Oskar stood aside with caps at the ready to collect change. When Kiana and Jaro took a break, the group moved to a quieter corner to count the loose change.

Lori groaned. "We need two more Lira." They moved to another location in the market area. Kiana and Lori began singing Italian songs. Jaro and Oskar watched the crowd. After twenty minutes, Kiana and Lori stopped singing. From the corner where Oskar was standing, he gave a nod. They had reached their goal plus a few coins more.

It was close to eight in the evening before they found a single room in a house. It wasn't a guest house as such but a room in an ordinary house. The old lady was doing her best to make ends meet. Renting a room or two out was her only source of income since her husband had died years ago. She had been supported by her two sons and daughter, but the war had seen her two sons die and the daughter permanently disabled when a bomb landed too close to the medical tent. Her grandchildren who are in their teens were doing their best to provide for her. The old lady didn't want to burden her grandchildren any more than necessary. Four people filling her house was an income. She directed the three men to the spare room and Kiana to another much smaller room. The old lady said, "The price includes soup and breakfast." That sealed the deal for the group.

When the group were about to leave the following day, the old lady asked, "I am happy for you to stay another night."
Oskar replied, "We don't have enough for another night. We did appreciate your hospitality."
The old lady wasn't going to leave her only customers for a month to escape. "How about you do some work for me and then you can stay an extra night."
The group looked at each other before Jaro asked, "What kind of work do you need to be done?"
" Painting my house so more customers will come. I did the front fence myself, but I can't do the house. I can't reach up and I am no good on ladders. I get dizzy. I have the paint, brushes and whitewash in the shed at the back." She clutched onto Jaro's arm and pulled him towards the back yard. "Come. Come on the rest of you. You can do it." Reluctantly the group followed.

As soon as she opened the door, assorted tools tumbled out. She pushed them aside muttering, "The grandchildren were supposed to tidy this up, so things did not fall out." She pointed to the large cans of whitewash. "There is the paint." She searched the shed with her eyes and pointed. "There are the brushes and the clean-up chemicals." She grabbed Kiana's arm and pulled her away. "That's men's work. Your work is inside the house." When the lady and

Kiana went into the house, the lady said, "Help me cook some food and then help me clean the house. The walls and ceiling are dusty. They need a clean. Then we do the floors." Kian groaned but didn't say anything.

Three hours later the painting was completed, and Kiana's work was done. The old lady looked at the house from the street. Although she could see some areas of whitewash applied unevenly, she nodded her approval. "Now you go out and enjoy your holiday. I will see you tonight at six. That is when dinner will be served."

The group scouted the town for information about the routes to Chiasso. The information was consistent. Germans ruled the roads to Maslianico and the alternative route to Cernobbio. They had check points at random locations along the roads on the Italian side of the border. Going off road and running parallel to the main road was also risky. It would draw suspicion. That meant the Germans would use them as target practice. Not an option. The only option was over the mountains, cold and unforgiving winds that made the mountains a frozen hell. They had already crossed out staying a few more days in the town. There was no work, and the locals could grow suspicious of them. They would go via the mountains. They planned their needs for a two-day crossing. With luck, they would cross the mountains in a day.

 The first night on the mountain saw the group huddle together in rocky gaps. The blankets and closeness only cut the edge off the cold wind blowing across the slopes. They ate a ration of food with near frozen fingers. Sleep was almost impossible. The snow slowed their trek by having to pull their legs up high over the snow and only to sink again.

 The next night wasn't so cold. They found some trees to shelter behind and wrapped themselves up as much as possible. As they shivered, a lone fox dawdled by. Lori looked at the creature that had turned its head to look at the group.

"That looks delicious. Too bad we have no guns or other tools." He gestured for the fox to move on. "Shoo, Shoo. Don't look at us like that. I doubt we will taste that great. Shoo. Shoo."

The next morning the sky had cleared. From their unofficial lookout, they could see the rooftops of Maslianico. "Just one more hill to go over and then we will be there." They packed their meagre belongings and headed for the town. They wanted to cover as much ground as possible before any new storm brewed.

Exhausted, they slowly climbed down the final slope. They stopped when they saw a barbed-wire barrier. Oskar swore at the obstacle, "Who the fuck put this here? This is still Italy. Why the wire on this side of town?"

The others groaned and offered no possible reason. They didn't have any tools to cut through the spiked wire. They had no way of knowing how far the wire stretched.

"Which way do we go?" asked Jaro as he looked around at the surrounding landscape.

Oskar replied, "Good question. The road to the town must be close by. I am going to climb that tree and see if there are any roads."

Ten minutes later Oskar was on the ground again. "The closest road is about two kilometres away. The bad news is Germans and Italians are guarding it for traffic each way. There is approximately fifty metres of no man's land inside Italy. The town of Maslianico seems to be surrounded by wire. I can't see much more than that. What do we wear? Italian uniforms or German ones? Civilian clothes are out of the question. It is a sure way to be searched and maybe taken as prisoners."

Lori climbed the tree and studied the distant activity. "I say two of us go in German uniforms and the other two in Italian. The two groups of soldiers are working side by side. It would look quite normal."

Kiana and Lori wore German uniforms while Jaro and Oskar donned Italian uniforms. They walked towards the road and to the checkpoint. On the way, they observed others going through and decided to imitate the actions. They gave a nod to the guards and continued towards Maslianico.

They reached the outskirts of the town, the first of many streets and stopped. Another checkpoint. They saluted the guards and walked through. They continued as if everything was normal. When they were well away from what seemed to be the final checkpoint, they relaxed. The town was swarming with soldiers from both sides but the division between the two armies was marked. Not many civilians walked in the streets and those who did walked hastily past with their heads down to avoid eye contact with any soldiers. Kiana looked around the near deserted street. She pointed to a tavern. "Let's go in there and see what is happening."

Still in their uniforms, the group entered the tavern. The very few Italian soldiers in the place looked up. Those who did immediately continued their private conversations. The Germans who bothered to look up to watch the newcomers, hailed them over to their group. Lori and Kiana gave a nod. Jaro and Oskar just looked on. Lori whispered, "I think we better grace ourselves. Maybe we can get some information." The group walked over to the seated soldiers.

The seated soldiers offered two chairs still vacant at the table and gestured for Oskar and Jaro to confiscate two from surrounding tables. The group introduced themselves with variants of their names. Kiana suddenly became Karl, Lori became Leo. Oskar adopted the Italian name Ottavia while Jaro took the Italian name Jacopo.

Twenty minutes later Lori, Kiana, Jaro and Oskar left the small German group who were becoming rowdier as the alcohol saturated their bodies. Kiana said as the group walked away, "Let's find a different place to stay but we need to change our clothes." The group found another tavern which was less crowded. Oskar stood guard in the short narrow hallway to the restrooms. Kiana checked the women's area by calling out if anyone was inside. She slipped into the room, found a cubicle and change into civilian clothes. The men rotated the watch for each other while Kiana made enquiries about work and accommodation at the main bar. While she was waiting for her drink order, she froze when she heard a voice behind her. She slowly turned around to see the German soldier who she brushed off in the bus going from Villach in Austria to Udine in Italy.

Louis said as he smiled, "We meet again fräulein. Fate has brought us together again for the second or is it the third time?"
Kiana just stared trying to collect her thoughts. Eventually she said without taking her eyes off Louis, "Believe what you want. I have --- no interest or intention to even speak to you." She took the drinks the bartender placed on a tray to a table with four chairs. She placed a beer at each seat. Louis followed her and placed himself on one of the seats. Kiana removed the drink and said, "That is not for you. Go." Jaro, Oskar and Lori were now in civilian clothes when they spotted a German soldier at their table. It was obvious to them Kiana was quite annoyed.

The trio walked over. Oskar said to Kiana, "Thanks sis for getting our drinks. Jaro and Lori placed themselves beside Louis to partially corner him. Louis saw the three men surrounding him with only an escape to move backwards. Louis said, "Why can't you men leave her alone?"
Oskar hissed, "My sister is my responsibility. She clearly doesn't like you. Move away."

Jaro stepped forward. "My cousins are not impressed with you. Please take yourself away."

Lori added, "My friends don't like you. Let's be civil in this establishment. Please just walk away."

Louis looked at Kiana's bodyguards, nodded and slowly stepped away. He looked at Kiana. "I will see you around. Maybe we can meet another time under different circumstances." Louis walked away annoyed. When he neared the door, he looked back at the foursome. He took note of their faces. His mind was ticking over. The same group of men were on the bus. One she said from before, her husband was gone. A pretty young widow somewhat over protected by three men. He noted they spoke flawless German and their Italian was spoken with a slight accent. His mind was ticking over as to who this group could be. He would keep watch.

This low set tavern had some accommodation. The group booked a family room. The room had four beds. Three singles and a double. Kiana opted for the bed closest to the door. She allowed the others to sort out who was going to have the other beds. They all sat in the room whispering their next set of actions. Too many soldiers on land. Maslianico was the last town in Italy before crossing the border. They recalled the mission to take two teenage girls across the border into Switzerland. Oskar pulled out the address and then referred to a very tattered map of the town hanging on one wall.

The map was nothing more than the city centre with arrows pointing to what could be villages or even suburbs. Oskar pointed to the arrow. "It looks like we go north to pick up the children. I wonder if we could even cross the border with extras to take care of. We have enough trouble doing it ourselves. No uniforms for these girls. It will pose a problem."

Jaro said, "I know this will sound unpopular, we go over the mountains and cross in a remote location and then double back to Chaisso to drop the girls off. We need better information. Better maps will help. Tomorrow, we scout for information about the mountains, the conditions and so on. Kiana, can you gather food supplies while we ask questions around town?"

The next morning, Kiana scoured the food shops and bought what she thought would carry well. She didn't want to be caught like before with matches trying to light moist wood. She purchased a mini can of kerosene. Then she recalled the barb wire blocking their pathway. She found a set of large wire cutters. She looked at the tool and whispered, "This should do the job. Now some gloves to protect our hands." Kiana jumped when she heard a voice behind her. Louis was there. This time she had no back up.

Kiana hurried to the counter, quickly paid for the wire cutters and the kerosene before almost running down the street. Louis was in pursuit. He caught up with her and pulled her by the arm in a bid to stop her.

Instinctively, she dropped the food and the kerosene she was carrying, swung around to clout Louis over the head with the large wire cutters. He stumbled backwards a few steps and then dropped to the ground. Kiana gathered her food, the cutters and can and ran as fast as she could to the tavern. She locked herself in the room. She shook with fear as she was expecting the police or some German military policeman to come knocking on the door. She thought to herself as she sobbed, *I am in really big trouble. I must warn the boys. How. I can't leave this room.* She swore at the situation she created for herself and the others.

An hour later, Kiana heard a key slide into the lock. She took cover and armed herself with the wire cutters. Then she heard Oskar talking to Jaro and Oskar. She relaxed and ran over to hug Oskar. She shook and cried. He pulled her back a little. "What's the matter?"

Kiana quickly explained what had happened. "I really don't know if I killed him or just knocked him out. Sorry. So sorry, I stuffed up so badly. Every time I heard footsteps outside the room, I shook with fear not knowing who was coming for me."

Jaro said, "I overheard some people say that a German soldier was attacked. He was carried away to the local hospital for treatment. I think we better start moving out of this place. When that soldier recovers, there will be a search."

Kiana said, "The soldier was Louis. I think he was following me. As I said before, it was instinctive self-defense. That guy scares me."

Lori started packing his belonging. "Start packing and get out of here. We can discuss our next move later."

Three hours later the group found a boarding house. There were no other guests. The family which ran the guest house welcomed them. Money was in short supply and any guests were welcomed.

The family had moved the children around. The girls were placed in one room which had two, two-tiered bunk beds. The boys were crammed in another room containing a single bed and a bunk bed. The baby's cot was in with the parents. The cramming allowed three bedrooms to be opened for renting.

In their new overnight stay, the group planned their movements. They would go Chiasso via the mountains. The teen girls would just have to brave it out. It would mean the trip would take two or three days although they could see Chiasso from Maslianico. It was frustrating, so close and yet so far.

They collected the two girls, Chiara and Fiorella from their mother, Alicia. The girls were surprised that they would be going via the mountains. Alicia phoned her sister, Maria to be at the chalet in two days' time. She warned it could be three days depending on the terrain and weather conditions.

Alicia drove the group as far as she could to the mountain bases. They passed through three check points. Passports as the only identification they had on them, was checked and photos inside were checked.

At the end of the road, Alicia unloaded the group. She checked their luggage, hugged her daughters one last time before watching them disappear into the trees at the base of the mountain range.

When Alicia returned home, immediately felt the emptiness of the house. She turned on the radio in a bid to quell the emptiness. She gasped with shock. There was a description of the young lady wanted by the police for assaulting a German soldier. She wondered if the young lady who was with the men and in fact the men themselves were criminals. Then she immediately changed her mind. Luca, her brother would never have given his trust to these people. She smiled as she considered the situation. Her daughters escaping to Switzerland, although be it via a dangerous route, was a load off her mind. Going by road, a much shorter alternative was significantly more dangerous. They had food. They had warm clothes and sleeping bags and an extra blanket. They were weighed down. She saw the slow walk towards the trees. She nodded to herself. *They are in good hands. Women don't attack men for no reason. A woman has a right to defend herself from an attacking man. The nationality was irrelevant.*

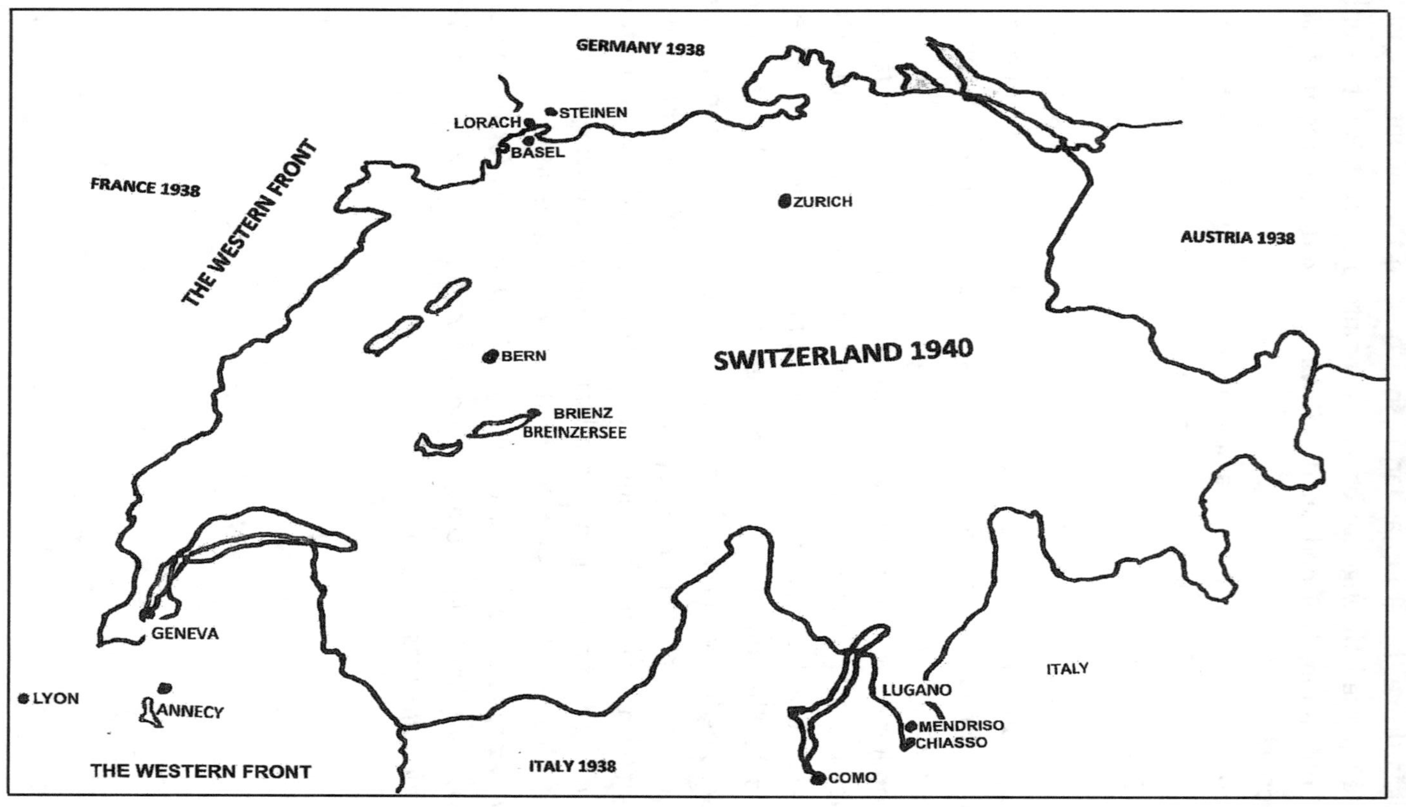
GERMANY 1938
LORACH
STEINEN
BASEL
ZURICH
FRANCE 1938
THE WESTERN FRONT
AUSTRIA 1938
BERN
SWITZERLAND 1940
BRIENZ
BREINZERSEE
GENEVA
LYON
ANNECY
LUGANO
ITALY
MENDRISO
CHIASSO
THE WESTERN FRONT
ITALY 1938
COMO

Chapter 21
Chiasso

On the first night on the mountains, the group of six huddled in a cave which was no more than three metres deep. They built a small fire near the entrance to heat up some rations. The smoldering wood was scattered to the sides of the cave in a bid to reduce the coldness coming from the cold rocks. A few smaller rocks were piled at the cave entrance as far as the found rocks would permit. Between the gaps, a blanket was draped. The make-do minimally effective wind barrier was all they could do. Kiana made the girls sleep closer to each other and to herself to maximize body heat. The men did the same. Through the night, the wind howled and snow fell.

The next morning, the group had to push away some snow blocking the exit of the cave.

When they all were outside, Oskar groaned. The ground was thick with snow and slippery. He cursed. *If things were not difficult enough, now it is slippery.* The group studied the surrounding for an easier route. It was difficult to make a judgement with so much snow covering the ground. Kiana pointed to a distant location. "Tell me if I am wrong. Is that smoke I see over there?"

Everyone turned their attention to the dark-grey plume. Jaro commented, "I think you are right, but it is a long way away."

Oskar looked at the compass he was holding. "It is in the right direction towards Chiasso. I have a feeling something happened over there. Let's start moving."

It was near the end of the day when they found what was burning. They gasped. It was a plane which had crashed. The parts and contents were strewn across the mountain side. Oskar cautioned the others. "I will go alone. Keep under cover. I will signal if it is okay to advance. If anything happens to me, run away. Go east. I mean leave me." He turned to Kiana. "Do you get what I mean? No screaming. Just run east."

Slowly Oskar approached the downed plane. He examined the debris as he went. Bits of metal here and there were strewn across the ground. Nothing of value or interest. The tail had broken off from the fuselage. Oskar stopped dead in his tracks when he heard a soft groan. He was on high alert. He squatted and then went into a crawl. He reached the main fuselage. A man wearing a British uniform and blood dripping from various parts of his body, looked blankly at Oskar. The man tried to smile when he saw Oskar. He mumbled. "The storm." The man puffed the next words. "Are you my contact?" Oskar didn't respond immediately. "No. I just happened to have seen the smoke. My curiosity got to me." The injured man spat out blood as he continued to gasp for air. The man's eye went glassy, and he stopped breathing. Oskar was silent not knowing exactly what to do. All he could think of was the two teen girls should not see this. He was wishing he had not seen what he had.

He dragged out the injured man and made a shallow grave; just layers of snow covering a badly damaged body. Satisfied all was clear and the girls would not see the dead man, he waved his hands to the waiting group. It was safe.

The group searched the plane. It was a British Spitfire which had been modified for aerial surveillance. Jaro looked at the semi-melted cameras on board. He wondered if the film was also damaged. He couldn't dislodge the camera from its mount as the heat from the fire welded the camera to it. He poked around it, pushing and pulling anything thing that could still move or looked it could be moved. One section came ajar but not enough to prise it open. He found a piece of jagged metal to insert. He twisted the make-shift lever to near breaking point. The slot suddenly sprung open. Film was inside with signs of melting. Jaro pulled out the roll and exposed the undeveloped damage roll to sunlight. Any images that were there, disappeared, or damaged to the point of being useless. Jaro spotted another camera attached to the underbelly of the plane. It was still smoldering from the fire. He used the lever again in a bid see what was on the film. The film compartment was like molten lava which poured out its contents. Jaro jumped back and shook his hand. The hot goo burnt his fingers.

Lori called out to the others in the group. "I have found something. A briefcase!" The others came running to the briefcase which Lori found some ten metres from the cockpit. He opened the bag. The documents were in English. Lori asked, "Can anyone read English?" The oldest of the teenage girls, Chiara said, "I was learning English in high school. I am not good at it. Can I try?"
Lori handed her one document. The others gathered around. She stumbled on some words and said she didn't know others. She formed a gist which she said to the others, "It may not be accurate. I think it says Hitler is going to break the treaty with Italy." She looked up and said, "Does that mean, Italy will be invaded too?"
Oskar replied, "The pilot must have been in contact with a spy to have such information. Not knowing everything in that document, I have to say yes." He looked to the others. "Do you remember what Colonel Morelli said when we first met? He guessed Hitler was getting tired of Mussolini's failures and could invade Italy. It looks like his deductions from all the disasters were correct. What do we do with these documents?"

Without hesitation Kiana said, "Put them in the brief case and bury them. We can't travel with that. If we get caught, we will be murdered as spies." Chiara placed the documents in the briefcase and closed it. She handed it to Oskar. "Here. Burry it. We are not spies and this makes us spies. I don't want to die as a spy." Oskar looked around for a place to bury it. He thought of the body he had buried earlier. "I have a place." He walked over to the dead pilot. He partially uncovered the body and slipped the bag under the dead man. *This is not ideal. When the snow melts, the man and the documents will be easily found. If the ground wasn't frozen, both would be buried properly. This is all I can do.*

The group searched the plane wreck a little longer. The younger teenage girl, Fiorella, lifted a lid of what looked like a chest. She called out. "I have found something. It is a full British uniform with a pistol."

Oskar was first to reach her. The girl held up the uniform. "I think it fits you." She handed it to Oskar. Fiorella dug deeper into the box. She smiled wildly at what she saw. "Yum! Chocolate and other delicious food." She pulled out three chocolate bars, two packs of peanuts and a packet of licorice. She rummaged for more, but no more food was found.

Oskar examined the chest contents again. He pulled out a small box of ammunition which was for the pistol. He pocketed the box. Oskar took the uniform and put it against his body. It was a near fit. It was a bit short on the arms and trouser length, otherwise it was okay. He forced the uniform, the pistol and ammunition in his backpack.

The group made it to some trees for cover when the plane circled back. Oskar was very worried. "Our footprints in the snow will lead them to us."

Jaro looked above his head. "I know this is inadequate and primitive but help me cut this small branch with leaves. I will walk behind the group and erase our footprints. Just walk in a straight line behind each other." The group which usually walked in pairs made a single file as they travelled down the slope towards the Swiss border. Although it was not perfect, Jaro swept the obvious trail away. He muttered to himself, "It had better snow tonight. My arm is starting to ache."

The sunlight was beginning to fade. The wind was starting to pick up. Oskar stopped the group. "We better find a place to camp."

Kiana pointed to a cluster of trees. "I will check the trees out."
Fiorella ran to join her. She said, "You people seems to know your hiking and camping skills."
Kiana smiled as thought of the mountain treks in Austria flashed back. "At first, we were hopeless, but we are all stubborn enough to see it through. When I think about what we did to survive, it is like another lifetime. Now it is second nature." Kiana stopped walking when she saw a semi demolished cabin. She walked over to check it out in detail. She wondered if it could stand up to another night of winter storms. "Go tell the others about this broken cabin. It may be the only option we have." Fiorella ran out of the trees and began yelling for the others to come.

Through the night the wind blew, and snow fell. The remains of the cabin shook. Kiana tried to comfort the girls who clung on to her as if she would disappear at any moment. Lori commented, "At least this storm is nowhere near as severe as the one last night. If it was, this cabin would be spread over the slopes." His eyes watched the timber rattle. Oskar told him to shut up as he was feeding the girls' fear.

The next morning the sky was crystal blue. The air was crisp. The group slowly emerged from the cabin. Oskar pointed north-east. We go this way. The border can't be that far away.

For three hours they struggled through the snow before coming to a stop. Barbed wire blocked their advances. Kiana dug through her bag to retrieve the wire cutters. Jaro took the cutters to begin snipping. When he was about halfway through, he handed them to Lori. Lori began cutting. The pieces removed were neatly piled about five metres away at the base of the barrier. Lori cursed as much as Jaro. The constant action of opening the cutters and squeezing the handle made their hands ache. Lori gave a sigh of relief when the last tenacious wire was cut. A doorway about a metre wide had been formed. One by one they filed through. When all were though and had moved away from the opening, they laughed and cheered. The smell of freedom filled the air.

Oskar pointed almost due east. "Chiasso is that way. How far, I cannot tell. Let's go and see how far we get before night falls. I really don't want another night in the open."

Two hours later they saw roof tops of a town. Kiana stopped the group. "Somehow, we need to join up on the road to look like we came the normal way. Let's be careful. One mistake can see us in trouble." As they neared the town, they stopped again to reassess the situation. Chiara said, "It has been a long time since I have come to this place. I am not sure if my memory serves me right. There is a hiking track which links to the main road. We should go to that point and act like we just finished a half day hike." The others liked the idea. Lori said, "Lead the way."

Within minutes the group were on the main road where they joined the trickle of other people. Some were refugees fleeing to anywhere which would accept them. Others were locals going about their usual chores. No soldiers guarded any road. The check point for the border was the only sign of any officialdom and that was well behind them.

The chalet where the girls were supposed to meet Maria came into view. The group slowly entered the busy chalet. Chiara's and Fiorella's eyes scanned the crowd. Fiorella said softly to Chiara, "It is a long time since I have seen Aunty Maria. Is that her sitting alone at a table near the big window?" Chiara squinted. "It looks like her." The lady turned. Chiara confirmed, "Yes. That is her. Come on." The group followed Chiara to the lady.

The lady stood up when she saw her nieces approaching with the unknown foursome following. Maria almost squealed her delight at seeing the girls. She gave them each a tight hug and kissed them on their cheeks. When she was satisfied that her embraces nearly squeezed the life out of them, she nodded to the group. "Please introduce me to these fine people."

When the introductions were done, Maria insisted on them to join her for a meal. She said, "Swiss and Italian food is available here. But the war has caused a lot of rationing. The meals are not as good or as generous as they used to be. But that is what happens in war; food supplies get cut or disrupted." She handed them a modified menu.

After the meal, Maria guided them to her parked car. She said, "Sorry. The car is too small. I will make two trips. Chiara, Fiorella and Kiana get in first. Gentlemen, I will be back in thirty minute to collect you." Maria drove to a small farm no greater than ten acres. She almost tossed the girls out before speeding back to the chalet to pick up the men.

The farmhouse suddenly felt small with six extra people cramming inside. Maria's husband, Marco returned that night from herding the goats. He brought in a bucket of goat's milk and placed it on the floor when he saw Fiorella and Chiara. Maria quickly introduced the strangers who delivered the nieces through what Marco called occupied Italy. Maria took the milk to the cook top to boil. She said, "I hope you don't mind goat's milk. It took us a little time to adjust to the taste. We no longer have sheep. Sheep milk is nicer. Our sheep kept disappearing. I suspect they were stolen and ended up on the chalet's menu. I have no proof. As soon as the local sheep supply was gone, the chalet took mutton and lamb off the menu." She gave a wink.

Marco gestured for the new arrivals to sit at the only dining room table. "Sorry for the cramping. We rarely get visitors. Now tell me. How did you meet, Luca?" Oskar took up the question and the related events until they reached the plane wreck. Then Chiara took over with all the enthusiasm of a teen involved in a great adventure. Marco nodded as he continually eyed the Austrians.

When the meal was complete, Maria ushered her nieces and Kiana to one bedroom. Seeing there were only two beds, Kiana immediately volunteered to sleep on the floor. "I am very used to sleeping on the floor and on rough ground." Maria gave a sigh of relief. Jaro, Lori and Oskar were told to sleep in the small lounge. They rolled out their blankets and sleeping bags to settle in for the night.

The next morning Kiana, Lori, Jaro and Oskar decided they should leave the family to travel deeper into Switzerland. When they were about to leave Marco offered to drive them back to the chalet. He said, "At the back of the chalet is a bus depot. There is only one bus going north. It goes to Lugano. Then you change buses to get to Bellinzona. From Bellinzona you have a choice of bus or train.

Whatever you decide, both go to the final destination of Bern in the northwest. That is much closer to the German border where the British-French and German front lines have their long battles. France has lost some of its territory. The alternative route by bus or train takes you to Zurich. That is closer to Germany, namely Munich.

"The Swiss government in the 1930's built three radio towers for the three main languages of this country, French, German and Italian. The original language still spoken by a very small minority does not have a radio station. In 1937, the Swiss government upgraded the German radio station in Bermomunster to short wave radio. One reason was the Germans were spewing out their Nazi propaganda. That is offensive to us. We spit out reality in defiance and also in accordance with our constitution and our doctrine of 'Spiritual Defense.'"
Oskar interrupted. "What is the doctrine of Spiritual Defense?"

Marco thought for a second as he tried to sum up the essence in simple terms. "It is the collective Swiss people's reaction to Nazi propaganda. The Nazis are trying to wear down the Swiss people and for that matter, the European people. There are four main bits which is a mix of our constitution and the Bible. Yeah, someone modernized and applied bits of the bible. I am not sure which parts. I think one bit is from: St. Paul's letter to the Romans, bits of Mathew, I think 26.41 and a few others. Anyway it says something like 'victory of the spirit over the flesh' and 'not based on race'. That means in Biblical terms, a clear refusal to the racist Nazi ideology. But the four main bits of our Constitution and parallels the Bible are:
*federalism vs. uniformity.
*equal rights and respect of minorities vs arrogance of race.
*tolerance and individual freedom vs state ideology
*multi-party democracy vs one-party dictatorship.
Put together, the Swiss Constitution and the Spiritual Defense make the 'Creed of Switzerland's Civil Religion.' Get used to it as you

will hear it everywhere by everybody. The Creed really upsets the Germans, and they struggle to do anything about it." He continued with his recent history orientation for the Austrian group.

"When you travel around Switzerland, you get different language radio stations: French to the west, Italian to the south and German to the north and central areas. I heard on the only radio station, the Italian one for this area, German and French aircraft were shot down for violating Swiss airspace. The countries, including Britain and America were warned planes flying over will be shot. Just be aware, some towns which were pestered by foreign aircraft from both sides, have eight p.m. blackouts. That is to mess up the navigation of foreign crafts flying overhead. Some bomb the wrong towns, while others crash into mountains. Whatever, our anti-aircraft force shoots first and then identifies the culprit. Sometimes, the anti-aircraft units force down any foreign plane. When down, the pilots are jailed. The plane is rebadged for the Swiss air force. We have a mix of planes from France, Germany which happens to be our main supplier, Britain, and America. They will all eventually learn Switzerland is a no-fly zone." Marco shook his head. "The world has gone crazy."

Marco pulled into the small car park at the chalet. He directed the group to the bus station. He bid them farewell and drove off. Marco knew he would have to return in a few days to pick up Luca, that is if Luca could cross the border in his Italian uniform. If not, then Luca would have to go via the mountains like the nieces. All he could do was wait for the call.

At the bus depot, Jaro, Kiana, Lori and Oskar studied the extra-large map of Switzerland covering half the narrow wall near the ticket booth. The booth itself was a glorified box which housed one seat for the ticket salesperson, a counter which swung open to be the door when the internal latch was pulled aside. There was only one price and one destination, Lugano. Oskar asked for the fare price and then asked if Lira or Reichmarks would be accepted. The salesperson shrugged. "Both are acceptable. Francs would be better." Oskar purchased four tickets with mixed currency. He accepted the Franc currency as change. He waved Oskar on. "Next customer please."

In Lugano, the group got off the bus. Their finances were low again. Jaro said, "It looks like the same routine, find work and accommodation. How much do we have?"
Oskar opened his wallet. "Six Lira, four Reichmarks and now seven Francs. Maybe enough for one meal. I suggest we don't do any thieving. They are quick to kick people out." As he said that, he pointed to a newspaper on a stand. The paper stated that Switzerland wasn't able to cope with the influx of refugees and would be excluding them from entry and deporting others to any of the borders. The closest border to anywhere was the way out for refugees. Oskar read another section of the newspaper. "It looks like Switzerland is conscripting all males to the army to protect its borders. ....And we are in the conscript age bracket. Don't be surprised if we get pulled up to do our duty to this country. They are paying soldiers eighty per cent of their civilian wages. We better find out what the wage structure is just in case we are pulled up for service."
Jaro and Lori were not impressed. "Is there a job section in that paper?"

Oskar took the top newspaper out of the honorary box and slipped the smallest coin in the slot. He flipped through the paper to the back section. There were two columns of advertisements in large print..
He read down the list. "Accountant, bank teller for the Zurich Bank in Zurich of course, some farm jobs. Now let's see that list: herding goats and sheep, general repairs, planting for the summer. That is it." His eyes went down to the bottom of the page. "Kiana. This could be for you. Nurse's aide required at the

local hospital. Duties include bathing patients, changing bandages, help feed patients, cleaning the wards. How does that sound?" "I can manage that, but it is a rather shit job especially if someone soils themselves. I am not sure if I could handle that bit. It has to be better than any bar work. I have had my fill with pulling beers and sleezy remarks or innuendos. What is the name of the hospital?" Oskar read out the name. "Lugano General Hospital." He looked at the street sign of the street they were in. "It must be at the end of this street. He looked up to see a cross barely reaching above the surrounding rooflines. He pointed. "It's down there. We can go together. Maybe we can pick up some other work like gardening or even cleaning."

When they reached the hospital, they went to the triage desk and asked for further information and directions about the job. The nurse who was prepared for such enquiries replied, "Go down the passageway and up a set of stairs. There is a sign which says, 'Job Applications and Training.' Knock on that door. Dr. Brucker. He is in-charge of recruiting and training."
Kiana thanked the nurse. The group walked immediately to Dr. Bruker's office.

Dr. Brucker was in his fifties. He looked at the application forms for possible jobs in the hospital. To Kiana, he quizzed her about her past work experience. He nodded thoughtfully at her experiences. "We have had two other applicants. We only need one. However, we can take in another as staff disappear to the areas which get bombed by both the Allies and the Axis." He scoffed. "Bombings explained as accidents always leave a mess and us short staffed. Can you start your training tomorrow?"
Kiana smiled. She asked, "I need to find accommodation. Can you recommend any place?"

Dr. Brucker looked over his spectacles. "We have vacancies in the nurse's quarters." He wrote down the address and rang the building manager to expect a new person to move in.

He looked at the next application. Oskar had written down orderly on one sheet and on another, gardening. Dr. Brucker looked at both applications. "We need full time gardeners. We have started to grow our own vegetables to help feed the patients. Rations are not helping patient's recovery. People need a variety of fresh food not a limited range of food on its last days. You are hired. Start tomorrow but for now, I will get our head gardener to show you around and where the tools are kept."
Can you recommend any accommodation places?" asked Oskar.
"Another person wanting accommodation?"
Oskar coughed. "My friends and I are new to the area. The other two are waiting outside. They are looking for jobs as well."
Dr. Brucker looked over his spectacles and then leaned back in his chair. "Bring them in."
After twenty minutes of discussion, Jaro was appointed to assist with the ambulance service for the town and Lori was directed to assist with general repairs and maintenance. All were recommended a guest house which frequently accommodated hospital staff.

For two months Kiana, Lori, Oskar and Jaro worked happily at their new tasks. They mixed with the locals but at the same time keeping their heads down. Then all three men received a letter. They were conscripted into the army. Training was to start at the start of next month. Oskar cursed. With Jaro and Lori, they fronted up at Dr, Bruker's office to explain their time of conscription departure. Dr. Brucker groaned. "You will have three weeks training and then a month at the borders or somewhere you will be needed. Then every year, you will be required to repeat that three weeks of training. You will get paid. Twenty per cent of your wages goes towards your army pay. It is Defense Insurance. Thank you for telling me in advance. It gives me time to find people to fill those places. When you come back, the positions will be available. The training is done in Zurich. I will see you when you come back." With that he waved them away. Dr. Brucker was visibly annoyed. *Staffing in these times is hard enough, now it is staffing of round-abouts.* He looked at his clock on the wall above the door. He stood up to begin his rounds.

Kiana wasn't impressed with the news that her 'support team' as she quietly called the three men, were going in a separate direction. She didn't protest. She had a job which she liked, except for cleaning up biological accidents as she referred to it. She felt safe in the dormitory with five other aides and nurses. There were no bombs and life on the run had come to an end, at least for now. When she bade Oskar, Lori and Jaro farewell, she felt sad. The separation from her team was going to be difficult. She knew she had to adapt. It was only going to be seven weeks. It will fly in a blink of an eye.

Chapter 22
Zurich.

The training at the army camp by comparison to the Italian army's training was a mix of fitness and using a range of equipment. To the trio, the food was superior, and the accommodation was non-comparable. Only four people were assigned to a dormitory and that came with fully working bathroom facilities. One corner even had two two-seater sofas. A luxury. Although the trio were split up in their accommodation, they were able to be with each other every other time. However, the crunch came on the second last night.

Sirens screamed overhead. Lights went out. Soldiers scattered to their designated dormitories. Going under their beds offered some protection from any possible debris from explosions. Bombs rained down and announced their arrival with evil screams before exploding. Each bomb seemed to be closer and closer. There were two exceptionally loud explosions. Both shook the ground. Oskar felt the ground shake beneath him at the same time a window exploded to spread the glass in all directions. Just as fast as it started, the bombs stopped. The smell of burning filled the air.

The dormitory where Oskar was only received the shattering of glass. One of the men in Oskar's group tried to switch on the light. No power. As the men slowly walked through the door to go outside, the sound of glass cracking beneath their feet broke the eerie silence. In the distance they could see the hellish glow of red. Something major was struck in the bombing. It couldn't be determined from tis distance.

Now outside, the men were instructed to gather in the exercise square. Roll call was taken and going from dorm one to twenty in order. Oskar heard Jaro's reply. "Here!" Oskar gave a sigh of relief. Then there were names called out for dorms nineteen and twenty. No replies. Oskar held his breath and listened for Lori's reply. None. Lori was missing along with ten other men.

A battery-operated spotlight from one tower turned on the square to reveal men with injuries. The light slowly turned to dorms nineteen and twenty. The buildings were flattened; the roof was sitting on the floor and the walls were like scattered sticks in the game for fiddlesticks. The men ran over to the wreckage and began to pull apart the structures. Hopes of finding anyone alive was slim. The sergeant screamed out orders to stop and listen every few minutes. Soft voices were heard. One by one the men were pulled out of the wreck. Three deaths and the rest casualties.

When Lori was pulled out, he smiled and coughed to clear his lungs. Oskar and Jaro ran over to him and gave the biggest hug. Lori coughed again. "Give me air!"
Jaro said, "We were worried sick. We thought you were a goner."
Lori wiped away some dirt from his face. "Close to. Obviously not my time. Ouch! May back aches." Jaro lifted up Loris's shirt and called out, "Medic. Over here!" No one came. Jaro said, "Climb on my back. I will take you over to the medical tents just being set up. You have some very ugly bruises on your back." Oskar took a quick look. "Not bruises just one jumbo one covering most of your back. Did your bed cave in?"
Lori gave a faint nod. "It could have been worse considering the bed buffered the roof from crushing me. Small blessings."

The next day military police and the local police examined the damage. One police inspector cursed. "Bloody Hitler and his propaganda bullshit. Accident. My Ass. This is neutral territory, and we get pounded again and again." The inspector wrote in his report which types of bombs was used, where it could have come from and where each landed. The edges of the army camp had left a gaping hole which could hide a tank. The power station took a direct hit. There would be no power for anyone to operate anything for kilometres around.

The next day, the soldiers were supposed to return home. Instead, they were rostered to different locations. Oskar contacted Dr. Brucker at the Laguna hospital. He relayed what had happened and they were now deployed to the northern borders. Oskar asked if the message would be delivered to Kiana. The doctor agreed. Lori, when recovered, would return to Lugano to resume his employment.

Chapter 23
Bern to Lugano.

Oskar and Jaro were transported to Bern in the north-west. It was much closer to the border than Zurich. Bern and the surrounding towns and villages suffered several bombings- many came from within the French border where fighting had raged for months. From there, the new recruits were split into two groups. Jaro and Oskar were assigned to the German-Swiss border town of Basel.

Their assignment was to assist the monitoring of German trains and trucks using Switzerland to access Italy and other countries of the Mediterranean. Oskar and Jaro frowned at the so-called neutral stand of Switzerland. Flying over was forbidden, yet trucks and trains with covered carriages were permitted. The Swiss officer supervising the German-Switzerland arrangement collect either a gold bar or Francs or Reichmarks as payment. Every two weeks, a Swiss truck loaded with gold and money went to the Bank of Switzerland. No questions asked. Switzerland's coffers were growing by allowing its major trading partner to use their roads and rail system.

Jaro and Oskar spent six weeks doing their expected supervision duties. When they were discharged, they didn't opt to return to Zurich. Instead, they put on German uniforms and rode on one truck going south.

The truck drove through towns and only stopped for a fuel refill. They pressed on passed Bern and stopped at the shore of Breinzersee, a large inland lake.

There were a few houses at the campsite. The locals were severely outnumbered by the frequently arriving German soldiers. In a bid not to stir up the hornet nest, as the locals referred to the Germans, they supplied the army with food. It was say nothing, hear nothing and see nothing. Keeping alive was the priority. Injuries meant a full day's journey to Bern. That was always expensive and time consuming for the locals.

Oskar was rostered to be on duty to watch over the trucks. For the first three hours he and four other soldiers stood guard around the trucks. Jaro would be in the next shift. The night was uneventful for the first two hours.

 A lieutenant and a captain walked towards the stationary trucks. The captain climbed in the back of one trucks. The lieutenant followed. They opened one box to check its contents. Then another box was selected at random. The captain said, "This box will do." He tapped an unopened box of bullion. They slid the box toward the opening of the truck. They jumped out and lifted the box out. They gave orders. "Soldiers close your eyes until we say when to open them." The soldiers obeyed. Oskar closed his eyes until the two men walked past him. Then he observed their actions.

The box was carried to the lake's edge where a rowboat was waiting. The men rowed no more than twenty metres from the shore. The box was heaved into the water where it sank thirty metres to the bottom. Gone for now but ready to be reclaimed after the war.

Back on shore, the two officers gave the order to open eyes. Stone faces stared back at the officers. Oskar grinned when the officers disappeared. *Bastards. I will have to learn to scuba dive to retrieve that. One bar would be nice.* Oskar's attention was snapped back to reality when Jaro asked, "Anything exciting?" Oskar gave a wink. Knowing anyone around could hear every word in the still night. he lied, "Nothing. Damn boring."

The next day the trucks pulled out of Brienz. They were heading south. This time each truck was carrying extra fuel. They would not stop at any small village or town. There was a timetable which must be met. When they reached the north-western outskirt of Lugano, Oskar and Jaro slipped away in the dead of the night. As soon as they could, they changed into civilian clothes.

 The captain did an unexpected roll call. On his records, Oskar and Jaro were not listed. The captain didn't notice but one soldier looked puzzled. He thought about what he had seen. The two newcomers did a runner. He wasn't sure if he should report the discrepancy, then shrugged it off. He pulled out a cigarette and contemplated the options. Hell would break out. The army was supposed to be invisible to the locals. Raising hell for two people not even listed on the roll was not worth the trouble. He would be questioned. Another reason to keep his mouth shut. *Good luck to them hitching a ride and then deserting. Gutsy.* He chuckled to himself and blew out smoke.

He walked away from the others to enjoy his private entertainment. He looked around wondering if he could also disappear and appear at will. *Ghosts or spies. It didn't matter. They came and went. The command didn't notice. I am practiced at playing dumb to any corruption. Going to the lake and being silent was good training. The bosses telling everyone to close their eyes was a joke. It made sure all were watching. Gold is being syphoned for later collection.* He grinned as the cigarette was coming to an end. *What Hitler didn't know didn't matter. I will try my luck after the war.* He stomped out the cigarette butt. *Fuck Hitler.*

Chapter 24
Lugano.

When Oskar and Jaro met up with Kiana and Lori, they noticed Lori had a limp. "Is that permanent?" asked Jaro. "Unfortunately, yes. I have made slight improvements. I think it is more nerve damage. The doctors showed me a picture of the bruising. It was massive. I think there is a crack. I was on my stomach for a long time." He looked over to Kiana. "She has been a wonderful help. I wasn't exactly the best patient." Kiana commented, "Some people I attended to are a lot worse. You still have to take it easy and that includes no lifting anything more than two kilos. Women handle pain better than men. Now tell us what happened in Bern?"

"Bern was just a stopover. We were in Basel. When our time was up, we were supposed to go back to Zurich. We hitched a very interesting ride on the back of a German truck. Let's go over to the park. Jaro and I will tell you what happened with the Germans." The group slowly walked to the park. Oskar and Jaro told their stories. At the end Lori asked, "Who will teach us to scuba dive?" Jaro and Oskar shrugged. "Knowing the lakes are being patrolled, is not an option for now. Too many onlookers and too many questions would be asked. Let's lay low and get on with living in peace. We have to leave the gold hunt for after the war, whenever that happens."

Oskar and Jaro were able to resume their duties at the hospital. They were relieved it gave them some stability of income and living.

Keeping a low profile and mixing with the rest of the locals was kept to a minimum. It was a balance between keeping to themselves and still being perceived as social.

One evening, Kiana was called into work. German soldiers were being transported into the hospital after their truck rolled on the mountain side. Kiana with many other off duty people rushed to the emergency room. Like other aides, she was ordered to assist with cleaning the wounds and where needed slow or stop blood loss. Ten soldiers with assorted injuries filled one ward. Most men had broken limbs. A few had punctured wounds. The doctors had removed the assorted objects such as bits of trees, gravel and metal from their bodies. The trophies were displayed by each of soldier's beds.

Days later most of the soldiers were released from the hospital. With their previously released soldiers, they set up a crude camp near the wreckage of the truck. They couldn't help but notice all the contents had been pillaged by the locals. They weren't going to try to question anyone about the missing contents. No one would answer and they were on neutral foreign soil. Diplomacy was in order, not accusations. The soldiers bought civilian clothes so they could meld into the local population without hearing verbal abuse assaults.

Those who were released, frequently went to the hospital to visit their injured comrades. Kiana was on duty when she noticed two new soldiers of rank visiting the men. One had a notebook and taking down notes. Her view of their faces was obscured by both distance and angle of viewing. Adding to the difficulty, their caps were drawn down to cast a shadow over their faces. She gave a sigh of relief when she noticed they appeared to be finished with their line of questioning. The men stood up, the notebook disappeared into a jacket pocket and the chairs were returned to their original positions.

Kiana didn't want them to see her as the men left the ward. She went behind the nurse's station and bobbed down to pretend she was selecting items for her work. She continued rummaging around but was forced to stop when one of the men knocked on the counter. At first, she ignored the knocking and continued her pretend rummaging. She couldn't avoid the men when one leaned over the counter and said, "Stop hiding. We need information about the men still in the ward."

Slowly and reluctantly, Kiana stood up. She thought, *Damn! Louis again*. She cringed. Louis recognized her and gave a smile. "Fräulein. We meet again." Kiana stared back. She said nothing. Louis continued. "When can these men be released?"
"I don't know. Only the doctor has that authority," she replied.
"Can I see the doctor?" asked Louis.
"Just a minute. I will see who is on duty." She left the men at the nurses' station and went down the hall.

While she was away, Louis said to his companion, Max, "I met this girl about two years ago. She was travelling on a bus from Villach in Austria to Udine in Italy. She spent the entire time looking out of the window and refusing to talk to me. When she got off the bus, she pretended to be getting married to a much older man. When I met her again, she said she was widowed. I don't believe word. She is being difficult to get."
"I must say she is very attractive. Any family?" asked Max.
"I know for sure she has one brother. She pretends the other men she is seen with are brothers or other relatives of some kind. She and her male friends are like glue. I suspect there is something more to their background. She and her male companions seem to be on the run. From what I don't know. I want to find out."
The men stopped talking when Kiana returned with a doctor and a nurse.

Dr. Brucker greeted them and listened to their requests. Dr. Brucker gave a sigh. "Two can be released tomorrow. But they still need some rest. The man down the back," Dr. Brucker flipped through the charts to find his ailments. "He can't be released for another week or more. Did you see the souvenirs we pulled out of his stomach?" Both men nodded.

"Well, that man can no longer be a soldier. He goes back to Germany whenever he gets better. I am not holding my breath. I have been assessing him every two days. He is not coping well. He has an infection which we are struggling to quell. He goes in and out of consciousness. Come with me."

Dr. Brucker led the German soldiers back to the man. The doctor groaned. He yelled, "Nurse! Nurse! Assistance." The nurse and Kiana came running. "He is unconscious again. Check his vitals."

The nurse said, "He is very low. Blood pressure dropping. Kiana what is his temperature?"

"Too high. It's forty and climbing." She ran to get an ice pack. When she returned, everyone was quiet. The man had died. Dr. Brucker said, "Now you can take him to Germany. It is safe for him to travel. I will have him in the mortuary until you come back. You have three days to remove him. After that he gets buried in our cemetery for foreigners. The average burial cost is five hundred Francs."

Louis looked surprised. "Okay. We will bury him. Can we have the paperwork?" Dr. Brucker unclipped the charts from the holder at the end of the man's bed and gave them to Louis. "You need a death certificate. I will do that now."

Dr. Brucker went to his office. He returned minutes later. He handed Louis the certificate. "That is all there is for this man." Dr. Brucker, the nurse and Kiana began to leave the room. Louis walked quickly to catch Kiana. He grabbed her by the hand and pulled her back. "How about a night on the town?"

Kiana pulled her hand back as Dr. Brucker and the nurse watched on in shock. "In your dreams. Let go of my hand. I am not interested." Kiana placed herself between Dr. Brucker and the nurse before walking off with her impromptu escorts.

Max said, "That went well. Another flat refusal. I think you should give up. Three nos, means no."

"Yeah. Damn cute. One day but not today or the near future, it will happen." Louis turned to his companion. "Am I that ugly that she refuses to go to with me?"

Caught off guard Max said, "No. Maybe it is the uniform. Maybe she has other reasons you don't know about."

"Like what?"

Max shrugged. "Ask her."

"She won't even talk to me. How am I supposed to get her to open up?"

"That's your problem. Let's get out of here."

That night Kiana met with Oskar, Jaro and Lori. She mentioned Louis was in town and asked her for a date. The men were initially shocked and then burst out laughing. "It's not that funny," she retorted.

Oskar said, "I would have loved to seen his face on the third rejection. You really know how to injure that guy's ego."

"There is something off with that man. Really off. Slimy."

"He was collecting information about the accident. He pops up every so often. He must report to some higher command. It is good to keep our distance from him," said Lori.

Three days later, Kiana was walking along the street to purchase some groceries. Her heart stopped when a voice behind her said, "Hello Kiana. We meet again."

Kiana began to walk faster. She was only few metres away from the shop when she felt a hand grab her arm. She glimpsed in at the window of the hairdresser to see where Louis was standing. She spun around and kicked Louis in the groin. As he fell to the ground clutching the injured area, Kiana ran into the shop and explained what had happened. The lady gave a smirk. "Come here." She gave Kiana a hug. "Gee. You are shaking like a leaf. Sit with me. When my son comes back from making a delivery, I get him will escort you back home." Kiana gave a sigh of relief.

In the twenty minutes period of waiting for her son to return, Kiana introduced herself and purchased the required groceries. Miya quickly explained the situation to her son, Elio. "I will look after the shop while you take her home." Elio accompanied Kiana right up to the dormitory gates. "You should be safe now. I will watch you until you go inside."

Elio walked back to the shop. When he arrived, Miya serving two men. All three looked up as Elio walked in. "She's home now. She's safe." Elio stopped talking. He altered what he was going to say. He directed the comments towards the men. He looked at the two men whom he suspected were the cause of Kiana's anxiety. "Men should respect when a lady says no. Not interested, it means not interested. The poor girl is traumatized." Louis and his companion walked out of the shop after purchasing some fruit.

Louis whispered, "Traumatized? My manhood is traumatized. I haven't been able to pee properly ever since. That girl can kick harder than a mule."
Max chuckled. "I didn't know you had been kicked by a mule. When did that happen?"
"Err. It hasn't. It just a comparison I made."
"Oh. And the plumbing is not working either? Is it going sideways?"
"Shut up." Louis gave him a clout over the head.
"Well, we now know it is not the uniform turning her off. It is you or she is not ready for a relationship." Louis ignored the comment.

When Kiana met with Oskar, Lori and Jaro that evening, she told them what had happened. Oskar pushed back his hair and screwed up his face. He and the others were comfortable in their current life. Reluctantly he asked the group, "Do we go on the move again? I am not going to demand anyone to come along. This place has been good to us."

Lori said, "I am still not physically ready to trek anywhere. I need more time to recover. I am improving. I can twist around more, and the bruising has disappeared. I am not ready to move on, but all of you can if you so desire."

Jaro added, "This place suits me. However, I will accompany you to the border if you decide to leave."

Oskar thought about the remarks. "Okay we wait until Lori is fully recovered and has regained some strength. But in the meantime, we should plan an escape in case things go south. We need maps. We need to pay more attention to the news regarding the war. That could determine what we do. This weekend, I am completely free. I would like to pay a visit to the Morelli's. Anyone interested?"

Kiana thought about her schedule. "I will need to make a couple of swaps. Maybe we can meet them in Mendriso which is halfway. It will give the girls a break from the farm and allow them to see more of this country."

"I like that idea. I will give them a call. They are one of the few farming families in the area which have a phone," said Oskar.

Chapter 25
Mendriso.

Oskar, Lori, Jaro and Kiana were waiting at the Mendriso bus depot for the Chiasso bus to arrive. The thirty-minute bus ride would stop at the Mendriso chalet. The chalet was bustling with activity.

Smiles lit up when Chiara, Fiorella, Maria and Marco alighted. Smiles turned to concern when Luca didn't appear. After the warm greetings, Oskar ushered everyone to a nearby restaurant. About halfway through the meal, Kiana asked Maria, "Where is Luca?"
Maria's eye welled up. She gave a soft sob. Marco's arm suddenly cradled Maria's shoulders as he drew her into her chest. Marco answered, "He was denied entry. He was one of hundreds who were told to return to their own country. We saw him through the fences. He was calling out to us, but border guards pushed him away. We received a letter stating he would try the mountains. We gave him details of your path and the hole in the barbed wire you created. We do not know if he tried the mountain path and died trying or gave up and returned to Italy where he could have been court martialed for assisting people to escape to Switzerland. We simply don't know."

Oskar thought about the response and tried to connect the events occurring in Italy as mentioned on the radio. "It would be very difficult for him to come across the border in the usual way. The mountain path wasn't exactly a walk in the park. I am sure Chiara and Fiorella will attest to that."

Oskar took a sip of his beer. He continued. "The Allies are sweeping across Italy with King Emmanuel's guidance and assistance. I have heard the northern towns and cities in Italy have sustained the heaviest bombing. Milano, Udine, Trento, Brescia, Vercelli to name a few have taken a major pounding."

Kiana chimed in, "It's a pity, the Vatican was spared. I would like to have seen some of the not-so-holy men occupying the place go to meet Lucifer. When I was there as a cleaner, I saw German trucks unload timber boxes. The boxes were small and heavy. Some larger boxes were shaped like they were hiding works of art. The Vatican was profiting. Not exactly a Godly act." Oskar gave her a kick under the table. She stopped talking. She apologized, "Sorry. The Vatican has bad memories for me, my pet hate."

Marco asked the group in general, "Are you going to stay in Lugano?" Lori replied, "We are uncertain. It has been good for us. Unfortunately, Kiana keeps being pestered by a German soldier called Louis. We may break-up as a group. Kiana and Oskar are considering moving on. Jaro and I have not decided."

The two groups left the restaurant and headed to the scenic areas around town in hired cars. At four p.m. the two groups went their different ways. Maria, Marco and the girls drove back to their farm close to Chiassio.

Oskar, Lori, Jaro and Kiana found a tavern for an overnight stay. They again crammed into a family room. Kiana grinned. "This brings back memories."

Oskar looked towards her. "You got used to the dorms. Do you miss the girls?"

Kiana replied, "I have become friend with two girls and just give respectful ways with the others. It can be fun at times, but one needs their own personal space from time to time. That doesn't happen at all. Just the walk to the hospital is all the personal space you get. Six to a room can be a crowd at times. Sometimes the numbers drop due to staff leaving. I relish those few days with reduced numbers. Are we going to stay here all night, or should we head out to see the long-playing satirical performance, Die Pfeffermuler (The Pepper Mill)?"

Jaro gave an enthusiastic, "Oh Yes. I was told it was equally as good as the Cabaret Cornichon. We all enjoyed that show."
Lori said, "If they roast the Hitler and cronies as much as they say Cabaret Cornichon does, then I am for it."

After the performance, the group laughed as they recalled overt ridiculing of the upper echelon of the German army. They clicked their heel and saluted in jest after recalling some of the dialogue.
Their laughter ended at the front door of the tavern. They headed to the bar for a night cap.

They were halfway through their drinks and a light snack when Lori nudged Kiana. "I see your boyfriend has just come in."
Kina swore and hissed at Lori's ribbing, "That asshole is everywhere. I think he is following us. There are too many coincidences." She slipped an arm over Lori's shoulder. Lori grinned. "This is not going to make you invisible. He already suspects Jaro and I are not related to you or as your boyfriends."
"I suspect that as well. On the other hand, you two are more than best friends. Family. And family sticks together to protect each other."

Jaro turned to the counter to see Louis and Max holding their drinks Max said softly, "Your girlfriend seems to have another love interest."
"Funny. Last time it was the other guy who is now looking at us. Maybe she is a bit kinky, two in the bed at the same time." Louis raised his glass as he looked at Jaro, *Cheers. You lucky bastard*. Jaro gave a smirk and reciprocated.

Louis began to approach the table. Max cautiously followed behind. Politely he asked, "May we join you?"

There was a chorus, "No"

"So be it." Louis slowly moved away. From a distance he kept watch on the group who were now whispering to each other.

"We have to give him the slip," said Oskar. "We go outside and circle the block. We hide in any place we can. When they disappear, we come back."

The group finished off their drinks and light snacks and went outside. They walked together around the corner. They came across a lane which ended at the backdoor of a shop. "In here," directed Jaro. "Kiana, let's swap some clothes. We are close the same size. Just the lower half."

Kiana grinned. "This sounds fun." The two quickly swapped half of their clothes. Jaro and Lori continued to walk in one direction with Lori's arm placed over his shoulder. Oskar escorted Kiana away to return to the tavern.

Louis and Max approached Lori and Jaro who had his head slightly bowed. In the darkness Louis could only see the skirt billowing in the growing evening breeze. He said with all the confidence he had, "Fräulein. I just want to speak with you."

Lori replied, "She has made that clear she doesn't want to be near you or speak to you. Do you need another attack in the groin to make it clear?"

Louis said, "Let her speak for herself."

Jaro squeaked, "Go away. I am not interested. Just leave me alone."

Louis and Max were taken aback by the voice change. "Let's see what we have here?" He pulled out a small torch and shone it in Jaro's face. Jaro and Lori responded by kicking Louis and Max before running away. Louis and Max swore, picked themselves off the ground before giving chase. They ran up the street before turning towards a row of small shops. With Louis and Max in pursuit, they deliberately ran towards a police station which was just closing its doors for the night. Lori yelled out, "Help! Stay open!" The two officers looked at the four men coming their way.

The older policeman muttered to himself, "Why does this have to happen at closing time?"

Lori and Jaro pushed passed the officers to enter the police station. To their surprise, Louis and Max followed with the police officers trailing behind. The younger officer locked the door from the inside while the older one tried to pacify both groups. He yelled out, "Sit. Shut up all of you!"

One by one the four men came to a stop. They were all panting. The older officer asked, "What is going on?"

All replied at the same time with different answers. The two groups were pointing to each other. The older officer slammed a book down hard on his desk yelled again, "Stop this now! You!" He pointed to Lori wearing a skirt. "Why are you dressed in a skirt?"

Lori puffed, "That man has been harassing my sister when we were in Lugano. Then he followed us here to Mendriso. Then he tried to invite himself to join us so he could get close to my sister. She has made it clear to all, she doesn't want anything to do with him. His friend is new to the scene. To ensure my sister got home safely, we switched clothes. Sure enough, the decoy worked. They followed us to a dark alley. Then we ran."

Louis fumed, "You bastards. You attacked us in the alley. See!" He pointed to a bruise forming on his chin."

"That is what you get for stalking women who clearly don't want to be with you. No means no! Dickhead."

Louis went to charge at Jaro. Max pulled him back. "Fuck you. Let her make the decision about seeing me."

"She didn't like you from the start when you sat beside her on the bus from Villach to Udine. That should have been enough. But no. You had to persist to satisfy your inflated ego." He whispered, "Kraut." Again, Louis raised his fist. The younger officer grabbed Louis's arm. "I think it is cool-off time. Spend the night in our wonderful cells at the back," said the older officer.

When the men were locked up, the older officer said, "Let's go home. They can sort themselves out. If they yell at each other, we don't have to listen to them carry on. I must say, if that guy dressed as a girl did that to make sure his sister got home safely, it worked. I have never seen a brother take his duty to look after a sister so seriously. That Louis guy must be having a hard time trying to get to know her."

The next morning, the two officers returned. The older officer asked, "Have you all sorted out your differences yet?" He heard four hisses and saw screwed up faces. "I guess no." He approached Lori's and Jaro's cell. "You two first. Give your statement. If the statements don't match up, you all will stay longer. Princess you are first." Jaro was guided to the interview room where he gave an account of past and present events. Then he was marched back to the cell. Lori was next. Louis and Max were last to be interviewed and returned to their cells. The older officer said, "The stories kind of match. They are close enough. Can you ring the tavern and ask for Kiana and Oskar to come. They better bring a set of trousers for the princess."

Kiana and Oskar fronted the older officer at the police station. Kiana gave her story about the switch of clothes. She voiced her concern of dislike for Louis. All she wanted was for him not to approach her. "There is a bad feeling about him. That is why I don't want to associate with him or him to be near me. I don't like how he pops up at different times and locations. That is it. There is something bad about him and that is all. I follow my gut feelings."

The officer said, "Then follow your gut feelings. We do that here when there is a crime. Now, tell me are all these men your brothers?" Kiana looked the officer square in the face. "Oskar is. The other two with Oskar and I have been through so much together. We consider ourselves as one family. What happens to one, affects all of us. We love each other as a close-knit family. Yeah, Lori and Jaro are my brothers by choice. No one is going to change that fact. End of story." "I see," said the policeman. "You are lucky you have such a strong bond in these troubled times. Where are your parents?

"Dead. Killed by Germans."

"Where?"

"Austria, just over three years ago. Oskar, Jaro and I are the only survivors. We met Lori on our journey to escape. He was running away too. He was with another unofficial brother, Paul. Paul died in Albania. He was trying to get them some bullets. They had no ammunition to defend themselves." replied Kiana.

"So they have seen some war. Are there any other relatives?"

"All dead. Killed by the Germans," replied Kiana. "When can we go? We have a bus to catch to Lugano."

The officer nodded. "Wait here. I will speak to your official brother, Oskar. Then you can go."

Ten minutes later, Oskar was joined with Lori and Jaro who had changed back into trousers. Oskar said, "We have to hurry. Everything is packed and at the tavern. The bus leaves in one hour."

The older officer purposefully waited for thirty minutes before speaking to both Louis and Max. He gave a stern warning, "Leave her alone with her brothers. They don't like Germans and you are Germans. Germans wiped out their families."

"So that is the reason she avoids me," said Louis as he accepted the revelation. "Not all people wearing German uniforms are killers or even German citizens. What a shame. So cute." Max gave a cough to remind Louis to snap out of his dreams.

Chapter 26
Geneva and the Western Front.

The days clicked over. Life resumed some form of normality as routines of work and home life became the norm. The new norm was shaken again. Lori, Jaro and Oskar were called up to do another round of border duty in the Swiss army. This time they would be away for three months.

The trio went to the barracks assigned to them in the notice. Then the mixture of new recruits and past seasoned border guards filled square. Everyone listened to their names being called out. Loud voices saying here or yes rang out from random locations. The officer in charge called out for all the new recruit to go to the far-right side of the square. The rest were directed to another section with different orders.

The new recruits which included Lori, were ushered into the cabins where they would stay as a unit. The officer in charge noticed Lori's limp. He called Lori over. "Will you be able to keep up?"
Lori said, "I am not sure. I will have to find out myself."
The officer nodded. "How did you get injured?"
Lori lied, "Italy had a habit of recruiting anybody and everybody into their army. I saw action in Albania. That is where I got this permanent reminder - a gift from the British."
The officer nodded. "In that case you can join the other group. I will give you a note for you to be with them." The officer scribbled on the note:

He has had military experience. Hence the limp. Take him.

Lori showed the note to the commanding officer who had the bulk of the soldiers.

In their two groups the troops were immediately direct to a train which took them to a camp base just outside Geneva.

Jaro and Oskar smiled when Lori sat with them for the two-hour train journey. The group was intact. Unpacked and in their barracks, the soldiers were given a short time to orientate themselves with the surroundings. After lunch, all the soldiers were required to be in the mess hall. The commanding officer stood on an empty fruit box to make an announcement:

"Tomorrow all the soldiers who have done military service before, will leave with their mentors for their designated border patrol locations. All the very new recruits will remain and do your required training. Then you will be transported to the border to assist the soldiers already on duty. The new recruits can leave now and go onto the square to meet the officers who are going to train you." He waited for the men to leave the room.

He continued with the announcement:

"When I say your name, stand up and go with your appointed mentor. Your mentor will explain what you have to do, and if necessary, show you how to do things like repairing barbed wire without getting multiple scratches. He will in effect, be responsible for your training. He will be with you for one week before he goes home. This is to make sure the transition from new to old staff goes smoothly. Take this opportunity to meet your mentor for the next two hours. Ask questions about anything. Pack your bags to be transported to the front line at four p.m."

Jaro, Oskar and Lori with their new mentors were frequently on night duty. When they were on dayshift, they spent their time repairing any barbed wire, and observing the distant war. They were recording what planes from any side flying past and dropping bombs or any other material such as propaganda flyers or even food drops to isolated villages. That was the easy part of the job.

At night, all one could do was try to count the drone of engines and the dropping bombs on the French side of the border. At time parachutes were observed. The white chutes formed sinister descending clouds. They were also recorded. At night screams of men, women and children could be heard. All Swiss soldiers froze at the blasts followed by blood-curdling screams carried by the wind. It was carnage which they could not do anything about. Every Swiss soldier wondered when a stray bomb would hit their side of the border. The nagging thought always returned at night, the darkness blotting out the clear border lines as seen by day.

For Lori, Oskar and Jaro, the night shift was always spookier. Bombs couldn't be seen, just heard. There was no way of telling how far they landed until they exploded. To them it was nerve wracking. Being on high alert for anyone trying to escape to Switzerland through the barriers was mentally fatiguing. Any sound was regarded with suspicion. That meant all guns were pointed and the finger on the trigger. Every so often, gun shots were heard. Who shot their gun and at what was never disclosed. The curiosity added to the uneasiness of the night.

One morning saw the Swiss soldiers on high alert. Visibility was not much better than the night. Wind swept dust smelled of gunpowder and smoke of burning villages filled the air. More screams, more bombs rained overhead from the German occupied side of the Western Front towards any of the French towns. The Germans were advancing at an alarming rate.

Within days, Oskar, and Jaro had observed the bombs and audible gunfire had died down. Smoke from captured villages blew to Switzerland. The bombs dropped by German bombers were now visible. When each dropped and exploded, Oskar and Jaro closed their eyes in a bid to block out the carnage. Their imaginations would conjure up images of the destruction. Flashes of what they recalled of their home village of Haltzweg going up in smoke filled their heads. Anger filled their bodies. Their mentor, Julian saw the distress and held them back by pulling them to the ground. He said softly, "We cannot do a thing. We cannot interfere. If we do, we are dead. The Germans may start invading us. We must remain neutral. That is the only way to survive."

Oskar and Jaro began to calm down. They sat on the ground with their guns pointing to the barbed wire. "War is hell. It serves no purpose. It destroys families and souls," said Oskar.
"That is very profound," said Julian as he held out a hand to pull Oskar up. "I have a philosopher on my hands." Then he extended his hand for Jaro to be pulled up.

Oskar gave a sardonic grin. "No. Jaro and I have seen our home senselessly destroyed. It makes you see things in a different light. The only thing still standing in my village is an obelisk. I feel like that obelisk, a sentinel with a heart of stone, yet fragile to the surroundings. I am always watching, waiting and guarding ghosts of years past. That is me."
"And your friends, Lori and Jaro? Are they obelisks too?"
Oskar nodded. "We are all obelisks, relics from the past. We are just a memorial or a nod to what was once and can never be again. War only displaces people with lost or shattered souls or both."
Oskar and Julian turned their attention to a noise coming from behind. Jaro screamed at the sky, "Just what did those people do and what did we do to deserve to be annihilated?

Julian pointed out the reduced near-by war activities. "The villages are being burned by the Germans. There are less cries and screams and less bombing in this area. Most of the action appears to be over the hills to the right."

Jaro said, "I heard news reports, but I don't know what is true or more propaganda. The Germans have advanced into France by several kilometres in parts and only a few in other parts. I am going to guess Paris will be attacked within six months."

Julian gave a friendly slap on Jaro's back. "Are you fortune telling? I have my doubts. The French and the British are too strong."

Jaro butted in, "And too spread out. Their lines are thin. They will have to bring in soldiers from other countries. The British will bring in soldiers from their empire and I bet those soldiers will fight on French soil."

"See what I mean. A fortuneteller," Julian said as he chuckled. "I can see why you two are friends. I have the philosopher, and a fortune teller guarding me. Your friend Lori, what is he?"

"Pissed off," said Jaro with a broad grin across his face. "Actually, if you use common sense and put the facts together, you do not need to be a war strategist to know what will happen."

Julian felt surprised. "Just how old are you three?"

"Twenty going on seventy," replied Oskar.

That evening for a rare no border patrol was called for one hour. Lori took the opportunity to sit with Oskar and Jaro. "Something must be up. No patrols for an hour."

Before either Jaro or Oskar could reply, the commander walked in front of the gathered soldiers.

"I will make this quick. We can't leave the border unattended for too long. We want volunteers to cross into France and gather information." The commander looked around. No one put their hands up. He sighed. "I was hoping to avoid this." He held up a black drawstring bag. "I have coloured bits of straw. If you draw out a red straw, consider yourself as a volunteer."

The bag was given to one of the mentors on the far-left side of the front row. Twenty natural-coloured yellowish brown straws were pulled out. The first red one came out. The man went white and began to tear up. More straws were pulled out. No red straws. Lori pulled out a red straw and cursed loud enough to be heard by those around him. They all turned with sadness in their eyes.
Oskar swore to himself, "Fuck."

Gingerly, he put his hand into the bag. He pulled out a yellow straw. He gave a sigh of relief. Jaro was next. He pulled out a red straw. He swore a bit louder. The bag continued. Two more red straws were drawn. Julian glared as he held the straw. He cursed. "I am supposed to go home tomorrow." Dismay and anger crossed his face.

When the bag was returned to the commander, he asked for the red straw holders to come forward.

Julian was in the process of standing up when Oskar snatched the red straw from Julian's hand and quickly shoved a yellow straw into Julian's hand. Oskar whispered, "Do you think I am going to sit back and watch my friends cross enemy lines? Just promise me one thing, if we fail to return, tell my sister Kiana, a nurse's aide in Lugano General Hospital. Promise me."
Julian gave a nod. "Promise. Thanks."

Chapter 27
South-East France.

Led by the base second in commander, Captain Henri Meyer, Oskar, Lori, Jaro and the first to draw one of the red straw, Corporal Alfred Suter, silently under the cover of darkness crossed the border into France. It was a twenty-kilometer hike going up the Borne Mountain Range to the first stop, Plateau Des Gliers.

While they rested, Captain Meyers watched the surroundings. The town of Annecy, which was dubbed the Pearl of The French Alps, was still sleeping. German vehicles and tanks dotted the streets. Captain Meyers sighed. "Blast. Too many Germans. They have occupied the town."

All gave a start when a sound from behind them made everyone spin around. A man holding a rifle at the group said, "What do we have here?"
Corporal Suter stuttered, "Don't, don't shoot. Swiss army."
The man still pointed the gun. "Now, that is not exactly believable. Why are you in civilian clothes?"
Capatin Meyers spoke, "Gathering information. We are getting too much propaganda. We want the truth not some NAZI garbage. I will show you my orders. I will put my hands in my jacket and pull out the instructions." Slowly the Captain placed his hand in his inner jacket to draw out a piece of paper. Slowly he handed it to the man. The man took the paper but struggled to read it under the night sky.

He pocketed the paper and waved his gun for the group to stand up. "Follow me."

As they walked dawn broke. The man ordered them to stop. He pulled the paper out and read the contents. "I am still not convinced." He gave a whistle. From out of the woodwork more men appeared. All held guns at the group. "They say they are Swiss trying to get information about the Germans." The leader of the resistance group came forward and took the note. "Keep watching them while I get this verified." The man walked away taking the note with him.

Twenty minutes later, he returned. "Let them go. They are legitimate. My contacts verified them, and our border patrol saw them leave Switzerland. Our patrol followed them to their resting spot." The guns were lowered. The leader of the resistance group led by Lieutenant Dario Payet said, "Welcome to our little resistance group. We call ourselves The Silent Knights. What do you want to know?"

Captain Meyers said, "I will introduce my people. Corporal Alfred Suter, Privates Oskar Grat, Lori Binder, Jaro Bauer. The Germans are swamping Switzerland with propaganda, especially in the North. We have other small groups scouting for truthful information so we can counter the rubbish insulting our ears."
Lieutenant Payet said, "The town is occupied as you gathered from your observations. Nothing gets in or out without German inspection. They are thorough. Families are checked at random for numbers. Our houses are checked for anything and anyone. They give us hell and we do our best to stop them or slow them down."
Meyers asked, "How many are in this resistance group?"
"That's classified," said Payet. Meyers nodded. He knew his curiosity which wouldn't be immediately or never satisfied.
"As you can see, our mission is to get good information. We need to get into the village."

Lieutenant Payet burst out laughing. "Be my guest. It is suicide. The Germans know everyone and everything that happens. You wouldn't get more than two metres into the town before you are dead."

Oskar, Lori, and Jaro grinned. "Suicide to go in dressed like this. It is not suicide to pretend to be Germans," said Lori.

"Oh yeah. Young euthanistic people end up dead," said a soldier standing behind Lori. Lori turned his attention to the speaker. He grinned. "Oskar, Jaro and I have had a bit of firsthand war experience."

"Where?" asked the two captains at the same time. Lori gave a quick glance to Oskar and Jaro as if he knew he overstepped the mark. Oskar and Jaro nodded. They took off their back packs and emptied them out.

The people around them gasped. Three German and three Italian uniforms fell onto the ground. One British uniform laid on top. Oskar said, "All of us are deserters who were forced to join the German army. All of us saw the Germans murder our relatives. We went to Italy where the Italians were so desperate for soldiers, any one from anywhere were forced into the army. We served in Albania before we deserted the Italian side. While on the run to Switzerland, we came across a downed British surveillance plane. There was only one uniform that we could poach. In Switzerland, we act like Swiss people and be law abiding. We are doing our time in the Swiss army. When we finish our time in the Swiss army, we will resume our Swiss jobs. We have no intention to run away from the Swiss army or have an excuse. Switzerland has been good to us. It is our decision to stay."

Captain Meyer blew out a puff of air at the revelation. He was stunned for a sort while. "Well, that makes the decision easy. These three men go with one or two of yours to scout for information. What is your view on this?"

"I will need to discuss this with our Captain," said Lieutenant Payet.

The next day Lori, Jaro and Oskar were teamed up with Antonie Payet, Lieutenant Dario's brother, and Jean Roux. Jean and Antonie wore civilian clothes while Oskar, Lori and Jaro wore German uniforms.

As they neared the town of Annecy, the group walked past the small patrol on the outskirts of the town. No one was suspicious. Antonie pointed to the main street. "Turn left. The Germans have taken over the main motel, Haute Savoie. They like their luxuries. I am going to visit my family which I haven't seen for four days. Jean will take you to the motel and will continue walking towards his home. You go into the Haute Savoie by yourselves. If we go, we get shot."

Jean continued walking past the motel. Lori, Oskar and Jaro stopped outside. They drew in a breath before going inside. They pretended to be familiar with the surroundings. Lori nodded his head towards the restaurant which was now a buffet set up. Soldiers walked in and out at all times of the day between five in the morning and eight at night. "Let's get something to eat before we wander around trying to find anything useful."

Oskar, Loris and Jaro completed their meal. "That was so good. Where shall we go next?"
Oskar said, "The bathroom. I have to go. It is surprising what you hear in the bathroom. Many people put their guard down."
Lori thought about the surrounding. "I will head up to the next floor and see if there is an office or a communications room."
Jaro said, "I think I wander around to see what and how many soldiers are housed. I have noted the reception desk is not always attended. Their books may say who is living in which room. We should meet at this restaurant at four this afternoon."

Oskar was in the restroom when two soldiers walked in. The men were laughing and bragging about their conquests with the local females. "The younger they are, the more innocent or naive they are. They are the best ones to go for. They know nothing. I believe I got one pregnant. She was covered in bruises from her irate parents," said the younger man.

"Is she still pregnant after the beating?" asked the other.

"I am not sure. It doesn't matter. The kid will always be bastard, and I am not putting my hand up for any responsibility," said the first man. Oskar was furious. He wanted to bust out of the cubicle and smash the soldier's face in. It took a lot of restraint.

After several of men coming and going without saying a word, Oskar was about to leave when older voices were heard. "I will organize another house search. We haven't done one for a week. We may be able to find the missing men who are a part of the growing resistance group. I hear they call themselves The Silent Knights."

"Yeah, let's shake up the locals. We do a search tomorrow," said the other voice.

Oskar left the cubicle after the unknown men left. He waited for the others to meet him at the restaurant. Jaro was first to appear. He gave a smile and whispered, "I know which rooms the captains, lieutenants and higher ups are in. There is a colonel and a general on a visit. They are here to supervise the house inspections which will be on tomorrow. It is a snap inspection."

Lori returned. "There is a communications room on floor two. The operators' roster is pinned to the wall. Those men come and go as they please. They left the room unattended. A message came through. I took the call. I have details of a shipment of arms coming through in two days' time. I wrote down the road on which they will be travelling. We better get out of here."

At four-thirty that afternoon, they went outside. Jean was walking towards them and then continued to go past. The trio followed and turned the corner where they met Antonie.

Antonie asked," Did you find anything?"

"We certainly did. There is going to be a surprise house inspection tomorrow. They are looking for absent men. They know about the resistance group and its name, 'Silent Knights'. A general and a colonel will be supervising. I guess it is to make sure all procedures are followed and to catch any man in the resistance group. Also, spread the word, the soldiers, well at least the privates and corporals are deliberately luring young girls into sexual activities. Making them pregnant seems to be a trophy. Warn their parents to educate the girls."

Lori chipped in, "The radio room is on the second floor. It was empty for a few minutes. I took a call. There is a truck of ammunition coming this way in two days' time." He handed over the details. Jaro said, "Floor three is the home of captains, lieutenants, colonels and now a general. It seems that floor is allocated to VIPs and other bullies of the regime." Jean and Antonie were surprised at the amount of information. We better get back to the camp and let people know they must be home for the inspection."

Oskar said, "I want to stay and see how they do the inspections. Jaro and Lori go back with Jean and Antonie. There is no pint in all three of us getting caught." Lori and Jaro began to protest. Oskar raised his hand for them to stop. "I need someone to look after Kiana if I don't get out of here. That is final. Go all of you."

When the group of four were well away, Oskar returned to the Haute Savoie. He sat in the lounge area trying his best to read the French newspaper. His eyes darted back and forth across the room at random times. Sometimes he struck up a conversation with other German soldiers. He was doing his best to blend in. When the restaurant closed, he left the lounge. He asked at the desk which rooms were vacant. He played the randy soldier trick. "I want to bring one of the local girls in. I want a vacant room. I have a nice young lady lined up." The soldier gave a broad grin. "Lucky you. Room 412, fourth floor is one of these purpose rooms." Oskar accepted the key and went upstairs.

The following morning the motel was bustling with activity. A string of trucks was lined up. Six men climbed into the back of each truck before they sped off to the designated streets. The truck Oskar was in, pulled up at an intersection. Three soldiers went down the left side of the street and the other two and Oskar went down the right. They knocked loudly on the doors until it was opened. Delays were met with the doors being smashed. Scared residents, many were in their night attire, were lined up outside. While one person did a roll call, two entered the home.

The soldier who was with Oskar said, "You can do the outside first. Check all sheds and anything under the houses especially if you see any access doors." Oskar gave a nod. Oskar opened a shed containing gardening tools. He looked carefully at the array. He closed the door. He checked behind a tree. Then he checked the unruly garden going down both sides of the house. Nothing.

He spotted a trapdoor close to an external tap. He carefully opened it. He got down on his knees to enter the under-house cavity. He heard a sound as if someone was shuffling deeper into the shadows. He stopped moving and listened more. Silence. He saw a piece of white fabric which glowed in this torchlight. A cat zoomed out giving him a start. He looked again and tugged on the fabric. It was just a rag. He checked further. Nothing.

At the next house, he started with the upper floor. Two children's bedrooms and a bathroom looked very normal. In the master bedroom he felt something was there. The wardrobe thickness didn't match the interior. He thought, *There has to be a secret door*. He pushed and tugged at different locations. Slowly the back panel slid open. In the gap, a middle-aged lady stared at him with fear.

Oskar raised his finger to his mouth. "Shhh." He closed the door again. A soldier's voice from downstairs filtered through. "All clear." Oskar responded, "All clear." He walked down the stairs and hoped the frightened lady could breathe with comfort for another day.

When the inspection of the street was clear, the owners of the house raced upstairs. They opened the secret panel. The lady gave a sigh of relief. She gave her sister a hug and quickly explained what had happened. The brother-in-law said, "It must have been the Austrian man who gave us intelligence about the sudden inspection."
The lady said, "He saw me and just said shh. He closed the door and said everything was clear."
"When I go back to the camp, I will see if it was that man. If it is him, he may have information as to how to get you to Israel."

The next day at the camp, the man asked questions about the newcomers. He was pointed to the direction of Jaro who was slowly becoming anxious about Oskar's delayed return. Minutes later, Oskar appeared and began ripping off the German uniform to replace it with civilian clothes. "Good to see you back. What took you so long?" asked Jaro.
"Sorry. I told you to go back to Switzerland with Lori Why are you here?"
"To make sure you go back," replied Jaro.
Oskar continued, "After the inspection, I was rostered into being a butler for a day. The general's butler was ill, and I was the replacement. Where's Jean and Antonie?"

Oskar called out their names. Both men walked over, "No more shouting. The wind carries your voice. What is it you want?"
"The truck with the ammunition was blown up by another resistance group or was it yours?"
Antonie grinned and said nothing. Oskar nodded then he added, "Three more trucks are coming. The soldiers are doing a rotation

and food is on its way. Three trucks in all. Same road as before. That will be arriving in three days."

The man who wanted to speak to Oskar edged his way forward. "You were on inspection duty, weren't you. You found my sister-in-law hiding behind a cupboard. She said you didn't report her." "Why should I? I am not a fan of Germans."

The man continued, "My sister-in-law is Jewish. She has been on the run since her family was taken away. Is there a safe route to Israel?" Before Oskar could reply, Jaro said, "There is no safe way. Don't expect the Vatican to assist. They only help Italian Jews, and the Germans frequently visit with what we suspect are boxes of gold or other valuables. The Vatican is housing items for the Germans." The people around them gasped. Antonie asked, "How do you know this?"

Oskar said, "My sister was made to work in the Vatican. She saw what was happening."Oskar looked at Jaro. "We better leave this place."

Jaro replied, "Lori, Alfred and the Captain went back to Switzerland. Alfred said he will wait at the border for our return."

"I want to leave as soon as possible," said Oskar.

Jean looked intently at Oskar, "We can use a person like you full time. Are you sure you want to leave?"

Oskar nodded. "Next year when I get called up to the Swiss army, I will pay a visit. I am not sure of the size of your group, but I guess it is formidable. I will place a bet now. The Silent Knights will be the first resistance group to defeat the Germans. The German command has made a mistake and placed nearly all their men in one building. Let's say, a lot of eggs in one basket. Keep that in mind. I am sure Jaro has told you of the floor layout of the Haute Savoie. It will be up to you to defend yourselves. Your government is concentrating its forces further north. Basically, you are on your own except for the watchful eye of Switzerland."

BERLIN
POLAND
NETHERLANDS
GERMANY
COLOGNE
BELGIUM
KARIOVVARY
COLDITZ
PILSEN
ROZVADOV
CZECHOSLAVIKIA
AMBERG
VOHENSSTRASS
NUREMBERG
FRANCE
AUGSBURG
MUNICH
BOBINGEN
SALAZBURG
LORRACH
STEINEN
ELSBETHEN
AUSTRIA
DELLE
AUDINCOURT
OBERSEE
WEGHALTZ
BONCOURT
BASEL
ZURICH
BERN
SWITZERLAND
GENEVA
ITALY

Chapter 28
Switzerland and Germany.

L ater that night, Jaro, and Oskar were dressed in their Swiss army uniforms. Under the cover of darkness, they went back to the Swiss border. Alfred and Lori met them at the entry point. Lori gave each a hug. "Good to see you all back safely, the Captain is wanting to see you in his office. Be there later this morning about nine a.m."

Oskar gave a sigh of relief. "Good, I need to get some sleep. Six hours sleep won't be enough but a start. I am so hungry. Are there any snacks available? I am not sure if I can sleep when I am so hungry."

Lori handed them each an orange and two slices of buttered bread. Jaro looked at the meagre meal. "It's better than nothing."

"Sorry, that is all I could get. The food supply is short now," said Lori. After filling in a report of the extra days in France, Captain dismissed the group.

In his office he reread the report, not once but twice. *These men work brilliantly in a team. I wonder if they could infiltrate the Germans again and get more information.* He drummed his pen on the table. *I wonder.* He picked up his phone and called higher command.

One week later, Lori, Oskar, Jaro and Alfred were in the Captain's office. A Colonel was sitting beside the Captain. The original report and a copy were placed neatly in front. The Colonel said after the men were instructed to sit, "I have read the report. It is not often we come across men who can slip into foreign camps and walk out. All you are required to do is gather information to counter the propaganda assaulting our ears. What do you say to this?" Oskar was first to break the mini silence. "Extra pay and back at home in five weeks. No more call ups in the future. Someone to tell my sister if anything goes wrong like one of us dying. I would like the balance of my pay if I were to die before that time, to be paid to my sister, a form of compensation."

"Alfred, what about your family? Who do you want notified?"

"Err..my parents and fiancée, need to be notified. Also, home in five weeks. And if I get called up again, no more border crossings. I will consider I have done my share of crossings."

"That is settled. Your pay will be fifty per cent more on this job," said the Colonel.

Jaro said, "No. Double pay. It is double the danger."

"I only have clearance for fifty per cent more," said the Colonel.

Lori said, "Then you better tell whoever it is, to make it double pay. If they disagree, tell them to join us on this information gathering mission. Let them see our worth firsthand. We take no responsibility for their death."

The Colonel glared at the four men. "I will see what I can do. Be prepared to be sent to Basel. That will be your new base. That is where we hear all the worst propaganda."

Three days later, Oskar, Lori, Alfred, and Jaro were in Basel. The sound of German planes threatened to drop bombs on Basel. Some did fall to cause chaos in the streets. This was followed by a weak German apology and the national anthem. "Good grief!" said Lori. "What a load of rubbish. Hearing that music makes my ears want to throw a tantrum."

Jaro grinned. "The Germans emit major gas from their mouths. It needs to be plugged up."

"It looks like we head for the radio stations. How many stations suffer from mindless verbal trash?"

"I don't know. We need to do some homework," said Alfred.

Again, under the cover of darkness, Lori, Alfred, Jaro and Oskar wearing German uniforms crossed into Germany. Lori pointed to a German jeep on the side of the road. The group looked around for its owner. The owner couldn't be seen. Lori edged closer. The keys were still the on the seat. Lori guessed the owner didn't realize the keys had fallen out of his pocket. He clicked the engine over and looked at the gauge to see the indicator showed half a tank. *It would have to do*, he thought. In first gear, he drove the jeep onto the road. The others climbed in. The jeep sped away.

When they came to outside of the town of Lorrach, they changed into civilian clothes. They found themselves an inn to rest before scouting the town for a possible radio station. None was found, but a shop was selling radios, Volksempfanger (people receivers). Jaro nudged Oskar.

"I bet this place has a small radio reception booster of some description. I think a fire may help the locals not having their brain dumbed down with the propaganda. What do you say?"

"It's an idea. Let's go inside and check the place out. Pretend to be customers," said Oskar.

The shopkeeper approached the group and greeted them. The group reciprocated.

Oskar asked, "Show us the best and most powerful model."

The man hesitated. "The standard model is the Volksempfanger. It is the best. Cheap too."

Jaro pointed to another model. "What about this one?"

The shopkeeper walked over. "That is expensive. You have to be careful using it. Herr Gobbles has made it treason to listen to foreign broadcasts. Sometimes foreign broadcasts can be heard. It is more powerful, and the clarity is so good for German broadcasts."

Jaro nodded. "Thank you. I will consider that information. "

Alfred was next to ask, "Is there a post office or other place in town where we can send telegram messages back to our families?"

The man smiled. "Here. I have a small unit. Like everywhere else, I charge by the word."

Alfred nodded. "I will have to draft a message carefully. I will book a time tomorrow to come in to send a message."

Oskar said, "I will buy one of these Volksempfangers. Can I put it on a weekly payment scheme?"

The shopkeeper said, "Most people do. The lowest is 2 Reichmarks per week."

Oskar replied, "I will come back tomorrow with a deposit. The rest will be payment per week." He held out his hand to seal the agreement. As the group left the shop, they chattered with excitement about the impending purchases to make sure the shop owner felt a sale or two would happen tomorrow.

At midnight, the group left the inn. The town was silent other than a stray cat mewing for attention or a feed. The dog telegraph was working. Barks were relayed across the town. When their message was done, the next mut would relay the sequence of barks. Oskar said, "No dog has barked at us passing in the street. We are still clear."

Lori picked the lock on the back door and entered the shop. The entrance contained a less than basic kitchen cabinet with a wash basin. A power point with a small electric jug, a new invention of the times, was connected to the only power outlet. Oskar opened the door to the next room.

A high-powered telegraph machine was clicking away with its tape spewing out a message. When the transmission stopped, Lori snapped the tape and pocketed it. Oskar pulled out the store of tapes and unwound the reels to make a mess on the floor. Every so often he would rip a section just to make any salvaging would make the owner annoyed with the shortness of the tape.

Oskar looked at the small machine he had never seen before. The machine started to operate all by itself. To his amazement, a letter with varying grades of print quality came out of the unknown machine. When it stopped, Oskar whistled. He read the information: PREPARE FOR NEW BROADCASTING PROGRAMS. MORE TRADITIONAL GERMAN MUSIC, MORE THIRD REICH MUSIC AND NEW WAR PROGRESS. WE WILL BE ADVANCING ON FRENCH SOIL TOWARDS PARIS AND ALL SURROUNDING AREAS. ALL TANKS AND CAVALRY ARE TO BE REDIRECTED NORTH AND ALL AREAS OF THE WESTERN FRONT.
THERE IS LITTLE FRENCH RESISTANCE TO THE ALL-POWERFUL THIRD REICH.
HAIL HITLER.

Oskar pocketed the letter as Lori and Jaro looked at the now silent machine. "Well," said Lori. "What technology is that? Letters by-passing the postal service. That is a bit scary."

Oskar looked at the machine in detail. It plugs into electricity. I have an idea. Cut the power lines and machines like these will fail to operate. I wonder if they use the same radio broadcast towers? Or do they use the powerlines?"
"We will find out later when we leave this place," said Jaro. "We better continue doing our job."
Alfred said as he ripped the plug out of the wall for the machine, "Give me something to cut this cord." Lori handed him a pair of scissors. Alfred tried to cut it. The cord frayed bit by bit. Alfred then cut two wires inside the cord. He tossed the cord to the ground. "That should stuff up the communications."

Jaro began sprinkling kerosene around the floor. "Time to leave."
Outside they laid a small trail of kerosene to be a fuse. The fuse was lit. The fire crept towards the shop. The fire was engulfing the shop as the group split up and took different paths back to the inn.

It wasn't until mid-morning did the group 'learn' of the fire. The upset receptionist relayed it to all her customers who were the biggest users of the telegraph system. Alfred said, "What a shame. I was going to send a message home. Oh, well, nothing can be done about that now. Is there another telegraph shop in another town?"
The receptionist said, "There could be one in Steinen"
Oskar nodded. "Thanks. It is in the wrong direction. Our rest period is over by the time we get there and back to the base. We must get back to our unit on the Western Front."

Oskar, Lori, Alfred and Jaro went deeper into Germany. They were going towards Steinen. Alfred pointed to the barely visible tower to the distant left. "I think that is a tower." The others stopped walking and turned their gaze to where Alfred was pointing out. Lori grinned. "It is a tower, and it doesn't matter which type it is. It goes down. They left the road and pushed their way through bushes to the tower.

At the base, they looked up shielding their eyes from the late morning sun. "Does one of us go up? Or do we blow it up?" asked Alfred.
Jaro examined the tower by walking slowly around. "Too many wires. One would need training to know which wire needs to be cut. Cut the wrong one, it will make for a very messy body." Everyone in the group stopped. A truck was coming in their direction. The group scattered for the cover of the bushes.

A maintenance crew got out of the vehicle. Some equipment was pulled out of the back of the truck and laid out in the ground in an orderly manner. Oskar was the closest to the truck. He crept towards the truck's rear and climbed inside. He put the only stick of dynamite he had in the truck and attached a cable to dynamite before rolling it out. The cable was perfect for a fuse. He got out as fast as possible.

The men drove away with the cable rolling out behind the truck. Oskar lit the cable. The lit cable followed the truck to the next tower which was just over one hundred metres away.

The truck was at the base of the second tower when the it exploded. The tower shook and was damaged on the side of the exploding truck. The integral strength of the tower was severely compromised. The tower still remained upright. When the group reached the site, they examined the damage. Lori advanced first. The soldiers were dead.

The truck was smouldering. Its surviving contents were strewn over the ground. Others were welded into a solid mass worthy of some modern sculpture. A large toolbox managed to survive the blast. The lid was misshapen but still permitted itself to be pressed open. Lori took advantage of this to open the box. He called out to the others, "Hey we struck gold. Tools to take down the rest of the tower."

The others came running. The assorted tools were examined to see which could complete the tower's demise. Alfred took a saw and began working on the most compromised tower support. Jaro took a sledgehammer to slam away at the same leg. After ten minutes, the remaining metal gave way. All four pushed on the structure. There was swaying but more needed to be done.

They attacked the second support leg which was not as badly damaged as the first. After twenty minutes, the support was cut. Oskar swung the sledgehammer as hard as he could. It bent the lower section of the support. Still the tower held up. Lori took the sledgehammer and went back to the first breached support. He slammed it against the more damaged upper section. With both legs having a section bent and not touching the base, the tower was now at its weakest.

Alfred, sorted through the scattered rubbish for cables and ropes. He tied them to the tower. He gave an order, "Pull as hard as you can. Let's get this tower down." No matter how much they pulled, the tower remained but now there was a bend that stretched to overhead cables. Oskar said, "Let's try two more times. If the cables at the top break, we have done our job. Nature can do the rest."

They pulled one more time. The top cables seemed to stress under the new tension. The second pull saw two cables give an almighty cracking sound similar to lightning in a major storm. Sparks flew everywhere. The live cable made the group run. Two live cables hissed and whipped in all directions like injured angry snakes. The wires on the other side of the tower also snapped. More sparks. The tower was not operational. The group reformed several metres away from the lashing monster. Then there was a loud bang. The tower collapsed smashing over the truck below. Lori nodded. "That looks like the tower fell on the maintenance crew, a freak accident. Let's get back to Switzerland before a posse comes after us."

Chapter 29
Lugano, Switzerland.

For three weeks, the Swiss people did not receive any German propaganda. Instead, the German people were able to hear Swiss broadcasts without German technology blocking out any Swiss programs. Freedom of the airwaves came to an end when the tower was replaced, and cables repaired. The German command in the area were on high alert for more sabotage and for the elusive resistance group. There were no more sabotages, and no group were found. The German people in the area were subjected to greater restrictions and stepped up propaganda.

Alfred went back to his home in Bern and as promised, was never called to do border duties again. Instead, he was assigned to be a spotter for German trains and trucks traversing the country in a special trade agreement which occurred just before the war. The Swiss government wanted to double check the numbers of covered train carriages and covered trucks to ensure the German government was paying the right amount of fees.

Lori, Jar and Oskar returned to Lugano in the south. They were disturbed when Kiana mentioned Louis was constantly showing up again. There were days where he did not appear but when he did, his presence was obvious. She said for the final two weeks of their absence, she always had a male escort or two women from the dorms whenever she left the building. She never left at night to go to any gathering at any location. She didn't want Louis to seize a chance to approach her for whatever reason.

Oskar made it a point to escort Kiana to and from work. Sure enough, Louis would disappear behind some structure as they walked. When Kiana was at work, Oskar approached Louis. "What is your problem? Leave my sister alone."

Louis stared Oskar in the face. "This is a free country. I can do as I please."

Oskar said with growing anger, "You are not free to terrorize or stalk people."

"There are no laws for that." retorted Louis. "I have checked. Lori, and Jaro have been put in the family or friend zone. That makes the door wide open for me to approach her. If I can get to know her, I think she would be the kind of girl I would marry." Before Louis could say another word, he found himself on the footpath nursing a bruised cheek. Oskar wanted to punch Louis again but held back. A crowd was forming. He said in a loud voice for all to hear, "Keep away from my sister. She doesn't like you. She is scared of you. The local police know what a bad citizen you are. If anything happens to her, they will know who to go after. Just stay away." He held up a fist to warn Louis.

Days went past. Oskar, Jaro and Lori were always at Kiana's side. She was always protected in any public area. At a local inn, the night was progressing well. The local guitarist played assorted folk songs and some of the newer songs heard on the radio.

Kiana excused herself to go to the rest room. She had done this so many times before without incident. As she was leaving the room, Kiana felt a hand over her mouth and her an arm being twisted behind her back. Louis' voice whispered in her ear. "Don't make a fuss. I won't hurt you." He pulled her backwards into the staff's change room.

"You must be the hardest woman on this planet to get to know. I won't hurt you if you don't scream or carry on. Do you understand what I am saying?"

Kiana nodded her head and gave a muffled, "Yes." Slowly, Louis released the hand holding her mouth closed. Kiana took the opportunity to bite hard on the side of the palm. She drew droplets of blood. With the grip on her twisted arm slightly loosed, she tossed him over her shoulder. In the confined space, Louis hit some shelves sending their contents on top of him. She opened the door and ran to the table where Lori and Jaro were sitting. She puffed out what had happened.

The trio ran down the street and directly into the police station.

The policeman who knew about Kiana's situation took notes. Proudly she said, "I only got away because I bit him hard and drew blood. He dropped his grip on my other arm. I tossed him over my shoulder. Stuff on the shelves fell down on him. That helped me escape."

"What do you want me to do since you bit him, demolished the room and escaped?" asked the perplexed policeman.

"Arrest him for attempted kidnapping," replied Kiana.

"He may press charges of assault. You bit him and buried him under shelf contents."

"That wouldn't have happened if he didn't try kidnapping me and constantly stalking me."

"Look I am not mediator of any kind. Why can't you two sort things out?"

"Why should I? I never wanted anything to do with him from day one," replied Kiana.

The policeman gave a sigh. "Have it your way. I will tell him you are a no-go zone."

"Good," replied Kiana as she picked up her handbag off the policeman's desk. She said on her way out, "If I disappear, you know who to go after. That man is crazy." The policeman thought, *two crazy people make for a poisonous relationship.*

Louis was absent for almost a week after the incident. That was soon to change. Kiana cringed when she was told a group of men from a convoy had been admitted. The truck they were driving was in a severe accident on the mountain road. Kiana was directed to work in the emergency ward for the day. A doctor called out to nurses and nurses' aides, "These men need Xrays. Wipe the blood off their faces and clean them up as much as possible. Remove all metal objects on clothing before taking them in the Xray rooms."

Kiana rushed to get a number of bowls with temped water and sterile cloths to wipes the men down. She placed all the equipment on a trolley and wheeled it into the emergency room. She handed out a set of equipment to the staff. Then she collected all the dirty equipment and returned with clean sets. She walked past one man groaning on a bed ready to be wheeled towards the Xray room.

 She glanced over and saw it was Louis. He was waiting for his turn to enter the Xray room. Kiana approached and grinned and then whispered to him, "God works in wonderful ways. What a pity he didn't send you to hell."

Louis recognized her voice. "God works in wonderful ways. Now you have to look after me."

He tried to grin. Kiana responded by throwing a cloth over his face. "Lucky you. I haven't had training to go into operation rooms. If I was there, I would make sure something like a swab would be left inside." She squeezed his broken leg.

"OUCH!"

"Did that hurt? I didn't feel it," she said with the bitterness in her voice filtering her whispers. She pressed a hand on his shoulder. He called out again, "Ouch!" Then he whispered, "Take the cloth off my face. Bitch."

Kiana smiled. "Your face looks better covered up. It takes a bastard to know a bitch. Welcome to hell." She strutter off to attend to other patients.

The next day Kiana was assigned to the ward where half of the men from the accident the day before were recuperating. She attended to the first three men. The last was Louis.

She drew the curtain around like she had done to previous patients. She looked at him and said, "I will do you temperature and blood pressure, but I am not doing anything else. I am not changing any catheter etc. You can enjoy the discomfort and smell. It is a part of hell." She took the readings and recorded them. Then she looked over her board and studied his expression. Louis knew he was helpless. He said, "What torture have you devised today?"
"Oh, I can give you a bit every day, just like the torture you have been giving me." She swung his suspended broken leg.
He yelled out, "That hurts. OUCH!"
Kiana responded loud enough for the other men to hear, "Don't be such a cry-baby. I haven't even begun. Shall we try again?"
"Don't touch me! Don't.... Fuck that hurts!"

"Stop fighting me and stay still. Oh, I give up." She opened the curtains to allow the other puzzled men see Louis grimacing. His leg swung with every movement he made. The more he tried to adjust himself, the more his leg swung. At the end, he threw a pillow at her but missed. Kiana picked it up and threw it back. It landed on his lap. "I don't take any nonsense from any patients." She looked around the room. "And that goes for all the rest of you." She noted three surprised looks. "Just pray I am not rostered here tomorrow." She stuttered out of the room. When she half closed the door, she watched the men inside questioning Louis. She noted his pride didn't allow the truth to spill.

It was two days later when Kiana was assigned to the ward again. She attended the first three men in the most professional way.

When it was Louis's turn, she said with a grin, "Ah! My favourite patient. How are we today?"

Louis said in a soft voice, "I was doing well until the nurse from hell walked in."

She corrected him. "Nurse's aide." In a louder voice she said, "Darling, Lucifer is knocking on your door. Do you want me to open it?"

"Is there another nurse's aide?"

"Sorry. Not today. It is me all day long." She gave a gentle swing on the suspended leg. Louis was determined not to scream out.

Kiana said, "You made some improvements. You didn't scream this time. Or was it the pain killers the doctors gave you helping with pain management?"

Louis turned his head away from her. He wanted to scream out his frustration and annoyance. When he calmed down, he said, "Well, my dear when I get out of this place and fully rehabilitated, I have a surprise for you."

In a loud voice for all to hear, "Really? Can I guess another attempted abduction? More stalking? More intimidation? More bullshit?"

She called out, "Hey Lucifer! What door do you have open for this bastard?"

Kiana sensed the other men were looking at the drawn curtain." She paused as if listening. "Okay. I will wheel him down to the mortuary. Number 666 cabinet. Got that." Kiana unclipped the leg and drew back the curtain. Louis began to scream out, "I am not ready to go anywhere. Stop! Stop this crazy woman from wheeling me out of here." In full view of the other men, he placed his hands in a pray position and started muttering any prayers he could think of. In his panic he jumbled many up. The other men were not sure whether to laugh or feel scared.

He was halfway out of the room when the doctor came in to do his rounds. "Where is this man going?"

"To the mortuary to formally identify a body. He is the closest relative to a carcass," lied Kiana. Louis laid in shock and wanted to blurt out exactly why he was going. Kiana adjusted the pillow under Louis's leg. The pain stopped him from talking.

The doctor hesitated for a few seconds. "Make it quick."

In the mortuary, Louis laid helpless on the bed. Kiana adjusted the bed so Louis could see what was going on. One by one, Kiana rolled out the trays in the cabinets. When a body was located, she left the carcass out. One empty tray was left out. Soon she had ten bodies on display. The smell began to assault their noses. Kiana asked, "Do you recognize any of these people?"

Between gritted teeth, Louis said, "No. What is the point of all of this?"

" I just wanted you to see what I saw when Germans raided my village and destroyed my family. Not exactly nice, is it?" Kiana pushed all the bodies back into their cabinets. The empty tray was the only one not returned. It was cabinet six. She jumped on the tray. "Yep, this looks like the right size for you. There is space on both ends to accommodate you." Kiana climbed down and took a measuring tape. She then measured Louis's height and then the tray. "Yes. A perfect fit. Lucifer said cabinet 666 but I don't see it." She looked at Louis, "Lucky you. You live another day."

Louis hissed, "Get me back to my room."

Kiana looked at him. "What is the magic word?"

"Oh now I get it. Not just a bitch but also a witch. Just wheel me back."

Kiana stood her ground. "What's the magic word?"

Louis rolled his eyes. "How do I know?"

"A clue? It has to do with manners."

"Oh! Please, wheel me back to my room," pleaded Louis.

Kiana gave a wicked smile. "Gee that took a long time." She slammed her hand down on the broken leg. "OUCH!" Beads of sweat instantly formed on Louis's forehead. He puffed as anger took over.

Kiana purred softly, "I think I am even now. You're going back to your ward. Just remember, any more shenanigans, you will have another taste of my nursing aide style." Louis took in a deep breath. Defeated now but he now had time to scheme.

When they returned to the ward, the other men looked on. Kiana could see they were bursting to ask him what had happened. They had to wait until Kiana was out of the room. They eyed her with a mix of amusement and earned respect. Kiana noted she was being watched and surmised the mix of emotions. As she left, she addressed all four men, "Keep smiling the world is a difficult place. It also makes people wonder what you have been up to." No sooner did the words leave her mouth, the three men who stayed behind, burst out laughing. She gave a cheeky smile and blew them a kiss. Only Louis wasn't laughing. He glared at her as she exited the room.

Two days later, Kiana was reassigned to the ward with Louis. She treated them all equally. Louis was not jibbed anymore. Max, Louis's friend came to visit. "I hear that your girlfriend is looking after you," he said with a smirk. Word had got out that Louis who was notorious for womanizing and always getting his way with women. This time he had bombed out big time. He looked at Max with some embarrassment. "That bitch has guts. She wheeled me down to the mortuary and pulled out all the bodies for me to see. Then she measured me up to see if I would fit in the cabinets. The only thing she didn't do was order the coffin."
Max laughed. "I think you found your match. She is someone who can keep you under control and make you honest."
"I am done with her. I am not going to watch her again or chase her ever again."

Max laughed. "I bet you, after six months away, you will be chasing her again. She can see right through you and can counter each move. She is your equal who can challenge you. Life would be interesting for you."

"She's the nurse's aide from hell," replied Louis.

Max turned to the other men in the ward. "Hey, that nurse's aide, Kiana, what is she like?"

There was a chorus of responses. Max held up his hand for them to stop talking at once.

"Hans, you go first." Hans looked over to where Max was standing. "She's really cute. Very nice. Smells nice too. She is gentle but at the same time firm. If I wasn't stuck here, I would take her out."

Max looked to the next patient. "Mark. What is your opinion?"

"Much the same as what Hans said. When she comes close, my blood pressure rises. She is hot. She has lots of guts. Nothing seems to phase her."

"Karle. What is your opinion of Kiana?" asked Max.

"She has a very unique way of getting things done. She is so funny in both words and actions. Taking Louis down to the mortuary and a measure up was the funniest thing to happen for a long time. I wish I was a fly on the wall when they were down there."

Louis retorted, "Yeah, very funny. The stench filled the room. I see those images just about every night I go to sleep." He shuddered at the recollection. "Ten bodies. Then she looked at me and the empty tray which she had slid out earlier. She jumped on it. She said, this would be the right size for me. Hell, she brought out a tape measure to double check my body length. As she puts it, to check that I would fit in the cabinet."

Max laughed. "I think she was measuring you to make sure there was enough room for your ego."

Louis gave him a dirty look. He continued, "She looked for cabinet 666 but couldn't find any. Then she says, I will live a bit longer. I was lucky."

The others, including Louis began to laugh. He then realized Kiana played him in a way that he couldn't even dream of. She played on his fears and insecurities. She could read him. That was unnerving. He didn't like that feeling and vowed to himself to keep away. His self-image and that he portrayed to others had collapsed. It was a shell that was going to be hard to rebuild. He tried to justify it in his mind, *those who didn't know me, will be none the wiser. Just the immediate group knew, and war would keep their mouths shut.*

One by one, the men in the ward disappeared. Most resumed their duties. Louis was the only one left. He rarely saw Kiana and that suited him. He went to physio once a week for checks and lessons. The rest of the time it was up to him to rebuild his leg. When he was able to walk with a frame he was discharged. His speed of recovery depended on him.

From the balcony of the house he was staying, he saw Kiana frequently walking to and from the hospital. She was unescorted. She took advantage of his down time to live a carefree life. He shook his head to get rid of the thoughts suddenly crowding his mind. He shook his head, *Bad habits die hard.*

Two months later he was walking with a slight limp. He resumed his duties in the German army. Trucks from Germany passed through Switzerland and down to the Vatican. New orders came. No more trucks to go in that direction. Too risky as the allies had completely captured Italy and Albania. The trucks were to go east from Munich through to Poland to a yet unknown destination. He had to plan the routes, the safest routes. The routes had to be under the cover of darkness.

Louis studied the maps going through Germany, Switzerland, Austria, and Czechoslovakia just in case he had to make massive detours. He listened to the propaganda and was convinced certain roads were more suitable than others. These trucks would carry food, guns of all types and ammunition for the ever-extending German eastern front. All road conditions were unknown: bitumen, dirt, narrow, wide, targets of frequent attacks. These were the words racing through his mind. He felt uncomfortable. He had never travelled on these roads before. The roads from Germany to Italy were easy. Even as a child he had travelled many of them, but this was unknown territory.

His mind fluttered to Kiana. She and her brother and adopted brothers, were from Austria. They would know the roads. Then it occurred to him, Kiana's gang were in their teens when they left Austria. Just how did a group of teenagers survive. Then he chuckled to himself when he recalled what Kiana said to him and the other men when they were hospitalized. *Smile, the world was a difficult place.* The sassy young woman was right. It is a difficult place. Then he chuckled again, when he recalled the air-blown kiss. *It makes people wonder what you have been up to.* He shook his head. *Why am I thinking of her?* He drummed his fingers on the map of Austria.

Chapter 30
Lugano, Switzerland.

Louis had orders to leave the southern Swiss area and to be permanently stationed in south Germany. His new base was Lorrach, the German side of Basel. From there he would assist to control food and weapons which would follow the German side of the German-Swiss border. The trucks would stop at Salzburg, Austria then turn north into Prague in Czechoslovakia. Another crew would ferry the goods to the next location. He returned to Lorrach where the spelled soldiers and the mildly wounded would be dispersed to their homes or hospitals. The round trip took three days, give or take a day.

 After doing four round trips, Louis realized just how much he disliked the job. Driving on bad roads was one thing. Dodging machine gun fire and sniper attacks was another. Swerving around potholes created by bombs almost saw his truck and others roll onto their sides. It was hair raising. Dodging bombs added to his discomfort. He rarely encountered that on routes between Germany via Switzerland to Italy. But here it appeared to be every two or three hours through each day. He saw trucks overturn when the drivers were shot. He saw the drained men desperately trying to hide from the onslaught of fresh gunfire. Many had survived the frontline only to be killed in transportation. *Unfair*. He thought to himself, *The chances are I could be next. My life is worth more than this.*

When he returned to Lorrach after his fourth trip, he feigned illness. The convoy went without him. While the team was away, he packed his bags. He was deserting.

In civilian clothes, Louis travelled back to Lugano. When he arrived, the German presence was gone. He felt he was the only German left in the area. In his mind, the war was over. He knew if he was caught, his life would be over at the pointy end of a firing squad. Desertion was instant death.

He stayed at an inn for two days to sort out his new life. He rarely ventured outside. He had to earn money. He had to keep a low profile. It dawned on him, Kiana's gang were trying to do just that, heads down and blend in. All he did was a good attempt to expose them. Now he felt annoyed with himself. Like them, he was displaced; his displacement was by choice, not by circumstances.

Louis emerged from his self-imposed exile and waited in a corner of the tavern he knew Kiana's group would eventually come. It was a Thursday night when he saw Kiana, Oskar, Lori and Jaro enter the venue. He watched them from his corner before building up the courage to approach them. He was nervous. The history between him and the group had not been good. He had to take a gamble. If he failed, he would disappear to another Swiss town.

The group of four had four glasses of beer and some finger food on a small plate on their table. Louis walked over carrying his own beer and a fresh plate of finger food. Before anyone could say anything, Louis said, "I come in peace, and I am not going to pester Kiana. I know my place." The group looked stunned. Louis continued, "I am going to eat a big piece of humble pie. I apologize for my rotten behaviour in the past. I will not repeat that ever again. May I sit down?"

Oskar and the others looked at him cautiously. Oskar slid over to make room. He warned, "One false move, and your dead." Louis nodded. "I totally understand."

Louis lowered his voice, "I was away doing my job driving supplies to soldiers. The new route was so dangerous, I told myself this is not worth my life. Call it selfish. I made food and ammunition deliveries and returned with broken men. Broken both physically and mentally, ghosts or shells whatever you want to call them. I lost count how many times I was coming close to look like them. I didn't want that. I feigned illness and cleared out. Hitler can have his war. Like you I am on the run."

The others looked on stunned by the revelation. Kiana was first to speak, "Did the dead bodies I showed you play a part in this decision?"

Louis nodded. "Actually, I didn't sleep well for a few nights. Driving trucks for skeletons and ghosts was worse. Bullets whizzing by isn't much fun either. Fuck Hitler. He can go to the front line himself and get dirty. I no longer want to be a part of that."

Lori, Jaro, Oskar and Kiana were stumped for words. It was a complete turnaround. They still didn't trust him. Words were always cheap.

The group was quiet for almost a minute. To Louis, it was the longest minute ever. Jaro asked, "Why should we trust you?"

"When the other drivers get back, if they get back from hell, they will see I deserted. I do not know if any of them will report me. If they do, I am a dead man. Actually, I am dead inside as well. Is that something you people went through when fleeing Austria?"

Oskar nodded. "I call it the Obelisk syndrome. You look solid and strong. In reality you are dead, cold and fragile on the inside. You chip easily on the outside creating little holes that sometimes expose the vulnerability of the interior. It takes one adverse incident to make a mess of your life and another lifetime to repair. We have been through that trauma. We are displaced and shattered souls; the walking dead who can never restore what we had. If one thing hurts one member, it hurts us all."

Louis nodded at the information. He could relate to it. He had let go of the rope he had and was grasping for another. His potential lifesavers were there before him. It was their decision for them to hand him a rope. Louis politely excused himself. "Thank you for listening." He downed the remainder of his drink and left the group. When he got to his room, he felt much better. The weight somehow was lifted but the uncertainty remained. He knew he had to accept whatever came next.

A week later, Louis found a part-time job driving a delivery van. With the meagre wages he moved out of the inn into a boarding house several blocks away from the town centre. The quiet suburb suited him. He slipped into a routine. Everything was going as smooth as it could be.

Months passed. Louis concentrated on work and keeping a low profile. He was now doing two part-time jobs, the second as a shop assistant starting late in the afternoon going to early evening. He only ventured to the inns on Thursday and Saturday nights. He switched the venues on a weekly basis as to not to establish a routine. Occasionally, he met with Kiana's group but kept his time limited as not to intrude. Sometimes it was just a hello and move on.

On one such brief visit he said to Oskar when both were waiting at the bar to be served, "I want to take Kiana out on a date. You or one of the others can chaperone us if it makes you feel better."
Oskar turned his head towards Louis and then to the group. "I will check with the others especially with Kiana. If she says no, that will be final."

Louis agreed to the situation. He waited near the bar and sipped on the new beer. He glanced over every so often to gauge their body language.

Soon he was signaled over by Oskar and Jaro. Kiana and Lori adjusted their seats to allow Louis to place a chair in the group. Kiana said, "You can join us a few times until we feel more comfortable with you. And no spying on us in the meantime."
Louis nodded. "Those days are over. I am not going to spy on anyone. I now understand what this group is all about. Again, I apologize for my past behaviour."

A few weeks later, Kiana and Lori met up with Louis. The evening went well. The trio stopped at a late-night café for a light snack before walking Kiana back to the nurse's dormitory. They were one block away in a well-lit area. The trio was crossing the road. Kiana waved and called out to two nurses being escorted back with their partners.

Suddenly, a fast-moving van roared up the street. Louis pulled Kiana back from the road at the same time gunfire sprayed out of the back of the van. Both Lori and Louis were shot. Both were dead on the side of the road. Kiana screamed and was pulled into the van. The onlookers were shocked. When they came out of their stunned state, the two nurses ran to assist the men in the street. Kiana was gone. She was kidnapped in front of their eyes. One of the men ran to the police station to report the murder and kidnapping.

When Oskar and Jaro were told of the news, both were initially shocked and went into a rage. The policemen tried to restrain Oskar and Jaro. They fought with the policemen before being subdued. One officer said, "We have witnesses to the incident. Two nurses who lived at the same dormitory and their male companions witnessed the incident. They are also shocked. One gave a partial numberplate number. We have begun searching the files for the numberplate. I am not expecting any results for a few days. Please come with us to make a formal identification of the bodies." Slowly Oskar and Jaro stood up. Tears were rolling down their faces. Anger simmered inside ready to explode with the slightest cause.

At the station, a nurse which Oskar and Jaro met once before approached them. She was still sobbing. "I am so sorry. It was just so quick. It was a matter of seconds. Both men dropped and Kiana just vanished. I am sorry." She gave him a hug. The other nursed approached Jaro. She sniffed and wiped her nose on a handkerchief before speaking, "The tall man I have never seen before pulled Kiana back. She would have been hit by the speeding vehicle. I think his actions protected her from the gunfire. God it was just so fast. I am sorry for the loss." She also gave Jaro a hug. Jaro just broke into tears again. The watching policemen ushered Jaro and Oskar to the interview room.

The next day the news of the double murder and kidnapping aired on the radio and then details were published in the newspaper. Oskar and Jaro stayed in their home to avoid the press and to allow time to think. The anger grew into bitterness. Oskar said, "It had to be Germans chasing Louis. But why did they have to kill Lori and why kidnap Kiana? It doesn't make sense." Jaro spoke with the same bitterness, "Collateral damage. They were in the wrong place at the wrong time. What do you want to do next?"

Oskar drank from a glass containing beer. He wiped his mouth on the back of his hand. He looked up. "I am not sure yet. I know for sure; I have to leave this place and go searching for Kiana and just maybe find the bastards who killed Lori and Louis. Louis knew they would be after him, but he expected that to happen if he travelled north. His so-called friend Max must be behind this. He must have spilled the information as to where to look. This time, I must travel by myself. No arguments.

I want you to stay. One of us has to survive this war."

BERLIN
POLAND
NETHERLANDS
GERMANY
COLOGNE
BELGIUM
KARIOVVARY
COLDITZ
PILSEN
ROZVADOV
CZECHOSLAVIKIA
AMBERG
VOHENSSTRASS
NUREMBERG
FRANCE
AUGSBURG
MUNICH
BOBINGEN
SALAZBURG
ELSBETHEN
AUSTRIA
LORRACH
STEINEN
WEGHALTZ
AUDINCOURT
DELLE
OBERSEE
BONCOURT
BASEL
ZURICH
BERN
SWITZERLAND
ITALY
GENEVA

Chapter 31
Germany,
Netherlands, Belgium.

Oskar said good-bye to Jaro. Oskar carried a new backpack containing the three uniforms: the German, the Italian and the British. Two sets of civilian clothes were also jammed into the bag. Jaro gave Oskar a hug. After several debates between Jaro and Oskar, Jaro was to remain in Switzerland just in the remote chance Kiana was found. At least there was someone to be with her on her remote chance of return. Jaro's other task was to receive and keep mail whenever it managed to get through on Oskar's search. Any incoming mail or correspondence outside Switzerland would be difficult. A letter now and then would all either of them could hope for.

For months, Oskar searched all the places they visited and all the surrounding areas. He lived like a scavenger taking what he could whenever he could. He showed people a picture of Kiana. All shook their heads. No. No. No. Never seen her were the usual replies. He even placed advertisements in the local newspaper and spoke on the radio, hoping someone somewhere knew where Kiana was. After exhausting all possibilities and leaving flyers at railway and bus stations, he wrote a letter to Jaro explaining he was going to Basel to cross the border at Lorrach into Germany. Oskar knew this would be the last letter he would send for a long time.

Germany.

In his German uniform, Oskar traveled from town to town showing the now heavily crumpled picture of Kiana. He hitched rides on German trucks going between towns. The journeys were never straight forward as the drivers zigzagged to avoid bombs raining from the sky and dodging craters left by past exploded bombs. Spasmodic gunfire from the sides of the roads made any movement perilous.

Oskar blended in at the barracks. He wasn't there to socialize but to get a free meal or some resemblance of a good night sleep. Gunfire, fires, and bombs saw sleep was always interrupted. Oskar slipped in and out of barracks in his German uniform and changed into civilian clothes when walking through towns searching for Kiana. His appearances and disappearances were never questioned. He said he was transferred between units or was on leave of some description.

Oskar noted Hitler was initially more bent on fighting on the Eastern front. Poland and the eastern countries took a NAZI hammering. More soldiers were deployed there than on the Western Front. Oskar was puzzled by the tactic and wondered if Hitler was crazy enough eventually to attack Russia in the bitter cold. Louis had told him of the living skeletons coming back from the eastern front line. Winter made sure food, clothing and transport were in short supply as roads were blocked by heavy snow. Soldiers had to shovel the snow off the road before any vehicle could pass. Trucks and trains being attacked didn't help the situation. Men were fighting and living on empty.

He recalled what Louis said, trains with Jews were going to Poland for ethnic cleansing. Oskar considered the idea of going to Poland to check out the camps of extermination but deemed it too risky. The Western Front offered greater survival chances although he doubted Kiana would have been taken to the west. But he had to try to eliminate the western side before trying to go to the eastern countries. He would start searching the Netherlands before turning south to Belgium. He planned his route and methods of getting to such places.

Netherlands and Belgium.

After crossing the border into the Netherlands, he replaced his German uniform with civilian clothes.

Winter was biting into his body. He didn't have enough warm clothes. He shivered as he walked the streets. People hurried past doing whatever they needed between the outbursts of ariel attacks which the Germans had perfected. The sound of Junker Ju 87's which sounded like millions of seagulls announced their arrival. Anti-aircraft guns were not responding. The Netherlands was out of ammunition for such artillery. The Junker Ju 87's did as they will; screaming through the sky to terrify citizens and drop a bomb or two. People scattered anywhere they could for shelter.

It was on one such emergency dash, when Oskar took shelter in a garden shed which was five metres away from a house. The owners believed they could hide in their house. A bomb exploded on the other side between this house and the next. Families inside both houses died. He survived but was in state of shock. The shed had partially collapsed. He had to claw his way out from under the debris. He knew no one was going to come to his rescue. That was a given. Just like the past in difficult situations, he could only rely on himself.

It took about twenty minutes for Oskar to free himself. Small cuts on his fingers and on other parts of his body mixed with dirt made him appear like a zombie. He stumbled towards a group of people trying to desperately dig occupants out of the fallen houses. One young lady rushed over to assist him to a chair which was earlier pulled out of the rubble. Not long after, men in a car loaded him into the back and drove him away to an overcrowded hospital where he stayed for a night. After bath and fresh clothes, the staff saw the injuries were minor. He was discharged after receiving basic first aid.

Oskar returned to the shed to retrieve his backpack. Then he entered the small near empty grocery store to buy some food. When he was looking at the near bear shelves, two German soldiers entered.

Oskar turned his back and lowered his head while grabbing a potato. He watched the German soldiers walk around the shop taking what they fancied. Oskar walked past one and lifted a wallet from a rear pocket. The German soldiers walked out without paying for their goods. The elderly man looked in horror but was much too frightened to challenge the blatant shoplifting.

Oskar approached the angry and scared man. "How often does that happen?" he asked.
The old man replied, "Those two do it all the time. The others pay the full amount or some of the amount." The man looked at Oskar. "You are not from here, are you?"
"No. Austria. The Germans wiped out my home village. Bodies everywhere. My sister was recently kidnapped by Germans. I am looking for her."

The old man nodded and gave a loud sigh. "You may have to go to a prisoner of war camp. People disappear all the time, especially Jews." The man leaned over to Oskar and said in a whisper, "Don't go near the police stations. Some police have been bribed and are continuing to be bribed for names and addresses of Jews and strangers. Most police are honest. It is only the few who are being traitors." The man pulled back and spoke in a normal voice, "Some girls have disappeared in different towns. Sometimes they are found. They are a mess mentally and physically. They are put into a building and abused by German soldiers, especially the higher-ranking ones. If they become ill, the girls are shot, and bodies discarded on the side of the road. Very few escaped to tell the truth."

The man wrote on a piece of paper the address. "This is one address I know such activity takes place. I am sure there are more."

"Thank you for your assistance," said Oskar.

Oskar replaced the potato he was holding but collected other vegetables and a few pieces of fruit. He aimed for food which could be eaten raw. He approached the counter with his selection, took out the German wallet and paid for his supplies. Oskar then gave the old man extra money, Reichsmarks.

Oskar apologized, "Sorry I only have Reichsmarks. "

The old man nodded. "I take any cash these days. No choice."

Oskar handed over the cash. "How much did those Germans take?"

The old man rubbed his head. "Maybe twenty or thirty Reichsmarks."

Oskar handed over fifty Reichsmarks, the old man protested. Oskar leaned over the counter and whispered, "I stole the wallet from one of the soldiers. You gave me helpful information. Take it."

Oskar left the shop. From the corner of his eye, Oskar saw through the shop window the man smiling.

Oskar stopped outside the shop and emptied the remainder of the wallet. It was only ten Reichsmarks. He tossed the wallet on the ground and half buried it in the snow. Oskar looked into the shop window to see the man watching him. Oskar gave a wave and held a finger to his lips to indicate silence and then disappeared.

Oskar found the location of the house where Kiana could have been taken to. He watched from the street for a short period of time. No movement. He went into a local bar which had been open for less than an hour. German soldiers were there guzzling the local brew. He walked to the restrooms where he changed into a German uniform. He walked directly out of the bar and to the 'residence' on the other side of the road.

The bell on the door announced Oskar's entry into the building. A man in a German uniform came out of a room behind the reception desk. Oskar approached cautiously. "What can I do for you?" asked the man. Oskar wasn't sure. He gave a cough. The man interrupted it was Oskar's first time in the place. "Most of the staff are sleeping. A couple do a day shift." He brought out a book showing the ladies. He flipped through the pages and stopped about midway. He swung the book around for Oskar to see. Oskar looked at the pictures. He asked the man, "May I look through this? I may come back later if I see what I like and happens to be on night shift." The man shrugged and watched Oskar carefully. Oskar turned each page slowly as if considering each female in turn. When he completed going through the book he asked, "Is this the only book?"
The man was taken aback. "Err yes. Are you looking for someone in particular?"
Oskar nodded. "I met this really cute girl last month. She said she worked at one of these places. She is about eighteen, green eyes, short hair. I can't tell you what the true colour of her hair is because she would put different colours through; red, blonde, brown, black. You name it. Once she made a colour error and came out purple. When she tried to fix the error, the hair went grey." Oskar gave a chuckle. The man on the other side of the desk gave a grin. "Well, that girl is definitely not here. Try these places." He wrote down three more addresses. Oskar thanked the man and moved on to the next address.

By ten at night, Oskar had visited all three addresses, and another supplied to him via one of the females who was waiting for her next client. All drew a blank. Oskar went into a bar and to the restroom to change into civilian clothes. He had been in the German uniform all day. It was useful for hitching a ride from venue to venue and for gaining information. But now it would become a liability.

After changing into civilian clothes, he walked down the street in search of a place to stay. An air raid siren filled the air. Lights all around him were turned off. Junker Ju 87s quickly made their presence known. Oskar placed his hands over his ears as he ran down the street. He was running blind. He heard bombs dropping in the distance. He looked up to see a Junker Ju flying overhead. He cringed as the plane dived almost vertical and then pull up. Instead of a bomb, leaflets rained down.

He picked up a flyer knowing all too well it would be propaganda. He picked up a number of them and stuffed them down the front of his jacket to help to insulate himself from the cold air. When he found a shed in a garden, he ran inside. He stayed the night.

When the sun rose, he slowly stepped out of the shed. He was confronted with the property owners. They stared at him. Oskar put his arms up to surrender. He said in broken Dutch, "It was cold. No home." The family stepped back as Oskar picked up his backpack and left the property. Oskar now considered leaving The Netherlands and go to Belgium, another neutral country occupied by the Germans.

Oskar hitched a ride with a German personnel truck going to Belgium. It went straight to one of the hastily built barracks. He mingled with the other soldiers when it came to food and board. When it came to moving to the front line, he did his best to dodge the deployment. He was sitting in the truck waiting like the rest of the group for the driver. The driver was longer than normal. Oskar said, as he stood up, "Let me out, I have to go to the toilet." Before anyone could stop him, he was out of the truck and heading towards the sleeping quarters. He stayed in the room until there was another group of soldiers entering.

He walked out knowing the movement of men. at the gate would be counting trucks and making a quick inspection. He posed for a few minutes as a head counter and inspector before slipping to the next truck outside the gates. He gave the signal to the gate guard all was clear. The truck moved in. Using the cover of the truck and a bit of dirt that blew up with the restart of the truck's engine, Oskar disappeared into to bushes at the side of the road he and ran as quickly as he could towards one of the villages he passed when going to the barracks.

Just outside the village, he found a cluster of bushes. He changed back into civilian clothes before entering the village. He didn't know what to expect or what to do. He just looked around. The village layout reminded him of Weghaltz. It seemed like a lifetime ago. Oskar slowly walked to a grocery shop. Like the one in The Netherlands, the shelves were almost bare. He bought a few items of food. He realized the shop owner was watching him as he left and moved down the street.

Suddenly, four men jumped him. Oskar tried to fight back but was overpowered almost instantly. They dragged him behind a shop which included a residence. In here, the unknown men tied him to a chair. The four men emptied his backpack and stared at the assorted uniforms. Suspicion overtook his captors. One named, Uli who could speak German punched him a few times in the stomach before grilling him.

"Where are you from? What is your name." asked Uli.
"Oskar Grat. Austria."
"You're a long way from home. What are you doing here?"

"Looking for my sister. She was kidnapped. We were living in Switzerland for nearly two years. She was kidnapped. There were witnesses to the murder of my Austrian friend and a German who deserted the German army. They witnessed the kidnapping as well. I have searched all of Switzerland, most of The Netherlands and just started to search here. There is a picture of her in the outside pocket of my backpack. Look for yourselves."

One of the other men, named, Arvin, opened one of the two pockets. He emptied the contents. No picture. He opened the other pocket. He pulled out a crumpled picture now protected in a small frame.

Oskar said, "She's been missing for nearly four months. She is the only family I have. The rest were murdered in my village and the village was set alight. The only thing standing is an obelisk, a memorial to fallen soldiers who died in World War One. The mayor painted on 'and WW2' before we evacuated. Everyone was hunted down and shot."

"How did you get the German uniform?" asked Uli.

'I stole it. My sister stole one for herself and my friends stole one each. We used them to cross borders and to hitch rides."

"What about the Italian uniform?" asked Cario in broken German. Cario was standing behind Oskar ready to restrain him further.

"We went to Italy thinking it would be safer. Germans had taken over Austria. We were forced into the Italian army and served in Albania. One of my friends died trying to get us ammunition. When we saw an opportunity to desert, we did. In this time my sister was trained to be a barmaid. She was then forced into the Vatican where she was working like a slave. We got her out of there. She said the place was riddled with dirty men and corruption. Then we went to Switzerland and lived there minding our own business."

"How did you get the British uniform?" asked Uli.

"We were crossing the mountains from Italy into Switzerland. There was a severe storm that night. The plane crashed in the storm. After the storm, we went to investigate the downed plane. The pilot was dead. No other passengers. We took what we wanted which was mostly food. I took a spare uniform that was in a box."

There was a pause in the questioning. The men walked out of the room but kept a watchful eye on Oskar.

Ten minutes later the four men returned. The questions started all over again. Oskar never changed any detail. Uli asked, "Did you serve in the Swiss army, at the border?"

"Yes. Two terms. One for each year. The first term was for four weeks after some basic training weeks and the last term for three months." replied Oskar.

Cario gave a nod. "I lived in Switzerland for a while. At first, they only had three weeks. When this war started, it was three months. He is telling the truth."

"Just tell us, what you did for a living in these years?" asked Bari who also spoke broken German and spoke for the first time.

"Anything we could find. Carpentry, roof repairs, farming, house cleaning, pick-pocketing if needed, when money was short and no jobs were around. Anything to get a meal and a place to stay at night. In Switzerland, we had stable jobs and a quiet life. That is all I want. But my sister disappearing has put an end to that. I am on the move again. This time searching; not running away."

The men left the room again. Oskar couldn't hear clearly what was being said. When the men returned, they untied him while another pointed a gun at him. There was an uncomfortable silence. All four sets eyes were watching Oskar, checking his next move. Oskar asked, "Can I please have a glass of water and something to eat?"

The men continued to look at Oskar. No one moved. Thinking he wasn't going to get even a drink of water, he started to pack his backpack. A foot stepping on the first item of clothing stopped him. Oskar looked up thinking, *What now*?

"Where are you going?" asked Uli.

"I thought you had finished the inquisition," replied Oskar suddenly feeling trapped.

"Wait here. The village is crawling with Germans. They do inspections every so often," said Uli.

"Tell us about being in the Swiss army in the south," asked Uli.

While in the Swiss army a group of us crossed the French border to get information about the Germans. Switzerland was being flooded with so much propaganda, no one knew what was really going on. We met with people from Annecy"

Bari who was holding the gun asked, "Did you meet with Jean Roux and Dario Payet?"

Oskar nodded. Bari lowered his gun. "Give Oskar what he wants. Jean told me of young Austrian who was able to get information about the Germans. You went on a German raid, didn't you?"

"Unfortunately, yes."

"You found a Jewish lady in a cupboard. You told the others in the search team all was clear."

Oskar nodded.

"Those people asked you to stay but you refused. Family was the excuse. Is that right?"

Oskar nodded again. Bari reconfirmed, "He's safe. I got a letter from Jean last year. He told me two young Austrians who gave them valuable information after walking into Haute Savoie, a motel which was taken over by the Germans. They also told the group of a convoy of food and ammunition coming to town. The Payets and friends attacked the convoy. Oskar, here is a natural spy against the Germans."

Bari turned to Oskar. "To survive here, you need to be in some form of resistance group. You have a choice, join us or go it alone." Oskar didn't say anything for a period of time. He mulled over the options. Finally, he said, "I join you on the proviso I can leave any time to continue my search for my sister."

"Agreed," chorused Uli and Cario.

"We have a dangerous task coming up. The more men the better. We are still getting details."

"Give me a hint," asked Oskar. "On land or water?"

"On the land. France. We go into France to make a mess and support the underground there. That is all for now."

Oskar wasn't feeling that pleased with the idea. He didn't say a word as a plate of food and a jug of water was placed in front of him. He began to eat the meal. After the third mouthful he asked, "Do you have a map of where we are going?"

Arvin who hadn't said a word, went to a cupboard to bring out a map. He spread the map across the table. He weighted down the corners with the salt and pepper shakers. He pointed. "Here is the German activity. We want to blow the area up."

Three nights later, Oskar was accompanied by ten men who slipped out of the safety of the residence behind the shop. They silently moved towards the outskirts of the town where they were met by Group G, a very experienced and successful group of university students who had caused the Germans millions in sabotaged bridges and railway lines. From here they were driven to the border.

"It is time to change into uniforms, German ones," said one of the students riding in the back with Oskar and his group. While they were changing clothes, they were given details.

They were driven through a German check point. The guards looked in the back of the trucks and noted the soldiers headed for the front line. They were signaled to go through.

They drove through the French town of Lille and then turned north towards the river Rio Lys. The truck went off road to be hidden in dense overgrowth. The men got out of the truck and unloaded the ammunition, bombs, and detonators. Guided by the two resistance groups, Oskar followed all instructions.

They came across a wooden bridge that clearly had signs of a hasty rebuild. Oskar with three others were guided to cut the supporting timbers and remove some of the braces. It was just strong enough for one car to pass or any foot traffic. Heavy vehicles and tanks would ensure the bridge would collapse. Pressure bombs were attached to the places where braces were removed. They would explode when the braces gave way. Then the group moved on to another location.

Further into France, the groups were guided by two of the local French resistance to a farmhouse. The rest of the ammunition was left at that location. The locals were preparing to ambush three trucks of German soldiers headed for Paris.

It was close to the early hours of the morning when they reached Lille again. All dressed in German uniforms, they were able to pass through the check point.

Back in Brussels, the group dispersed.

Two nights later, Oskar was approached again. "This time," said Uli, "We go through Germany and blow up a few radio towers and bridges. We are going to Cologne for the first time."

"That far into Germany? I have been to the southernmost edges only, Lorrach and west to Steinen. A few of us who were in the Swiss army, brought down a radio tower and burned down a relay radio station in Lorrach." said Oskar.
"So you know the area?" said the man.
Oskar nodded. "A bit. I got tired of the German propaganda, so a few others and I decided to turn it off for a while."

Uli smiled with delight. "This time we cross the border and go to Cologne. We have contacts that are going to get us that far. Did you know, there are up to ten thousand Germans who dislike Hitler? They have been instrumental in getting Jews and anyone out of Germany to Britain. They have been sending good intelligence to the British and the French. You won't see these people's faces. They wear balaclavas or are invisible. No one knows exactly who they are, but they are effective in helping people escape and getting information. It will be rare for them to get people into Germany. Once inside, we do not contact them until we are ready to leave. We have one day to get there, one day to do our job and one day to get back home ready for a house inspection the following day."

Oskar said, "In my private time in Brussels of searching for Kiana, I was told many women and older children were forcefully taken to Germany to be slave labour in the German ammunition factories. When I get to Cologne and help with whatever, I will leave you to start searching the ammunition factories."
Uli warned, "Just be careful. Any one new to any area can be called rightfully or wrongfully a Jew. Then it is straight to the gas chambers which are mostly in Poland. Trust no one while in Germany. Yes. Hundreds of women and children from this country and Holland have disappeared into Germany."

Arvin added, "King Leopold the Third, was incarcerated in his Belgium castle at the start of the war. He was totally ineffectual as a war leader, but I do give him credit for being a skilled negotiator. He did stop over 500,000 women and older children from being forcefully transported to Germany to be slaves in their ammunition factory.

"Another word of warning, there is some sweetheart deal with the Vatican and the NAZIs. The Catholic Church in this country has sided with the Germans. They are not the only group who have done so. The Rex, as they call themselves, like the authoritarian NAZI concepts of government. Rex and the other groups have divided Belgium in a way when the war is over, it will be difficult to regain any form of monarchy or democracy. The Rex is the main group. Look at it historically. The Catholic Church has always been authoritarian, autocratic, and patriarchal in nature over the centuries. They are just doing what they have done for centuries; side with the bullies or be the bully."

"When are we moving out?" asked Oskar.

"Tomorrow at sunset. Be ready," said Arvin.

"Since I will be in Germany, I will leave this group. I will search Cologne first before heading to Berlin or Munich." Uli slowly shook his head. "I am not sure exactly where the ammunition factory is, I think it is in the south of Germany. Just be careful. Being alone has made you desperate. Be careful." Oskar said in a sardonic tone, "If I am not shot, I just may disappear with thousands of others."

In civilian clothes, the group walked to the outskirts of Brussels. The truck was hidden at the base of a hill which was covered in thick bushes and trees. Here they changed into German uniforms before moving out. There was only one way to the location, a narrow dirt road barely wide enough for the truck to pass. The road came to a sudden end with trees and smaller bushes blocking the visibility of the dirt road. The truck made a sharp left turn to drive over low shrubs which almost concealed the truck's tracks. The truck zigzagged over the area to avoid making any ingrained path. Another five minutes, they were on the road.

Germany.

The group came to the first tower. Explosives were set one third of the way up. A timer was set for four a.m. Two more towers received the same treatment. In another district, the towers were set with bombs at least two metres high up. The timer was set for six a.m.

Then they crossed a bridge. A barrel of explosives was placed on the eastern side. The timer was set at six-thirty a.m.

When they reached Cologne, the group set up small bombs to create chaos. The administrative buildings were targeted. There was a small elite school which brainwashed the children with Hitler's dogma. The school's administration building was booby trapped for the start of school on the Monday. The children would be safe, the administration block wasn't.

It was after this last job, that Oskar parted ways with the Belgium resistance group. He was on his own again, venturing into the unknown. After spending a few days in Cologne, Oskar saw in the newspapers more propaganda about the wonderful women workers in the German ammunition factory. The picture showed smiling healthy women. Oskar scoffed at the photo. He muttered, "Bullshit."

He put on his German uniform and hitched a ride to Munich.

Oskar searched the city's outskirts when he realized that any ammunition factory would not be in the city itself. It was both a toxic and dangerous industry where people died from the inhalation of toxic fumes. The super fine dust would enter the body via the nose, eyes and skin. The death rate was high. If there was an explosion, it would make sense that factories would be well away from other industries and towns.

Eventually, Oskar received word there was a factory in Bobingen. He caught a train to the Augsburg, the largest town closest to Bobingen. Through the day, he slept in garden sheds or found a ditch covered in vegetation which would offer cover. At night, he showed the picture of Kiana to anyone in the streets. Through his questioning, he was able to find the exact location of the factory.

The factory was fenced off with a two-metre-high chain wire security fence. He climbed a tree that grew beside the fence. From there he could see the layout of the complex. He realized he was closest to the residential area. From his vantage point, he waited quietly.

It was late in the afternoon when he saw some activity. The closest houses which looked quite comfortable in both sizes and outside presentation, seemed to belong to officials or administrators. Their flashy cars gave the hint of officialdom. Across the road, the houses were closer together and less opulent on the outside. Oskar surmised, middle management. Kiana would not be in any of these homes. Still, he waited to see what else may happen. Nothing. These houses always had an occupant, the wives or families of the officials or management. Then he moved to another tree which was almost three hundred metres away.

From the second tree, he could see low class accommodation for workers. Three stories high, narrow buildings packed like the ammunition the workers were making. Under the cover of darkness, he climbed over the fence to go to each door. He was asked to join the people for a meal. He hesitated when he noticed the rations would mean one person would miss out on food. He didn't accept other than a glass of water.

 A door was left ajar when a girl no more than fifteen walked out with the aid of a walking stick. Gaunt, frail and very looking much older, she slowly placed herself at the only table. From his seat, Oskar could see the beds were bunkers; three bunkers tall and two sets crammed into a tiny room. Oskar was angry at the conditions, but he was powerless to do anything. He showed the picture of Kiana. She wasn't there. After visiting each room, a squat, as Oskar preferred to call the worker's quarters, he left the complex.

He would now make the hazardous journey back to Switzerland. The border was just over an hour away by car, but by foot, maybe a day.

Chapter 32.
Switzerland, Lugano.

In Lorrach, Oskar was in his underwear when he crawled through a stormwater pipe he found by accident. He smiled when he knew he was in Basel, Switzerland. After cleaning himself up the best he could, he walked to the post office. He sent a telegram to Jaro asking for money to catch a fare home.

In Lugano, Oskar and Jaro spent the night sipping beer. Jaro mentioned the usual routine of work, keeping watch for any form of news about Kiana. Then it was Jaro's turn to question Oskar about his travels and searches. They spoke for hours; both falling asleep in the early hours of the morning.

Jaro was the first to wake up. When he realized he was already one hour late for work, he ran out of the door and down the street. Oskar was left to sleep.

Oskar spent the next two days going over all the locations and information he had collected and mentally stored in his head. Kiana wasn't in any of the German occupied areas to the west. He poured over a map of Europe. He crossed out all the cities, towns and villages he visited. When he looked at the area, then it dawned on him just how extensively he travelled. His coffers were dry. He had to go back to work but wonder if he could be given his old job back. All he could do was try.

For three months he worked at his old job. He repaid Jaro for the travel fare from Basel to Lugano. At that time, he saved diligently. He knew his next round of travels would be extensive and equally dangerous. He looked at the vast area of Europe. She could be anywhere or in any place he had already covered. He still had to try.

But for now, he needed rest. He was mentally exhausted. Hiding, sleeping rough, and a poor diet did not help.

Winter had set in. It was the start of 1944. The allies had taken a hammering. The Axis received as much as they gave out. To Jaro and Oskar, nowhere appeared safe. In their view, both sides were guilty of double standards and double speak. What was true and what were lies had blurred lines. What was said was equally as loud as what was not said. Whispers and hushes made the world murky. No trust could be given or assumed. Honesty was something reserved only for nuclear families.

It was dystopia. Even within the Swiss borders, dystopia, especially of the airwaves and the Germans continuing to use Swiss roads to go from A to B. The skies were still out of bounds but a stray aircraft from any side occasionally found its way over Switzerland. Hollow apologies followed. Shortages of anything and everything was the norm. However, there was no shortage of words and ammunition. To Oskar and Jaro, the world had got its priorities upside down or back to front.

No matter which way they looked at it, the future was bleak for the Swiss citizens but rosier than all the surrounding neighbours. When other governments were going bankrupt from the war, the Swiss government was prospering. The German's were paying fees to the Swiss for the use of the roads and rail tracks. German money was hidden somewhere in Switzerland. The banks would not divulge.
The dichotomy prevailed at the local level. Shortages meant rations on one hand. On the other, the wealth of the government and the banks were embarrassing.

Oskar pulled out the map of Europe after not looking at it for several months. Winter had ensured many roads in any direction was hard to travel. Combined with rationing, Oskar decided to stay put.

However, that decision came to an end. He and Jaro were called back to border duty. "So much for keeping promises," said Jaro who wasn't impressed. "Wasn't that escapade into France via Geneva your last duty?"

"Not quite. Downing radio towers near Steinen was. Either someone stuffed up or reneged or there is a shortage of men for anything.

"Eighteen months reprieve, doesn't cut it," said Oskar who was not at all interested in seeing more aspects of the war.

One week later, Oskar and Jaro were at the barracks outside Geneva. They settled in with the other men. It was the same routine a before; a refresher course and then border duties.

On one evening, when Jaro and Oskar were watching the darkened landscape which was spasmodically lit up with distant bombs and fire, Jaro saw a movement. He aimed his gun in that direction. Taking cue from Jaro's action, Oskar raised his gun. "Take cover," whispered Oskar. Both men slipped behind a rock wall. Their eyes were barely over the top observing the approaching figure.

The man in the darkness raised his arms. He called out in French, "Silent Knight, resistance."
Oskar lowered his gun but kept it at the ready. "Your name?"
"Jean Roux," came the reply.
"Welcome my friend. What brings you here?" said Oskar as he slowly stood up.
"We need help. The SS is swarming Annecy. They have killed ten of our men. More are in for execution in two days' time. Help is needed to free them. Is there any way I can speak with an officer?"

As the man neared the border, Oskar could see it was indeed Jean Roux. Oskar offered him assistance over the border. Jean was surprised to see it was Oskar. Then he saw Jaro. Jean's faces beamed.

"Come. Let's get you to the barracks. Just a minute." Oskar called another Swiss soldier over. "Guard this gap. I need to take this man to the captain." The man gave a puzzled look and noted the three men talking like long lost friends.

In the barracks, Oskar and Jaro took Jean to the captain. The captain wasn't impressed with the disturbance. When he saw Jean, he was surprised. The surprise gave way to a smile and a hug.

Jean filled the captain in about the SS activities. After some deliberation the captain said, "The SS are not on the good boy's list. I can spare you five men and some ammunition. Oskar, Jaro will be there for sure. I will need time to select others." Jean was thankful. The captain said, "Get Jean some food. He must be hungry after travelling by foot over the mountains." With that, the captain tossed Jaro a set of keys. One of those bigger keys opens the kitchen. Come back in thirty minutes."

Jean, Jaro and Oskar were back at the captain's quarters. They returned the keys. I have three people who can go on this rescue mission. "Please meet Sergeant Charles Dubois, Private Claude Hauser, and Corporal Gabriel Hofmann. They aren't fans of the S.S. after they saw Jews rounding up and being transported to Poland by train." The captain added, "Rest up tonight and move out at dawn. I will make sure your kits are ready. Corporal, take Jean to your cabin. There are spare beds there. I will see you all before you leave."

It was close to midday when the group arrived back at the Silent Knight's camp. Advanced plans for the attack were marked on the map. Black chess pieces were the known locations of the SS. The only white piece was the location of the men being held for execution. Dario Payet explained the plan.

Chapter 33.
Annecy, France.

Just after sunset, four groups of six who were going to be decoys led the mini army. Two groups were assigned to the northern part of the town and two groups headed for the south. They were to start fires. Fires were common in the summer, but not so in the winter. The only places dry enough were the surrounding forests scarred by a dirt road built by the Germans to link villages surrounding Annecy. The groups waited until eight-thirty p.m.

The other groups were larger. In groups of twenty, they would attack the Haute Savoie after placing bombs on major structural locations. It was hoped the bombs would make the building collapse inward in a bid to spare the surrounding buildings. Those escaping the collapse would be shot. Other official buildings were targeted in the same manner.

A tavern where more Germans than locals visited was on the list. The locals were warned to be out of the building no later than eight forty-five p.m. That was fifteen minutes earlier than most would have left. It would have looked normal. The bar staff were prepared for an escape. One by one they would disappear through the back door but would tell the partying German soldiers they would be getting more beer from the cellar. That would take a bit of time to refill the barrels they were removing from the front bar.

At eight-thirty, one of the fires started with an explosion. Bombs causing fires were common. Petrol was sprinkled into an area near rocks to ensure the fire jumped the natural barrier. The men at the scene would circle and pretend they came from the town to assist to put out the fire.

The second fire was started by lighting the bushes. A campfire was made much too close to some overhanging trees. Empty bottles of alcohol were scattered around. Again, petrol was scattered around to ensure the fire spread. Again, the group circled and acted as if they came from the town to assist in putting the fire out.

Distracted by the two fires the locals working with the supervising German soldiers rushed to the two locations. To the makeshift fire brigade, it was an inconvenient but common occurrence. No questions asked. The fire was slowly being fanned by the growing winter winds. It was starting to go out of control. They had a fight on their hands.

In the city the red glows on both sides drew the attention of citizens and Germans alike. Those in the German army and lived at the Haute Savoie, began to gather to assist those fighting the growing fire. Too late. The bombs around town exploded simultaneously. Trapped Germans suffered varying degrees of injury or just died. The SS staying at the Haute Savoie, were buried under the rubble. The Haute Savoie existed no more.

The tavern was partially damaged. The area where the patrons gathered was severely damaged. Bodies laid in the rubble. Only two Germans escaped with minor injuries. The town's people rushed to put the fires out. Many carried the handful of injured civilians to the small hospital. That was planned. Fill the beds with locals first and then the German soldiers. If need be, the soldiers lined the corridors while waiting for their turn for medical assistance. A few more German soldiers died from the delays. Most bled out.

The remaining soldiers who were scattered around town gathered in the town square. Seeing they were significantly outnumbered; they dropped their weapons. The locals led by the Silent Knights had armed themselves with assorted knives, assorted guns, ropes and lumps of wood. They made threatening gestures towards the outnumbered Germans.

Dario Payet stepped forward to address the crowd as an empty German truck arrived on the scene. "Get in the truck and go home. Don't come back," he said in a loud voice. The truck driver who was one of the many in the resistance, jumped out. The motor of the truck was still running. The driver said, "Get in now. Get out of town." A corporal tried to protest, "No. You are under German control." Everyone laughed. The corporal felt small when he truly realized, the Germans were no longer in control. He tried to save face by demanding, "We need to collect our personal belongings. Then we will go."

Again the crowd laughed. Dario yelled, "Your personal belongings? What personal belongings other than the uniforms you are wearing. In your so-called house inspections, food and household items disappeared into your barracks and in the Haute Savoie. We are reclaiming our possessions, our daughters, or wives. Women step forward with your weapons."

The women stepped forward with lumps of wood and broom sticks. Dario ordered the German soldiers to stand in two lines. He spaced them out close to a metre apart. Then he gave the order to the women. "Ladies, here are some of the men who assaulted you. When you recognize a person who raped or deceived you into sexual relations, give that person a strike with the stick. Do not hit the person on the head. We need them to be able to talk. Start your revenge."

All the women present looked at each German soldiers. When they saw someone who assaulted them, the soldier received a heavy blow. The arms and legs was the most common strike points. However, one raped lady who was now showing signs of pregnancy, used all her strength to strike the soldier in the gentiles. The man fell to the ground clutching his privates. She struck the man again breaking his fingers protecting his gentiles. She was about to strike again when her husband stopped the third blow. "I think he is permanently damaged." He bent over the man to remove his broken hand and fingers. He wasn't sure just how much blood related to the gentiles or to the hand. He took the lump of wood from his wife's hand and slammed it again into the same area. He flipped the man over and rammed the stick into the soldier's buttocks. The man screamed again as a mix of pain and sweat poured out of his face. The lady's husband snarled, "This is what you get for raping women. Castration." The man walked away after slamming the wood over the man's back.

At the end of the localized judgement day proceedings, only three German soldiers were free from any blows. As each soldier was escorted to the back of the truck, each was questioned about their activities. Those who didn't respond received a rifle butt to the mouth and then pushed into the truck. After seeing the severity of the mouth injuries, the other soldiers answered questions. The captors were disgusted at the replies: it was for fun, needed to relieve myself, she looked cute, she was ugly and must have been hard up, she didn't follow my orders, and swore at me were the most common replies.

The town's people were ordered to make sure all soldiers were loaded onto the truck. The truck was overcrowded, but it didn't matter. As long as the soldiers were on board, that was all it mattered. Silently the crowd watched the truck leave town. The people of Annecy cheered.

The cheering stopped when another three explosions were heard. Two German trucks full of soldiers coming to the town to quell the uprising were blown up just outside the town's perimeters. The third turned around to leave the town before it too was blown up. There was a short outburst of gunfire. Silence. The battle was over.

Oskar, Jaro, Gabriel, Charles and Claude had their guns pointed at more German soldiers who were hiding in the rubble and observing the serving of justice by the town's people. "What are you going to do with these pieces of trash?" asked Claude.
Jean walked over to examine the stragglers. "The same as before. Line them up for the women to punish their attackers."

Fifteen nervous soldiers stood in the centre of the crowd. The women lined up with their pieces of wood or broomsticks. Ten were identified and received blows. One girls' father approached one soldier who had received three blows. The man took the piece of wood from his daughter's hand and swung with all his strength across the soldier's head. The man collapsed. The father checked the fallen soldier. To the watching people he said, "He's dead." He looked at the body at his feet. "This is what you get for taking advantage of innocent girls. For Christ's sake she was only twelve. Only twelve and you give her a life sentence." He kicked the corpse as hard as he could. "That was my parting gift. Rot in hell." He spat on the dead soldier. He walked away from the body.

The rest of the soldiers were chained at the ankles. The end of the chain was tethered to a statue in the middle of the square. More soldiers were recovered. Some had injuries after digging themselves out of ruins or just happen to be in the line of flying debris. By dawn thirty more soldiers were rounded up. Embarrassed by their defeat and being displayed like some trophy, the soldiers remained silent. The town's people had left except for ten watching over the spoils chained to the statue.

It was midmorning when Jean and Dario ordered the night guard to leave and be replaced with twenty more. Jean said, "You soldiers are going to clean up the mess from the bomb blasts. That will be your job. You get food and drink when the job is done." Jean signaled with a head movement for the surrounding men to release the soldiers.

At gunpoint, they were directed to the tavern which had the front blown off. Piles of rubble were dumped in a truck for disposal. What was salvageable was neatly stacked to one side. The tavern owner checked the salvageable items. Some items were redirected to the rubble pile. By sunset, the work had stopped. The soldiers were given food and water. Then they were chained again for the night. The night guards were on duty again.

The next day it was the same but at the Haute Savoie. Because the Haute Savoie was so much larger, it took one week for the soldiers to clear the mess. When bodies were found, the locals took them away to be placed in a mass grave. If there was any identification on the bodies, it was recorded in an accountancy book, name, date and time of discovery. Nothing else was recorded.

When the removal of debris and any salvageable material was complete, the soldiers were given a final meal and a half glass of wine. They were loaded into a truck to be driven away.

The truck stopped ten kilometres out of town. The men were order to a cliff's edge. It wasn't a big cliff but big enough to ensure any who fell could end their life or seriously injure them. Jean said to the soldiers, "This is the short cut to that village over there." Then he lied, "We do this all the time. Climb down the cliff and walk over to the village." He pointed with his gun. "Start climbing down. If you reach the bottom, you are free to go. Just a warning, when you get to the village, keep running. The villagers aren't as friendly as us. Go!" Knowing the men were physically exhausted and well underfed, he knew only the strongest would make the journey. He watched as the men nervously started to climb down the cliff.

Not knowing where the footholds were or any good grip locations, half fell to their death. Several fell to be seriously injured. They laid without assistance at the bottom. They would have to save themselves. Four soldiers made it down the cliff face. They ran towards the village. When they reached the first farmhouse they were met with guns. They were shot. The farmhouse occupants gave a wave. Jean waved back to signify all the soldiers had gone over the cliff. It would be up to the farmhouse owner's discretion to check the base for the injured and the dead. Their attitude has always been, 'I'll do it whenever I feel like it.'

Oskar and the others from the Swiss army were led back to the Swiss border. The siege to liberate Annecy was a success. Oskar told the captain of the barracks, "It will go down in history. Annecy will be the first and maybe the only town liberated by their own resistance group or groups." The captain smiled and nodded. I will recommend you for a promotion. You have done things well above your paygrade."

Oskar nodded. "I suppose I have. I want to leave now and continue my search for my sister. I want to go into France and look in places I have not been to."

"That is dangerous. Most of France is overrun with Germans. You will be behind enemy lines. Sit the war out. Then go and search for Kiana. Is that her name?" suggested the captain.

Oskar replied, "I would rather die trying than sit and do nothing. If she is dead, then I join her. It is the only thing that motivates me to keep alive. Yes, her name is Kiana. She is my only living family. That makes her precious."

"When will you go?"

"A week after you permit me to have early discharge. Earlier would be helpful," said Oskar.

"I will see what I can do. Those above can be a bit difficult."

Chapter 34
The Western Front, France.
Behind Enemy Lines.

O skar crossed the border at a village called Boncourt, south of Basel. From the border, he could see the next village just on the other side. Delle looked just as small as Boncourt.

Again, he asked around for Kiana. It was a negative response. After two days in the village and his French speaking skills slowly improving, he went to the next town. Audincourt was at least twice the size of Delle.

On his third day, a young girl said, "She looks like someone I have seen but never knew her name. I am not sure if she is a nurse or is working at the nunnery in the same area."
Oskar's heart was jumping with excitement. A possible lead and the strongest one for over eighteen months. After receiving directions, he went immediately to the hospital.

Oskar's mouth dropped. It was the biggest hospital he had seen. He wondered just where to start. He walked to triage and feigned an illness.

He was admitted into the emergency area to wait for a doctor. As nurses walked by, he studied their faces. When he caught the eye of a nurse, he would show the picture. All were negative. After seeing a doctor who only prescribed eating a better diet, he moved on.

He walked the wards checking who was inside and stopping all he passed. Eventually a nurse said, "Yes. I have seen her. She works at the nunnery. She comes here twice a week to volunteer in the children's ward." Oskar gave a sigh of relief and smiled like a cat in a fish shop.

He went to the nunnery and rang the outside bell. He waited for what seemed like an eternity. An elderly nun using a walking stick came to the door. She asked, "Hello. What can I do for you?"
Oskar was too the point. "I have a picture of my missing sister." He pulled the picture out of his jacket to show the nun. "Does this lady work here?"
The nun looked at the picture and adjusted he glasses.
"She does look like Sister Margret. I am not sure."
"Can I come in to see for myself?" asked Oskar.
"You can only come to the Mother Superior's office. You will have to wait there," replied the old nun.

Oskar was led along a short path, through a set of heavy wooden double doors to a badly lit corridor. When he reached an office door he was directed to sit outside. The old nun shuffled off to disappear into another room deeper into the building. Minutes later, an equally elderly lady came out of a room. She greeted Oskar and directed him into the office. "I hear you are looking for someone. May I see the picture?" Oskar handed over the picture. The old lady studied it carefully. "It does look like Sister Margret." The old nun pressed on a buzzer. Seconds later a middle-aged nun appeared at the door. "Please bring Sister Margret here at once. She has a visitor." The nun nodded, closed the door, and walked as quickly as she could.

She found Sister Margret in the sewing room fashioning new clothes from old clothes. "You have a visitor. A very handsome young man." Sister Margret was puzzled. She wasn't expecting anyone. Since joining the nunnery, she was shunned by her family. No one came.

No one replied to her letters. No one ever did and if someone did come, then something serious must have happened. She followed the nun to the Mother Superior's office.

Oskar stood up as Sister Margret entered the room. They both frowned at each other. No recognition. Oskar said, "I am sorry to disturb you. You look very much like my lost sister. You could almost pass as twins or even as sisters. The resemblance is uncanny."

Sister Margret nodded. "Do you have a picture of her?" Oskar pulled out the picture. Sister Margret looked at it with surprise. "We do look like each other. "What happened to her?"
"She was being escorted by two of my friends after leaving a tavern in Switzerland. Witnesses saw my friends being shot. Murdered. The same witnesses saw men in dark clothing kidnap her. She was tossed into the back of a van. She disappeared. I have been trying to find her since then."

Oskar saw all the nuns do the sign of the cross. Sister Margret added, "I have heard of such kidnapping. Some women are taken to the ammunition factories in Germany or Poland. Many died from the chemicals. Two women who escaped from such hellish places came here but died soon after. I was helping to nurse them in their final hours. Chemicals cause horrific illnesses. Bless their souls. Other women are captured and forced into brothels. They generally die of diseases or commit suicide. Bless their souls."

Oskar said, "Thank you for your time. Now, I am a little embarrassed to ask this, where is the nearest brothel. If she is forced into such work, I will pull her out. If I have to, I will kill the person in charge." Sister Margret chuckled. "Good luck with that. Most are operated by the Gestapo or SS or some other high-ranking NAZI."

Oskar thought about the information. "Okay, they are above my abilities. Can any person walk in and ask for services? Err I mean, relatives can check up on the ladies?" The others in the room broke out into a small chuckle. The Mother Superior said, "Only Germans can enter such dreadful rooms."

Oskar stood outside a three-story building which had NAZI flags on poles adorning the outside. He studied the building for close to an hour. VIPs in fancy cars pulled up outside. Chauffeurs opened the doors and saluted "Hail Hitler" as the dignitary alighted. The person nodded his head to the chauffeur before moving into the building. As they approached the entrance, the door would be opened by a German doorman. Oskar itched to go inside.

He walked down an alley three buildings away. He hid behind a pile of boxes holding assorted rubbish. He quickly changed into the German uniform. Confidently, he approached the building. When he went through the door, he was met with guards. "Privates are not permitted here. There is a place four blocks away for sergeants and under." Oskar just gave a Hitler salute and walked out. He changed back into civilian clothes. He muttered to himself, "I will be very discriminating. Bang."

Oskar walked to the described building. He didn't bother changing clothes when he saw it was a bar open to all. He guessed there were rooms at the back for sexual services. When he entered, a lady offering cigarettes for a price came immediately to him. He waved her away. He placed himself in an alcove. Almost immediately he was joined by two 'hostesses.' He chattered to them in his broken French. After a while he showed Kiana's picture. More negatives. He had two drinks then left. He headed back to the building where he was prevented from entering. He studied the outside a bit more. He made a plan.

He found himself a cheap guest house for the night. His idea of a sound sleep came to an end when the air raid siren pierced the air. The owner of the guest house knocked on all doors and ushered people to the bomb shelter. Silently, all the guests sat in the much too small shelter. The sound of bombs screamed overhead and exploded nearby. The small shelter shook with each near explosion. The siren announced the raid was over. People crawled out of their shelters or from under rubble. One man had died when a bomb landed on his home. Others in the house suffered assorted injuries.

One lady came running down the street yelling, "There is an unexploded bomb in my garden! Help!"
Oskar with many others in the street slowly ventured towards the unexploded bomb. When Oskar saw the size he yelled, "Get out! Get out! It's alive!" People scattered. In less than five minutes later the bomb exploded. The lady's house was replaced with a crater.

Back at the guest house Oskar asked, "Why did the British bomb an ally?"
One man offered an explanation. "To scare off Germans. They occasionally miss targets. Today was an example of a missed target. The governments on both sides would have been on it. The bloody NAZIs have occupied most of France for much too long. Now we have to rely on Britain and its colonies to help us out."

Later in the day, Oskar returned to the building where many German officials visited. He cursed. The building didn't take a hit, but Germans were scurrying around like ants which discovered a bountiful supply of food. He watched the activity. Soldiers appeared out of nowhere to assemble in front of the building. Oskar knew the bomb which tore up the residents a few blocks away was intended for this building. However, he did note, a less than skeleton staff was left inside the building when the leaders and the soldiers were trucked or marched off out of the square. *Now is a good time to upset the Germans,* he thought.

Dressed in his German uniform, Oskar entered the building. There was no resistance. The bottom floor was manned by one person who was reading a book behind the reception desk. The soldier didn't even lift his eyes from the book. Oskar immediately went to the top floor.

Oskar found the cleaner's room and removed cleaning agents. He examined each room for possible cash or jewelry that could be sold. All the upstairs rooms had heaters. He turned the heaters on and threw clothes over the top. In other rooms, he placed candles much too close to curtains. He lit the candles. The evening breezes could blow the curtains towards the candles. In all rooms he doused with cleaning chemicals. He didn't know which would help to be accelerants. It didn't matter. In one wing of the top floor were vacant rooms. He wasn't sure if anybody inhabited the rooms or were used for services. One of the rooms was elaborate. He helped himself to an expensive bottle of scotch. He placed the bottle in his backpack. He sprinkled the rest over the floor. The remainder of the cleaning chemicals were sprinkled in a trail to the cleaner's room. He swapped the empty containers for fresh supplies. He went to the second floor.

He was halfway through the rooms on the second floor when he stopped dead in his tracks. There was no time to hide. He was caught red handed. A man who was wearing a German uniform came out of the laundry room. Both froze and then put their heads down. Oskar noticed the man was carrying laundry powder. The powder was making a trail across the floor. Oskar said, "Leaking." He pointed to the trail. The man grunted and placed his hand over the leak. Oskar grinned at the realization; the man had the same idea as he. "Let me help you. Fire the place."

The man was shocked. A German was wanting to assist him to set the place on fire. Oskar added, "I put chemicals around. Some heaters will burn clothes soon. We get out now." The man threw some black powder into the laundry powder mix. Oskar directed him to a room where the clothes were starting to smoulder. The man added the trail of powder at that location. Both walked out of the building as fast as they could through the front door. The receptionist looked up from his book, nodded and recommenced reading. Oskar and the man parted ways.

Minutes later, the building started to burn. The fire alarm went off. Two explosions were heard coming from the building. Oskar knew, the other man had planted the bombs. With the fire raging to all parts of the building, the fire brigade was desperate to prevent the fire spreading to other buildings.

Thirty minutes later Oskar and the man met up again to watch the fire brigade trying to put out the fire. Both had switched to civilian clothes. In French the man said, "Nice work. What a shame the bastards were not inside."
"The poor darlings are homeless," said Oskar in a sarcastic manner. The soldier introduced himself. "I'm Nigel Thompson."
Oskar said but feeling unsure but took a gamble, "Oskar Grat."
"Come with me. Meet my friends who helped plan this event. They are waiting at a café two blocks away."
Oskar wasn't sure. Nigel picked upon the hesitation. "We are on the same side. We can do more together than by ourselves." Oskar knew Nigel was right.

At the café, Nigel introduced Oskar to his assistants. They were a mix of British and French men. Nigel explained how they met and the common goal which bound them. The men looked at Oskar with some admiration. "How did you get a German uniform?" enquired one.

"I stole it from two dead men. One had a hole at the top and the other had a hole in the lower part. Mix and match."

Another quizzed Oskar, "Where are you from?"

"Austria." Knowing the men were going to ask more questions, he voluntarily added, "The NAZIs murdered all the people in my village. I escaped with my sister and a friend. We met with other Austrians who had a similar experience. Unfortunately, they are also dead. Last year, my sister was kidnaped by NAZIs. I have been searching for her. I have no other family. That is why I am here. Checking monasteries, nunneries, brothels and anywhere she could be hidden. I even checked a German ammunition facility. I wish I could have blown the place up. Too many guards and too much security."

"Do you want to join our group?" asked one of the men.

"I have worked with groups before. This time I want to be alone in my search," replied Oskar. After a pause, "I need to move on to another town. Then it will be back to Switzerland." Oskar felt some pressure to remain with the group. He resisted. He left quietly.

Nigel said, "Let's follow him for a bit. Let's see how much pork he served us. But I have to say, he made my job easier and more effective."

For two days, the group discreetly followed Oskar. They lost count of how many times he showed a picture of his sister to strangers. "I really think he is legitimate in his story," said one of the men.

"No one keeps asking day in and out the same question, 'Have you seen this young lady?'"

"Let's keep watching," said another.

One week later, they saw something that made them think twice. Oskar began to pick pocket in crowded market areas. "Okay, the man's a thief." whispered a French man to another French man. "I think we should pick him up again."

When Oskar was meters away from the guest house he was staying at, the group swooped on him. He was bundled into a car and driven away. Outside the town and in a heavily forested area, Nigel asked, "We believe you about looking for your sister. What is with the pick pocketing?" "I am short of money. That is how my friends and I survived when we had no work." "What kind of work did you do?" asked Nigel. "House repairs, house cleaning, bits of farming, ambulance driving, gardening, hospital orderly work. Anything to put food in our stomach and a roof over our heads.Thieving was always the last resort." One of the men grabbed Oskar's bag. "You never take this bag off your back. What is inside it?" As the man was beginning to empty out the backpack, Oskar said in desperation, "My survival kit. It changes with the season." By that time the items were on the ground. "What the hell is this? Three uniforms?"

Oskar closed his eyes. He tried to relax. "All stolen. The only one I don't have is the Swiss one. They collect their uniforms when a person leaves. Rarely anyone gets shot."
"How would you know that?"
"I got called up for service. The Swiss government calls all men up every year for a three-weeks stint and few weeks for border guard duties."

"Okay. How did you get the Italian uniform?"
"When we fled Austria, we went to Italy thinking it would be safer. It wasn't. We were forced into the Italian army. They were short of men. Any men from any age were enlisted. The police assisted in rounding up youths." Nigel said, "I had heard of something like that when Mussolini was running the place. I am sure they collected uniforms with no holes in them for recycling for soldiers." "Wrong. When money was scarce, soldiers had to buy uniforms and ammunition" said Oskar "How did you manage to keep your uniform?" quizzed another from the group.

"My friends and I deserted the battle grounds of Albania and went back to Italy to pick up my sister. She was separated from us and forced into bar work with added services. However, we found her being enslaved by so-called Mother Superior in the Vatican. We helped her escape. We went to Switzerland where we all got jobs. Living in Switzerland means border guard service."

"That doesn't explain the British uniform. How did you get that?" When we were crossing the mountains from Italy to Switzerland, there was a storm. A plane crashed. When we went to investigate, the pilot was dead. We stole his food and took a spare uniform from a box."

One man looked closer at Oskar. He studied Oskar's face. "Just how old are you?"
"Twenty-one. Twenty-two in two months,"
The man shook his head. "He has done more in his short life than most others. It looks like he has travelled almost everywhere in Europe to avoid the war. Take him back to the town."

Oskar was ready to leave Audincourt when he was met outside the guest house. Nigel and two of the men were waiting for him. Oskar groaned at the waiting reception. "What now?" asked Oskar with a voice that was full of annoyance.
"Just a little chat. Then we will drive you back to Delle."

Oskar was driven on a road which led back to Delle. The car pulled over into a side lane. The dusty lane ended at a house which had seen some skirmish activity in the past. "Get out," ordered Nigel. "We are here."
Oskar slowly got out of the car. He was ushered inside. He was pushed down on a chair.
"Sit," ordered a voice from the shadows.

"You are quite a traveler and troublemaker."

"What are you talking about," asked Oskar.

"Belgium, Netherlands, France, Italy, Albania, the Vatican, Switzerland. Did I miss a country?"

Oskar shaded his eyes from the strong powerful light. With sarcasm Oskar replied, "Germany. You missed that one. Do you want to join me? My next stop is Poland? If need be, Czechoslovakia."

"Enough of the sarcasm. What did you do in Germany?"

"I was checking out an ammunition factory in case may sister was forced to work there. Then I got out of the place as fast as I could. I wasn't impressed."

The questioning continued for another two hours. Oskar didn't change his story at any time. The light went out. A jug of water and a meal were placed on a table. He was ordered to eat.

The group had just completed their meal when bombs were heard falling close to the isolated house. Everyone took cover. Oskar took the opportunity and ran into the surrounding bushes to hide. The emergency was over in ten minutes. Nigel looked around. "He's gone. Find him!"

The men ran out of the house with handguns.

They searched the surrounding bushes. Oskar couldn't be found. Nigel swore. "I needed more information from him. Damn. He can't get far in the bushes. If he goes parallel to the road towards Delle, we can pick him up there. The village isn't that big. Marcus and Jim stay here in case he doubles back."

Oskar lay hidden just outside the house. He counted the men leaving. Four were going. Two were inside. Oskar wanted to go to Delle. The journey already took him halfway. The car was going to

Delle. It was not an option. Oskar pulled out a rough map he bought from a grocery store. He looked at the options.

More aeroplanes flew overhead. From his hidden position, he could just make out they were German planes. More planes followed. All were heading north. Oskar decided to stay put until no more waves of planes flew over. The pilot of the last German plane decided to have some practice with his machine gun. He fired on the farmhouse. Oskar wondered if the two men inside were alive or injured. This was not the time to start investigating.

At sunset, Oskar left the safety of his hideout. He went deeper into the bushes. He was going to travel south-east to cross the border at any feasible isolated location.

He pushed his way through the undergrowth. The terrain was sloping upwards to be a hill or mountain. Oskar at that stage couldn't really tell. There was no vantage point for him to get definite bearings. The night sky was obscured by the trees. He found himself a ditch to sleep in for the night. It was going to be cold. He wasn't prepared for this scenario.

The next morning, he woke up. He was aching all over. The cold air and insufficient clothing made his body ache. He gathered some wild berries. He collected pinecones. He recalled the tedious task of extracting the nuts. This brought back memories of four plus years ago when he, Jaro and Kiana walked for days to escape the NAZIs in Austria. He smiled at the fond memories and frowned at the hardship. Tears welled up. He was alone again. Isolated. *Just like the obelisk in Weghaltz*, he thought. Slowly, he pulled himself together. He had to move on.

For three days, he wandered in the wilderness before coming across what looked like a barbed wire fence. *Maybe this is the border*. He searched his bag for anything to cut the wire. Nothing. He decided to follow the wire hoping to find signs of a Swiss border guards.

Two more days passed. Oskar was now feeling the effects of dehydration with starvation. The food he was collecting was not substantial. He had no rifle to shoot an animal. No gun. No knife. He was resting more than he was walking.

He pushed himself to climb the rest of the hill he was resting on. When he reached the top, he knew he was exposed to everything. He rested his body while he studied his compass, the one that was stolen from a drunken German almost a lifetime ago. He could see more barbed wire at the bottom of the hill. No signs of any guards. This was an isolated spot.

The sound of German planes roared overhead. He laid down on the exposed site hoping he wasn't spotted by any pilot. A plane began circling. Oskar knew he was found. He scurried away for cover and down the hill. The plane circling above flew away. He sensed the pilot reported him. With new energy, Oskar backtracked for a kilometre before changing direction to the west.

He came across a farm. Cows were grazing away totally ignorant of the squabbles caused by humans. He approached one cow. The animal lifted her head while she continued munching. In a soft voice, "Easy does it. I would like some of your milk. Easy. Don't be alarmed. Good girl. Good girl."

Oskar filled a cup made from broad leaves of a bush with warm milk. He drank four cups before his hunger and thirst were partially satisfied. He retreated to the bushes and trees. At dusk, the cows headed down the slopes. He followed them. They would lead him to the farmhouse.

Oskar gasped. It wasn't a modest farmhouse but a substantial mansion. He would watch the activities from afar before approaching. Nothing happened at night. The lights went out just after nine p.m. At dawn the place came to life.

The cows were released from their shed. Horses were set free to graze and exercise. The hens were running in their compound. They were guarded by a rooster who announced his presence to all. The farmer and his wife were seen doing their daily routine. Three children emerged. The girl was assigned to collect the eggs and attend to the hens. The boys were assigned gardening chores. Crops were being planted. Nothing unusual.

It was close to midday when a car approached the property. A man in a British uniform emerged. He was followed by another wearing a French uniform. Oskar cursed. He wished he had a set of binoculars to see the arrivals more clearly. More British and French soldiers came. Something was going on in this isolated place. Oskar sneaked closer to the villar. Six cars had four drivers waiting outside. Two drivers returned with trays of food. Another two would go inside. Oskar put on his British uniform. With confidence, he walked into the villar where he was directed to the servant's dining area. He picked up a tray of food. He joined the other drivers. They were to stay overnight at the villar before returning to Lyon. Oskar hid his delight. Lyon was west of Annecy. Annecy was just a short walk from Geneva. Things were looking up.

Oskar joined the rest of the drivers at breakfast. No one noticed he was an extra. When the delegation left the villar, Oskar climbed into the back of a truck that arrived with supplies early in the evening.

The journey to Lyons was uneventful for the first two hours. Then the truck began to sway left, right, the groan of hastily applied brakes followed by more swerving caused Oskar some concern. He wondered if the truck was going to roll. He cringed when he heard the sound of bombs whistling down to explode much too close to the convoy.

There was an explosion followed by the sound of glass shattering. The truck rolled on its side. Oskar crawled out of the wreck. He went to the driver to see if he was still alive. He was dead. The car in front was history. The occupants were in pieces almost just as much as the car. Other cars in the convoy had come to a stop after receiving assorted damage and the occupants: Receiving assorted injuries.

Oskar pulled the injured free of the wrecks. He did his best to apply first aid with next to nothing to work with. He handed a radio to one man. Oskar wasn't sure if it would work. "Call for help," said Oskar in French. The man took the radio. It crackled. The man twiddled with the dials. It worked.

Oskar searched for more injured people. An English Colonel appeared to be uninjured but trapped inside a car. Oskar removed some of the debris. He eased the Colonel out. The Colonel limped to the line of injured men. Oskar slipped away into the bushes. He could see the outskirts of Lyon.

The General looked around for Oskar. "Who was that man who did this first aid?"
The others shrugged their shoulders. "He was at the villa. French, I think. He had a very slight accent. I don't know his name."
"I can't see him anywhere. He may have gone for help by going to Lyon," said the General.
The radio operator said, "He gave me this radio. I managed to call for help. It is on its way." The General was puzzled.

When the ambulances arrived, the Colonel asked, "Did you see anyone on the road going to Lyon?" All the men responded in the negative. The General was more concerned than ever.

Oskar reached Lyon by walking parallel to the road. On the way he saw the ambulances racing to the crash site. He ducked for them to pass. He reached Lyon in the early afternoon. He found a fountain in which he washed his blood-stained hands. He wanted to take his shirt off and wash it as well. People watching him and the cold air changed his mind. He walked to a tavern to check in for the night. He used cash lifted from the dead and injured soldiers from the day before.

The next morning, he bought fresh clothes, the first complete set in almost a year. Feeling like he now belonged in the human race, he chanced asking the locals if they had seen Kiana. Again negative. At the same time, he asked about transport to Annecy. He was directed to the markets on the other side of town. Here he found a farmer who lived in the general area.

Oskar paid the farmer a small amount of money for the ride to Annecy. The farmer stopped at a fork in the road. He pointed. "Annecy is ten kilometres that way. I go this way."
Oskar jumped out of the car and waved.

In Annecy, Oskar sort out Jean Roux and Dario Payet. They welcomed him with open arms. Exchanges of experience since their last meeting kept them up half the night. Dario warned, "The Germans have not returned to this town. They are like rats and snakes rummaging around trying to pick us off. We are going to flush them out. Do you want to join us?"
"What I need is rest and some good food. I have lost so much weight. He tugged on his trousers. "Look. Floppy. I just bought these. These

are the only ones in the shop that came near my waist. The belt holds them up."

Jean nodded. "You do look thinner. Then rest. The tavern which was half destroyed is fully functional. The Haute Savoie is being rebuilt with lots of modern features. That won't be ready for another six months, maybe more. It depends on the supply of materials. Damn war causes more shortage than you can think of."

Jean and Dairo led raids around the town. More German were rounded up. More were used for hard labour to repair the higher levels of the Haute Savoie, the town's sewer system and other works which no one really wanted to do or were categorized in the dirty zone. They had breakfast and dinner but nothing throughout the day except for water. They were locked in a specially built building. Bars only on the windows which were two metre high from the floor. They slept on the ground or on bunker beds. One bathroom served each overcrowded room of ten.

One week later when Oskar was fully rested, he joined the hunt for stray Germans. He captured two. He thought it wasn't bad for a beginner on the first night. He went on three more missions. No Germans. He wasn't sure if they became cunning or had disappeared from the area. Oskar.

Mylan and Leo who had worked with Oskar on night duty were assigned to take Oskar to the border. All was well until they were less than thirty metres away. Germans opened fire. Leo took a bullet to the back. Mylan took one to the arm. He played dead. Oskar played along at being dead. Two German soldiers came forward to check the spoils. Oskar shot one in the face. Mylan shot the other in the stomach. Mylan gave the soldier two more bullets. Oskar said, "Go. Let the others know. I will go the distance by myself. Come back for Leo." Mylan knew he had to get back to Annecy. He left without saying another word.

Chapter 35.
Switzerland.

Oskar was at the border. One of the guards recognized Oskar. "Let him in. He is one of us." Oskar passed through. "Take me to the Captain." The Captain saw Oskar and welcomed him. "You sure know how to live dangerously. You look well."
The Captain handed Oskar an alcoholic drink. "I think you deserve this. I had word you got a promotion. Congratulations. Corporal Oskar Grat."

Oskar said, "Thanks. I need to let my friend Jaro know I am back. Do you mind if I sent a telegram?" The captain said, "You can. I will give the operator a note stating it is okay." He handed the authority form over to Oskar. "Come let's go to the mess hall. We can talk there over a meal." One and a half hours later, they emerged. The Captain asked, "What are you going to do after the war?"

"Continue looking for Kiana. It may be easier without the threat of bullets and bombs. Then again, so many people have been displaced, it will be harder with that kept in mind. This war must come to an end soon. Germany is losing major battles to the west and soldiers are dying from cold and lack of food to the east. Where can I sleep for the night?"
"I think there is an empty bunker in building four," replied the Captain.

Oskar packed his backpack to travel to Lugano. He wanted to see Jaro and find out if anyone had reported Kiana. He knew the chances were slim.

In Lugano, Oskar looked at the surroundings. For now, his travels had come to an end. Kiana, could not be in the west. He dreaded the thought of going to NAZI occupied Poland. Poland was in a greater mess than Austria. Austria was merely a springboard to eastern Europe. For six months, Oskar worked in Switzerland. He needed to buy supplies and warm clothing to travel east. Only half the warm clothes of the past were serviceable. Oskar bought a new backpack. The one he carried through western Europe was falling apart.

Chapter 36.
Germany to Czechoslovakia.

n civilian clothes, Oskar travelled by train from Lugano in the south to Zurich in the north. Under the cover of darkness, he crossed the border into Germany. He found an abandoned farmhouse which had signs of being bombed.

He entered the weakened structure to change into a German uniform. He searched the place for food. One dust covered sealed jar of cherry jam was found near an upturned kitchen table. Cautiously, he gave a tastes test. It was still edible. He ate half the small jar.

In the distance, he could hear mortar shells and gunfire. The flashes of both guided him to another village, or what was left of the village, Bobingen. He had been there once before. Then there were buildings intact. Now half the place was in ruins. The ammunition factory was closed down. The women were shipped off to an unknown location, most likely, Poland.

A German personnel truck drove past. The driver yelled out, "Get in. Get in. Hurry."
"What is happening?"
"I am rounding up all stay soldiers. We have to get as many as possible to Munich."
Without hesitation, Oskar jumped in the back with six other soldiers. Oskar asked, "What is happening in Munich?"

"A shortage of soldiers for an assault on the eastern front. The British and their Allies are dropping bombs everywhere. We will be lucky to reach Munich in on piece."

"Then we pray we get to Munich in one piece," said Oskar who was now double guessing his own actions.

A soldier leaned back and pulled out a cigarette. He offered one to all in the truck. Only three took a cigarette. He and the others sat quietly blowing out the smoke as the truck bounced its way along a very potholed road. The truck swayed from time to time to go around bomb craters. Everyone in the back was forced to hold on and channel their strength to stay on board.

Munich came into view at dawn. The driver drove straight to the barracks. To Oskar, the man looked exhausted after having to fight the road and watching for any incoming artillery. Oskar and the rest of the men were ushered to the mess all for breakfast. Oskar looked at the poor rations: dry bread, something that looked like eggs, but Oskar wasn't sure if it was eggs and an uninviting lump of oats cooked in water. There was no salt or pepper or sugar. Something that looked like dirty water was poured into a tin cup. He was told it was coffee. Oskar mentally questioned the substance. Oskar was curious when he was handed a chocolate bar. Oskar was suspicious of the treat. No real food but a chocolate bar. *What was Hitler thinking*? One soldier said softly, "The chocolate keeps you calm under bad conditions. There is something in these Third Reich bars that keep you calm. If you don't want it, can I have it?"

Oskar gave the man the chocolate bar, thinking *I am not taking drug-laced chocolate. Christ Almighty, Hitler has stooped to drugging his soldiers. Maybe it is to help them erase bad memories or to numb any pain for injury or even to make the men feel brave and confident. What is the drug? It has to be some form of narcotic like crystal methamphetamine. Kiana said they were using that in place of morphine when supplies had run out. She said it calmed patients down. But to put it in chocolate? How low can a leader go?*

After breakfast, the men in the mess hall were ordered to assemble again. The lieutenant bellowed out, "Get in. Next stop is Nuremberg." He watched as all the soldiers slowly climbed in the back of the truck.

Again, the soldiers held on for dear life. They cringed when the sound of a bomb or gunfire was heard. They all wondered if they would be next. Only three kilometres outside Nuremberg, a bomb landed directly in front of the truck. The driver took the full impact. Those sitting towards the back fared no better. The truck flipped on its side. Oskar and four others crawled out of the wreckage. Like the others, Oskar ran for the surrounding bushes. While the others stood still and collecting their nerve and thoughts, Oskar kept running. No one noticed.

By sunset, he reached the town of Amberg. He scouted around for a place to sleep for the night. He found another garden shed. He slipped into civilian clothes. When the lights in the house were turned off, Oskar raided the small garden. By now he was getting used to eating assorted vegetables in the raw state. It was better than going hungry. At dawn he left the security of the shed and headed further east. Poland was close.

He managed to hitch a lift on the back of a horse drawn dray. The farmer had to resort to the slow mode of transport as fuel was now non-existent for civilian use. The farmer's car had been confiscated by the NAZIs for transport. The only way he could get his small range of produce to Vohenstrass was turning back the clocks. He also noted, planes from both sides ignored the old transport. He was never a target. Soldiers at times would stop him to inspect the produce and take a sample before allowing him to pass.

When they reached Vohenstrauss, it was mid-afternoon. Oskar assisted the farmer to unload the stock to a small market stall. Oskar then disappeared into the growing crowd. He found dead end street to change his clothes into a German uniform. He walked to the nearest barracks. He went through the gates with no questions asked. He stayed the night in the barrack, or so he thought he would stay the night. A rain of bombs saw the barracks attacked. Men were running in every direction to put out fires and to carry the injured to the first aid area. Osaka saw the opportunity to steal a motorbike. He was out and heading to the border.

The motor bike he was riding was waved down by a German car. A colonel stepped out. "You must be the courier I was expecting." "Sorry, if I am late," said Oskar as he bent down to open a satchel. Inside was a document in a buff-coloured sealed envelope. "I am surprised you made it through. Vohenstrass was severely bombed."

Oskar just handed the envelope over and saluted with "Hail Hitler." He got on his motorbike and sped off leaving the colonel to open the envelope.

Inside another barracks, Oskar refueled the motorbike before joining others in the mess hall. After a short nap, he zoomed out of the small complex. He wanted to cross the border just after dusk.

At the border he was stopped by a guard. "Stop. Papers please," asked the guard. Oskar opened up the satchel again. Down the bottom was a small leather wallet containing a description of the rider. The guard looked at the description and then at Oskar. He signaled for the gate to open. He was now in Czechoslovakia.

Chapter 37
Czechoslovakia

Oskar drove slowly along the road. He pulled to the side when a German personnel carrier rumbled past. Two soldiers gave him a wave. Oskar returned the wave. His attention was cut short when artillery from the bushes sprayed around him. The bike was history. Oskar scrambled into the bushes to see who was firing at him. It was the local resistance group.

Oskar watched the men cautiously coming in his direction. Oskar began to change into civilian clothes. He remained silent after covering his body with assorted branches and grass. One man walked towards him but did not see Oskar camouflaged just metres away from where he was standing. The men continued searching. After thirty minutes, they decided the German soldier had escaped. Oskar remained in that location until halfway through the evening.

He was disturbed by another round of gunfire. Oskar remained still although he was bursting to see who the new target was. When everything was quite for a long time, Oskar slowly moved out from his hiding place. Walking parallel to the road and keeping under the trees, he walked closer to the Czechoslovakian town of Rozvadov.

As he approached, he heard voices floating out of a window on a house close to the edge of the town. He listened carefully. Czech voices were mixed with English. He wondered if the resistance was using the house as a hideout. He peered through a window which was half closed and breeze softly blowing a curtain. Three men and a lady were inside. His heart jumped when he heard a car pull up outside the front of the house.

The lady walked to the door as if she knew who was coming. She ushered two British uniformed soldiers into the house. They were greeted warmly. The British soldiers spread out a map on the table. Oskar cursed. He couldn't understand a word they were saying. All spoke in Czech. Carefully, Oskar left the window to head for the bushes and later down the street.

As he walked, he noticed no German uniforms. He was in civilian clothing. He was now nearing the centre of the town.

 He grew more cautious. There was a distinct German presence. He noticed the Germans were checking identification cards of civilians. It was random. Oskar searched his backpack for the wallet. He only had the owner identification card from the previous stolen motorbike and his own from Switzerland. He hoped he would not be asked for any papers. He wasn't sure which to use. He decided to hide again.

This time he went to a tavern. He waited until it was closing time. Then he sneaked into the back where rooms were available for those too drunk to see their way home. In the past, it was for tourists. Now they were places to sober up. On the fourth try, Oskar found the room empty.

He entered. He woke up at dawn, tidied up the rumples on the bed before leaving the premises.

He was desperately wanting to ask the locals about Kiana. Here was not the place. Germans would get curious. The locals too scared to speak. It could draw attention. Instead, he sat on bench surveying the surrounds. For nearly two hours he was ignored. As the sun rose and more people entered the area, he slowly began to move around. Germans were patrolling. Citizens were skirting around them, the new normal for this place. He knew he was kidding himself while studying all the female faces. He had a hunch; Kiana was not in Czechoslovakia. It was an unexplained vibe.

If Kiana was in Poland, there were two likely places. One was an ammunition factory, and the others were prisoners of war camps he had heard about. He had to get to Poland. He bought a map of the country to study. He would head north to Poland.

He had to keep moving but first to an ammunition factory where women succumbed to the toxic chemicals. He had seen the effects in Germany. He expected the same here in Poland.

Oskar made plans to go deeper into Poland. He pondered how hewould make the trip.

Connecting with the underground wouldn't be easy. They would be suspicious of him, and he would be equally suspicious of them. Oskar Oskar decided stealing another motorbike would be the best way to travel. The Germans parked their bikes in front of every building, but occasionally at the side when the front spaces were full. He watched their habits. Many took their keys of their bikes inside. A few would be careless or falsely think no one would dare try to steal a bike. These Germans were his targets. Patience.

Two days later, Oskar noted three bikes were parked at the side of the post office which was under German control. One man left the keys behind. When the man entered the post office, Oskar took the opportunity to take the bike. He wheeled it down the side of the building before taking off at full speed. On the bike, he went to Pilsen which was just a few hours away.

At Pilsen, he refueled at a service station. He bought extra fuel just in case there were no other fueling stops. He went on the highway which was almost reduced to a winding dirt track and ponds due to the craters filled with overflowing water created by the recent heavy rain. From Pilsen he followed the road to the next town of Karlovy Vary. The town appeared empty. The citizens were either hiding or were shipped out. There was no fuel to fill his bike. The fuel can was now empty. He pushed on until the bike ran out of fuel. Oskar hid the bike by covering it with fallen branches after wheeling it about five metres off the road.

Oskar didn't realize he was being observed since he left Karlovy Vary. Oskar climbed a tree which offered shade and cover. He rested there hoping another vehicle would come by. One did.

A man driving slowly came to a stop just metres away from Oskar's tree. He opened the door and looked up. He gave a wave for Oskar to join him in the car. It was also the signal for those watching.

Surprised, Oskar was captured. He was tossed into the back of the car with two men pinning him down. He struggled but the men overpowered him in the confined space. Oskar now wondered what will happen next. Ten minutes later, the car turned off the main road to go down a dirt track.

Oskar was dragged out of the car and punched a few times. Oskar offered no resistance. He took the punishment. When the men had completed their session, they dragged Oskar under a tree. A noose was at the ready. Oskar groaned at the sight. He thought his minutes were now numbered.

One of the unknown men raided his bag. He pulled out the uniforms. "I see we have a spy in our presence," said the man who had been driving the car.

"Not a spy. A runaway. Deserter," said Oskar hoping his German was understood. He repeated it in Italian. It earned him another punch to the stomach. He said in broken English, "Not a spy. I am running from the war. Germans kidnapped my sister. I am looking for here." The driver by then was going through the outer pockets of the bag. He pulled out the framed picture. Then he noticed the wallet with the Swiss identification papers and the German identification papers for the bike; a messenger.

The man switched to broken German, "Explain these two identifications and uniforms."
Oskar went through his German and Italian experiences and how he obtained the uniforms. He finished with living in Switzerland and doing national service for the Swiss. The man translated as Oskar spoke. One of the men restraining Oskar placed a blindfold on his head. Oskar was now certain the noose was going to be placed around his head. Instead, he was bundled into the car again and driven further down the dusty track.

When the car came to a stop, the blindfold was removed. He was pulled out of the car and led by force into a war-damaged shed. "Sit," ordered one man. Oskar sat on a bale of hay. "Wait. Keep your mouth shut." Oskar obeyed. He heard one man going outside with a walkie-talkie.

Although it was only minutes, to Oskar it felt like hours when a car pulled up. Coming out of the car were two Polish men and the same British men who he saw through the farmhouse window outside Rozvadov. Oskar concealed his recognition.

Oskar went through another round of intense questioning until all before him noticed the stories never changed and there was no hint of rehearsed speech. Oskar then asked, "Just who are you people?"

The men shot their eyes to each other checking out confirmation of their thoughts.

"Amia Krajowa," said one.

Another said, "The three Kings."

One British man said, "AK or the Home Army."

Oskar knew he was with one of many resistance groups that had popped up in many countries.

Oskar gave a sigh of relief. "Nice to meet you."

"Now tell me, are you really looking for your sister?" asked the British man.

Oskar nodded. "She was kidnapped nearly two yeasr ago. She wasn't in the German ammunition factory. I have been there. I would like to blow the place up for killing women with chemicals."

"Exactly what is the layout and where is the factory?" asked the British man.

"In Bobingen in South Germany. I went back there not long ago. Bobingen was bombed out and the factory is closed. Before the recent bombing, the residence was one side and the factory the other. The factory is half underground. That is what the women told me. The area is fenced and maybe still teaming with security. It is not possible for one person to blow the place up. Maybe a team could do it."

The British man nodded as he absorbed the information.

"Would you like to do a job for us?" asked the Polish driver.

Oskar was silent for almost a minute. He was weighing up his options. The noose down the road kept looping in his mind. "What do you want me to do?"

"There are two German ammunition factories in this country. As you say the women are dying from the chemicals. But men are enslaved as well. Non-Jewish prisoners of war are forced to make all forms of ammunition. It is about time we caused a bit of havoc."

"As long it is the factory and we can liberate as many prisoners as possible, I will give it a try. I just hope my sister isn't there or becomes one of the casualties."

"Two days later Oskar was with a group of forty men who had crossed the border into Poland. They met up with another twenty from another underground group, Narodowa Sity Zbrajre (The National Armed Forces – NAF). The NAF was a splinter group within the army who first fought alongside the Russians and later the Allies. The NAF sent valuable intelligence to the British army and occasionally, to the French. The Three Kings men sent information via radio to their exiled king living in London.

With three British soldiers dressed in German uniforms and Oskar in his German uniform they approached the main gate. The guard looked at their passes before waving them in. They drove to the main building which was half buried under tree foliage to disguise it from the enemy aerial photographs.

They approached the front door. More checks were made before going further into the building.

Oskar was paired with a British lieutenant who was fluent in Polish and German. Oskar was ordered to act mute or only speak in German if someone addressed the group. They walked through the building checking out the layout. The signal to act was a gunshot.

Minutes later a single gunshot pierced the air. The outside guards and nearly every other soldier in German uniform scrambled to pre-set destinations. With guns at the ready, the German soldiers inside the main building locked the doors and ordered all to take cover. Suddenly furniture on the bottom floor was flipped to its side creating a shield. In the mayhem, Oskar and the Lieutenant picked up random files not tossed to the floor. All were stuffed into a courier bag.

Oskar pointed to an office which was now vacant. Oskar slipped inside and took two files sitting on the desk. He showed the Lieutenant who nodded. "Time to go," said the Lieutenant. He pointed to a rear door that was unguarded. They slipped out.

They went down a set of stairs and disappeared into the man-made forest. They waited until the mayhem died down. They were joined by the other two men in German uniforms. When things appeared to be normal, the group walked quickly to the car they came in. The guards thinking the people in the car were going to give first-hand reports to higher command, let them out without making any checks.

There was no expected explosion. That part of the plan failed. However, fifteen prisoners were freed. That was a lot less than expected. They were aiming for fifty. No one in the two Polish groups were injured but one of the men from the Three Kings was injured. All wished they were flies on the wall when the German command received the news of the attack. They would be looking for heads to roll.

Oskar stayed with the group for two more days before trying to move on to Warsaw.

Along the way, Oskar switched from civilian clothes to the British uniform several times. He wasn't sure just where the British and German battle lines were drawn. All he knew, civilians were not welcomed by either camp. The British side considered them a pest for getting in the way and for soldiers to remove them. The Germans considered any civilian as fodder for the ammunition factory or to be placed in a prisoner of war camp. It was in his crossfire and blurry lines of defense, Oskar was captured.

Chapter 38.
Auschitz-Birkenau, Poland

He was taken to the prisoner of war camp, Auschwitz-Birkenau. Here he was stripped of his belongings and given a prisoner's uniform. After this he was assigned to be in camp 2. Not knowing what was installed for him in camp 2, he was blissfully ignorant. He only knew countless Jews were gassed. He cringed at the thought and hope he would not be classified as a Jew.

On day two in the prisoner camp, he was dragged to the administration office. He was made to strip down to his waist. The commander said, "I am assigning you to Sonderkommandos (Special Detachment). Oskar knew to keep his mouth shut. He didn't know what Sonderkommandos meant but he knew he would find out soon.

Oskar was given a shovel and made to get on a truck. As the truck bounced its way, Oskar looked at the drawn and somber faces sizing him up. One man said, "Be ready for bad things that no human should ever see. Just follow orders. Do not say a word or show any emotion no matter how much you want to fight at the injustice. Break the rules, and it is a bullet. I have seen a number of newcomers get shot on day one."

Oskar nodded. He thought to himself, *It's a warning. Compose yourself and get through this hell.*

When the truck came to a stop, everyone climbed out with their shovels. They were lined in pairs and ordered to march into the forest. Here they waited in silence.

One of three trucks full of bodies arrived. They were tipped into the grave already dug out by a front-end loader. The seasoned graveyard burial diggers began to shovel the dirt over the bodies. At the end of the day, saplings of pines were planted. A disguise to make the bodies harder to relocate after the war. Oskar repeated the task every day for two weeks. Then there was a change of duties.

His group was taken to the gas chambers. Here they were ordered to remove the piled-up bodies and place them in the back of the truck. Naked bodies with contorted faces etched their way into his mind. The 'cleaning out,' as it was called, was done three times a day. Bodies treated with no respect were dumped in graves. With identities gone, proof as to who they were was made impossible. They were ghostly victims of ethnic cleansing; just numbers and nothing more.

When it was late in the afternoon on each day, the men in camp 2 were free to roam in their very restricted area. A wire fence divided the women in camp 2 from the men. It was a meeting place where husbands, wives, sons, daughters, and other relatives met. It also doubled up as a check-up system to see who was still alive or who had vanished into the depths below.

It was here that Oskar was introduced to a lady close to his own age. Her name was Hanna. Through Hanna, Oskar was able to establish Kiana had never been at the facility or not at the time of Hanna's arrival. Another blank. He was disappointed on one hand and happy on the other. He still had hopes that she would be still alive somewhere.

Oskar was in the camp for close to nine months. He had lost a lot of his health. He was transformed to the zombie-like men that he first met in the camp. Then one day before going to his usual routine of shoveling or collecting carcasses, there was an announcement in Polish. The war was over.

The German war machine had come to an end. Officials in the camp lit numerous fires to burn evidence of their misdoings. The gates were opened for prisoners to walk free. Oskar waited at the main gate hoping Hanna would meet him there. The women slowly followed the men through the gates. Tired smiles said it all; we won.

Hanna and Oskar teamed up. They first went to Warsaw to meet her parents. Only her father was alive. It was then that Hanna learned that her mother had died in from a prolonged illness which could have been cured if hospitals had medication. Oskar stayed for a couple of weeks to regain his strength.

In that time, Oskar observed the mass migration of displaced people. People leaving devastation and famine was rife. The migrations across Europe saw many wanting to desert their smashed homelands. Distant countries looked inviting. Just getting there was an issue. It meant long hours of walking from city to city. Earning money was difficult. Getting clean water and fresh food was more difficult.

Oskar said to Hanna, "I really must move on. I need to find Kiana. How, I don't know. I will start by going to Weghaltz. We had an arrangement we meet there if we survive the war. We have a place where we leave notes telling us where we will find each other. I would like to leave in two days."
"Can I come with you?" asked Hanna.
"What about your father? He needs you."
"I will ask them. If another sister turns up in the next two days, I won't feel so bad," replied Oskar.

The next day, Maji, Hanna's older sister appeared. Dressed in unwashed rags for clothes she stood at the front door of the house. Maji informed them her husband and children were dead. They were killed when a bomb smashed into their home in Lodz.

Oskar was convinced to stay until the end of the week. Just to make sure Maji had settled in, and her father was comfortable with the new arrangements. To satisfy her father, Hanna decided to remain. She would follow Oskar when he was settled into a new location.

Chapter 39
Weghalt, Austria and Lugano, Switzerland.

After months of walking and hitching rides on any form of transport, Oskar arrived in Weghaltz. He looked around at the skeletons of buildings fast crumbling into nothingness. He walked over to the place where he, Jaro and Kiana agreed to leave notes to find each other.

Oskar dug up the ground near the obelisk, the only intact structure. He stopped and wondered what he can find to put the note in so it wouldn't perish. He scouted the ruins for a container of some kind. A small jam jar with rotted contents was cleaned out, washed, and thoroughly wiped. He placed a note inside:

Kiana,

I arrived here on the 7th May, 1946. Kiana, I searched the last 2 years of the war for you. Please contact me by going to the address in Switzerland where I lived with Jaro. I am heading there now, Lugano Switzerland. I dug up the chest and the retrieved my birth certificate. Jaro's and your certificate will be taken to Jaro's home address in Switzerland. He will safeguard it for you while I try again to look for you.

Oskar.

Oskar buried the container in the hole halfway to the depths of the reburied chest. He looked around for another container in the ruins. He found another jar, much larger and cleaner than the one with the note for Kiana. He placed the smaller jar inside the larger one to ensure it was water proof. He buried the jars. He found a slab of timber and jammed it into the soil near the obelisk where he knew the townsfolk a lifetime ago buried their land ownership papers, marriage, and birth certificates. With a children's paintbrush, he painted a sign:

Weghaltz. Dig one metre down for the names of the residents.

He wondered how long the sign would stay erect. The old paint was concerning. *Would it withstand the weather?*

Oskar knelt beside the obelisk and whispered, "Like you, I am all alone. Unlike you, I have travelled far and have been in mortal danger. I am tired of moving. I am tired of searching. I am worn out just like the paint the mayor, Valetin Karner, of this village painted on you." Oskar read the engraving and the faded paint in silence:
In memory of those who had fallen in World War One and World War Two.

As he stood up, he said, "Good-bye my friend. Now I leave you alone just like I have travelled alone. We are alone in our feelings. Sentinels just watching and guarding. You guard the village contents and me, I did my best to guard my only living relative, Kiana. Jaro has become a brother. He is another I protected from following me on last part of this perilous journey. He protested about us splitting in my bid to find Kiana, but he soon saw my logic. Everyone needs a home to return to. You have your home and your place in the world. I will return to mine. Well Lugano is for me a temporary place. I have yet to find my home and my place in the world."

Oskar set out to go to Switzerland. He travelled to the town of Lugano where he left Jaro.

When he reached to old address, he found Jaro. He was still there but with a major change. He had married the young lady he met not long before he left to find Kiana. Maria was expecting their first child.

Oskar stayed with them for two weeks. In that time, he sent a telegram to Hanna for her to meet him in Switzerland. From there they would go overseas. Just where was not clear. Oskar was still searching for a distant place, well away from the ravages of war.

Hanna sent a reply via telegram: I can't come just yet. Send me another letter when you reach wherever. Dad is ill and is not expected to live much longer. Love Hanna.

Oskar went to Zurich. Here he went from embassy to embassy looking for assisted passage to anywhere. When he came across the Australian Consulate office, he was given what he was after. He was escaping Europe.

Chapter 40
Australia.

Oskar like many displaced migrants sailed from Athens to Egypt. From Egypt a passenger ship would travel for three months to Perth, the third refueling port on the way to Sydney.

In Sydney, Oskar was assigned to work on the Snowy Mountain River Scheme. In the years he was working on the site, Hanna joined him. When the Scheme came to an end, they moved to a country town in New South Wales. Hanna and Oskar settled in with assistance from migrants of different nationalities. It was in this period Oskar wrote letters to different embassies and consulates in Europe in a bid to find his sister. All came back as negative.

Jaro and his family sent letters back and forth to Oskar and his family. When on holidays in Switzerland, or Italy, Jaro would look at the women in a slim hope of spotting Kiana. Like Oskar, he too gave up with the firm belief, Kiana was dead.

Twenty Years Later.

Oskar opened a letter which came from Germany. It was a letter from Kiana. She wrote:

I tried to find you after the war. I wrote to many embassies and received negative replies. I gave up honestly believing you were dead, but my heart didn't want to acknowledge the most likely fact. After ten years, I tried again to write to all the embassies. Then someone said I should try the consulates for the smaller countries. It was the Australian Embassy who contacted me almost four months after lodging my enquiry. They found your file. Then it was a long search to find you. Letters take time.

When I was kidnapped, I was taken to the German ammunition factory, Bobingen, to be a slave working in the most dangerous working and living conditions. One day I escaped.

Unfortunately, I ended up in a prisoner of war camp in Trebinka, Poland. Six days after my arrival, there was a mass breakout. Three hundred men tried to escape. Only fifty did escape. The rest were shot when returned or shot on the spot of capture. Then days later the camp was abandoned with many prisoners murdered by firing squad or gassed. They were buried in mass graves by using a bulldozer. I learned I was going to be one of a few hundreds to be transferred.

In the transfer, I escaped again. Six of us climbed onto the roof of a train and jumped when the train was going over small low-set bridge. Two died on impact, two were injured. Two of us escaped. We dragged the two injured to the side of the road for locals to find. They never survived their injuries.

I was on the run heading for Switzerland when I was caught again. Because of my history of escaping, I was heavily guarded and placed in Colditz. In that old castle, only two people escaped. About ten died trying. I was one of the very few women in the place. Naturally, they made the women do many domestic chores. That is where I stayed for the last year of the war.

In that time, there was a German sergeant who was kind. Yes, I mean kind, not kind when compared to other German soldiers. We developed a friendship. He would smuggle in extra bits of food for me to have. Also, I was on so called relief roster. Now that was the disgusting part of my confinement. I was made into a prostitute for the German soldiers. When Peter Batchel found out all the women were placed in this situation, he would add his name on everyone's list. He never touched them. He just chattered. Sometimes we played with a deck of cards. That could go on all night. He wasn't impressed with the war and less impressed women were forced into such duties.

I soon learned that Peter was working secretly sending information to Britain. He was frequently on guard duty. Every week a new list of names was printed. If a person died, that was noted. When people arrived, he made sure he knew who the new inmates were or who was the new official. Somehow, he managed to send details to someone who relayed the information to Britain. He was one of Churchill's secrete army.

I have since learned many Germans were disgusted with Hitler. They did their best to smuggle Jews out of the country. They passed on information to the many resistance groups. Without their assistance, some of the battles the Allies fought would have been lost.

Oskar, I married Peter. We live in Berlin. I have two daughters, Lea Azra and Julia Mia and a son, Louis Peter. The name louis was named after his father. May they never know war like we did. I hope one day we can meet.

Love Kiana.

After reading the letter, Oskar was in shock. His mind was blank, yet millions of thoughts ran through his brain. Oskar burst out crying. She was alive in Berlin. That is all that mattered. The weight of guilt for not protecting her was lifted.

Upon learning the news, Oskar asked Hanna, "Do you want to take a trip to Europe. Kiana has contacted me after all these years. Also, it would be good for you to visit your family as well." Hanna gave a wide smile. "Peace at last. Do we go to Weghaltz to see this obelisk?" "Oh, I think that can included, that is if it still exists." Hanna placed a kiss on his cheek. "An obelisk always remains. Even when it falls, the base remains; giving a reminder something important was there. I'll book a flight."